THE real THE REAL WORLD

Written by Hillary Johnson & Nancy Rommelmann

THIS
BOOK IS
DEDICATED
TO THE
LIVING
MEMORY OF
PEDRO
ZAMORA

TABLE OF CONTENTS

This is the true story of seven strangers, picked to live in a house and have their lives taped to find out what happens when people stop being polite and start getting real...

New York 1992

THE REAL WORLD

Name: Andre
Hometown: New Brunswick, New Jersey
Career Goal: Music
Job: Musician
Living Situation: Divides his time between Detroit and New Jersey

ANDRE

Gouda

Name: Becky
Born: 7/8/67
Hometown: New Hope, Pennsylvania
Education: Buckingham Friends School, Friends Select School, New York University Film School
Career Goal: Writing and performing music
Job: Singer/musician
Living Situation: "In Colorado, with my boyfriend"
Favorite Song: "Monkey Gone To Heaven," The Pixies
Favorite Group: The Fluid, Frank Black, Violent Femmes, Psychic Penguin
Favorite TV Show: *Prime Suspect*
Favorite Snack: "Food"
Romantic Involvement: Boyfriend, John
Car: "I usually walk"

BECKY

Smokey

Name: Eric
Born: 5/23/71
Hometown: Ocean Township, New Jersey
Education: GED ("I left school early; it's a buncha bullsh*t")
Career Goal: "To create peace on earth through my audience"
Job: Host of MTV's *The Grind*, Actor
Living Situation: With Mom in New Jersey and in shared houses in California and Arizona
Favorite Song: "Man In The Mirror," Michael Jackson
Favorite Group: Michael Jackson, "Because I only listen to music with a message"
Favorite TV Show: *Shark Bowl*, on the Discovery channel
Favorite Snack: Peanut M&M's
Romantic Involvement: None

ERIC

Name: Heather
Born: 11/13/70
Hometown: Jersey City, New Jersey
Education: St. Peters College, NJ, and living life every day
Career Goal: Rapper/Entrepreneur
Job: Owns and runs Nubian Hair & Nails
Living Situation: Apartment in New Jersey
Favorite Song: I didn't write it yet
Favorite Group: None
Favorite TV Show: ESPN/*Sports Center*
Favorite Snack: Doritos
Romantic Involvement: Writing rhymes
Car: NJ Transit

HEATHER

Name: Kevin
Born: 4/24/66
Hometown: Jersey City, New Jersey
Education: BA political science/English minor, Rutgers University
Career Goal: Writer
Job: Senior editor at *Vibe*
Living Situation: Alone, in Brooklyn brownstone apartment
Favorite Song: "Strange Fruit," Billie Holiday
Favorite Group: Temptations, Nirvana, Public Enemy
Favorite TV Show: *Taxi, Three's Company, I Love Lucy*
Favorite Snack: Chips and dip
Romantic Involvement: "I'm in love–she's dope"
Car: None, rides the NYC subway

KEVIN

JULIE

Name: Julie
Born: 1/23/73
Hometown: Birmingham, Alabama
Education: University of Memphis
Career Goal: Dancer
Job: Dance teacher and working with handicapped kids
Living Situation: With parents
Favorite Song: "Blue Moon"
Favorite Group: Ani DiFranco
Favorite TV Show: *Seinfeld*
Favorite Snack: Peaches
Romantic Involvement: Not right now
Car: '81 convertible Rabbit

Name: Norman
Born: 3/6/67
Hometown: Williamston, Michigan
Education: Interlochen Arts Academy, Cooper Union, Yale
Career Goal: Entrepreneur
Job: Doing freelance artwork
Living Situation: Shares a "beautiful home" in Pacific Palisades
Favorite Song: "Coney Island of the Mind," Alan Ferlinghetti
Favorite Group: Wild Colonials, XTC
Favorite TV Show: *X–Files*
Favorite Snack: Pepperoni and mushroom pizza ("I ate it 5 times this week")
Romantic Involvement: None. "My friend slept with my boyfriend and I got dumped"
Car: 1986 Jeep Cherokee

NORMAN

EPISODE 1: We meet Julie and her dad at home in Birmingham. She travels to New York with dreams of becoming a dancer. At the loft, she meets the other roommates: Kevin, the poet/writer; Becky, the NYU student/musician; Eric, the model/actor; Norman, the painter; Heather, the rapper; Andre, the rock singer. They try to set house rules. They play with <u>Book of Questions on Love and Sex</u>. Julie comments on Heather's beeper, leading to a discussion on racism. Julie takes the subway and bums a ride on a Harley. It's all new to her.

Julie reacts to Heather's beeper: "Do you sell drugs?" (episode 1)

EPISODE 2: Eric does a commercial for Jovan Musk. It's too steamy for TV but snags him a spot on a morning talk show—in his briefs. Heather raps in the studio. She and Julie hang out, walk Norman's dog Gouda. Heather writes a "slang dictionary" for Julie. Eric talks about Missy, the girlfriend he had on Long Island. Julie takes aerobics class. Eric has a party. EPISODE 3: Julie takes dance classes. Eric's almost-nude shoot with model Karen turns wild, and they begin to date. Andre's band Reigndance jam in a New Jersey basement and are visited by the police. The group goes roller-skating at the Roxy. Julie learns more about Norman's sexuality. He, Becky, and Julie go see Andre's band play on Staten Island. They take a late-night ferry ride home. EPISODE 4: The loftmates are getting on one another's nerves. Becky parties at the Limelight in a homemade Dixie-cup bra. The house calls a meeting. They argue: Heather and Andre want to "choke" Eric; Becky insists she is "less

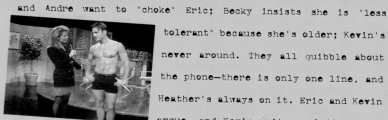

Eric goes on The Faith Daniels Show to discuss sex in advertising (episode 2)

tolerant" because she's older; Kevin's never around. They all quibble about the phone—there is only one line, and Heather's always on it. Eric and Kevin

Tension explodes (episode 5)

argue, and Kevin writes a letter to Eric. The loft reads it, and it causes a big fight. EPISODE 5: The animosity between Eric and Kevin continues. Kevin thinks it's a black/white thing; Eric insists he "admires the black race." We find out Eric is on probation for being caught with steroids several years earlier. We meet his mom; meet the kids he is working with as part of his probation. Eric and Kevin make amends and go to a Knicks game, where Eric's dad is a referee. Afterward, they meet Isaiah Thomas. EPISODE 6: Julie's virginity is discussed. She goes on a blind date, which turns out to be a hilarious disaster. We see Kevin at a poetry reading at the Nuyorican Poets Cafe. The loft decides they need to have another meeting and make plans for a Sunday dinner. Kevin doesn't show. They plan an April fool's joke on Kevin and switch identities: Eric is "gay," Norman a "hippie kleptomaniac," Julie a "slut," and Andre an "innocent bumpkin."

EPISODE 7: The joke backfires: Kevin is really shocked, especially with Julie's turnabout and is relieved to find out it was all a gag. Heather and Julie go to a basketball game, where Heather's idol Larry Johnson is playing. Heather, Becky, and Julie are informed they're going to Jamaica.

Julie's blind date is a bust (episode 6)

8

Heather hangs with her man Larry Johnson (episode 7)

Becky and Kevin have a fight in which he calls her a "racist." EPISODE 8: The girls are in Jamaica to meet men. They go to a nude beach where all the men are "fat and ugly." They complain there are no guys in Jamaica. Becky, however, does hook up with the show's director, Bill. Soon after, Bill resigns. Meanwhile, the guys hang in rainy New York. Norman meets and develops a crush on Charles. Back in New York, Becky and Bill hang out at the Dew Drop Inn. EPISODE 9: Norman and Charles continue to date, though Norman is unsure of their status. Norman becomes involved in Jerry Brown's presidential campaign, painting the loft with Brown's 800 number. Norman, Heather, and Becky drive to Washington, D.C., for a pro-choice rally, where Norman runs into Charles. Later, Andre and Julie come across a "Reaganville," where Julie meets Darlene, a homeless crack addict. She and Julie become friendly, and Julie decides to spend the night. EPISODE 10: Andre finds "the ugliest dog in New York" and

Painting Jerry Brown's 800 # on the wall of the loft (episode 9)

reunites it with its owner. Julie's mother and brother come for a visit. They are not pleased to find out Julie has been spending time with the homeless. Julie hears them out and tries to be a good hostess, but finds it exhausting. EPISODE 11: Kevin and Julie have a physical confrontation: she claims he

Julie spends a night with the homeless (episode 9)

threw a candlestick at her; he denies it. Julie is adamant: "I love this show, but I'm not going to a f**king funeral." A mob mentality forms against Kevin, but he simply avoids it by not showing up. Kevin and Julie finally talk, but it's still tender. Kevin and Eric decide to throw a party. Things get wild when Heather is queestioned by the police, ostensibly for pushing a guest. The cops take Heather away in the squad car, then let her go. EPISODE 12: Heather raps about the biz; she worries about when her album will come out. Andre's band perform a song called "Lazybones" and make a video with Bill, the former director, with whom Becky has broken up. At another Sunday dinner, Eric insists he's fed up with people being antagonistic to him; Heather says he brings it on himself. Julie and Eric pretend to take a shower together. EPISODE 13: "The party has to end," says Becky of their time in the loft. They each reflect: Becky says the experience was a "constant mirror," Andre hopes he gets

Kevin and Julie work it out (episode 11)

exposure for his band; Julie has mixed emotions, as her personal and career goals have not been met. They discuss the paranoia that comes with being around cameras all the time; explain that none of them ever got sexually involved because "Everyone is ugly!" (Heather) and because they all feel too much like siblings. They get drunk and have a slumber party. Led by Eric, they break into the control room. They switch roles with the production staff. They all discuss what an intense learning experience it's been. A lot of hugs and tears as they leave the loft.

New York City

Julie spends a night with crack addict Darlene in a homeless Reaganville in Riverside Park at 79th Street

LOX·AROUND THE CLOCK

BAR & RESTAURANT
6th Ave. & 21st St. NYC
(212) 691-3535 FAX: 727-3961

END HUNGER AT LOX!

Lox Around The Clock was the scene of Julie's ill-fated date

The "real" Real World–Kevin's home on 163rd Street and Amsterdam Avenue was separated from the Soho loft by more than just physical distance

Kevin read in poetry slams here (236 E. 3rd St.)

The loft

Gonzalez y Gonzalez was a favorite spot for Margaritas (625 Broadway at Mercer)

The Soho loft the roomates called home (385 Broadway at Prince Street)

Grocery shopping in New York City becomes a major hassle when a blizzard hits

Bill, the director, faces the other side of the cameras here on a date with Becky after his resignation (Greenwich & 7th Avenues)

Andre

"Andre is well rested.
Every time you get around him,
you know it's time to take it easy."

—Heather

April 1995
Andre's manager called to say that he was
"not interested in participating at this time."

"Andre's kind of an enigma to me. He's *very* laid-back, almost didn't want to be on-camera. After the show, I heard he turned down record deals. I thought he was ripe to be a star, but he's taking his time." —KEVIN

"Andre remained a mystery to the audience, and that seemed to only fuel their interest. His band, Reigndance, was pretty solid." —MARY-ELLIS BUNIM, EXECUTIVE PRODUCER

"Andre means very well and works very hard. He's a nice guy." —Becky

"*Andre represents the best of his generation. He's so incredibly tolerant, he listens to everybody no matter what, and he still tries to make his music. He's the ideal Gen-X guy.*" —Norman

"Andre, I felt he was doing the show for Reigndance. But at the same time, he was so ready to call the cards, to say exactly how it was. He was always really willing, and polite." —Julie

BECKY

Denver, Colorado • April 1995

"*The Real World*–as an artist, it's something you need to get over. I was 24, and I'd had a life. It was a landmark for me, it wasn't a beginning or an end.

"I had a friend of a friend who worked for the casting department. I was there one day, and they said, have her apply. I filled out an application and made a video. Free rent, that pricked up my ears. I had been an actress for a while, too, before the show. I heard that it was supposed to be a documentary, but also kind of a soap opera. I'd been to film school, so I thought, what's that about? Part of me also thought this could be the death of my music career. In the end, I reasoned that it would be a good experience, and it was only this little documentary and it would come and go. Then at the last minute I called my friend and said, maybe I didn't want to do this after all, but she said, 'No, they're already calling you their Annette Bening.'

"Once the cameras went on, the voices went up 10 decibels. I found myself doing it, too. So Norman and I decided to turn the experience into a Warhol event, camp it up, really rock everyone's boat. It didn't really work, but we spent a lot of time playing characters.

"There were these kids in Texas who had a cult about Norman and me. They called my mother's house and pretended they were old friends from college, wanting to get my phone number. Norman dated all of his fans. Norm had an entourage for a while. He wanted to be Warhol."

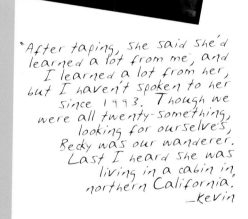

"When I got to LA, I did extra work on the Ben Stiller show. He was fascinated by *The Real World* and talked a lot about doing a skit where I'd play myself, but we never did. When *Reality Bites* came out, which Ben Stiller wrote, Norman called me up and said, "You're going to be really mad because it's about you. It's you exactly." Later on, Norman was in the same restaurant as Winona Ryder, and she refused to be introduced to him, saying she didn't want anything to do with '*Real World* people.'"

"After taping, she said she'd learned a lot from me, and I learned a lot from her, but I haven't spoken to her since 1993. Though we were all twenty-something, looking for ourselves, Becky was our wanderer. Last I heard she was living in a cabin in northern California. —Kevin

"I don't want to talk too much about what I'm doing now. I'm writing and playing music. I'm playing a lot with Gordon Gayno of the Violent Femmes. There's a part of me that's bored with the entertainment industry. It's a struggle, and it's a constant letdown. Part of me wants to go be a wacky performance artist, go seriously underground. I've been starving long enough, it's nothing new, so I might as well be happy. One of the things *The Real World* did was knock out any desire to be famous. That's an interesting experience to have had as an artist.

"I was just blown away by Becky. I thought, 'Man, she is so smart and mature.' Later, we figured out none of us were, but she could give you that idea. She was such a key element because of the mood she provided. She's kind of moody, and we'd have to go around that." —Julie

Eric

"They said, 'Look, there's this thing that MTV's doin'. Maybe you should check it out.' And I said, 'All right, cool.'"

"He's harmless, and such a nice person!" —Julie

"Eric was the one person I truly did not like. He was an annoying, egotistical, shallow human being. He got on my nerves—why do you exist? At least if you were psycho, there'd be something there." —Becky

New York, New York
June 1995

"I was in New York, and I was 20 years old, doing like modeling and some commercial work. And I was just trying to figure out what I was going to do with the rest of my life, and this project came up called <u>The Real World</u>. I found out about it through my commercial agent. They said, 'Look, there's this thing that MTV's doin'. Maybe you should check it out.' And I said, 'All right, cool.' I went back three, four, five times. Typical casting. But not 'cause you weren't really trying out for a part, you're just trying out to be yourself. I was the last person they cast.

"Being on <u>The Real World</u> changed my life completely and totally, 360 degrees. If it didn't change everybody else's life, they didn't get out of it what they were supposed to. It was a very serious and very special opportunity for me to work with six people who were nothing like me at all. Especially in a day like today—1995 in America is nuts! People are out of their minds. They don't know if they're coming, if they're going; if they're black, if they're white; if they're straight, if they're not. It's just a whole mass confusion. For me to get on to the show and to hang out with six people that are totally different, and be there with them, and live with them, was like a dream come true for me. It molded me into a perfect human being, and everything that you're supposed to be about.

"I think all my roommates are great. I feel the same way about everybody in the world now because of the experience that I had with my roommates. I have no grudges against anyone. No one. I love everybody that was on that show because they made me what I am today. I have to thank them for that.

"The show helped me out a lot because it taught me to be able to speak with people better. It made me aware of what goes on in the whole entire world. I've always been a curious person. If I see something, I'm like, wow, I wonder, why that is that way, or why is that or why is this? On <u>The Real World</u>, I had to do that with everybody. If Becky was to say something to me, or Andre was to say something to me, or Kevin or Heather, and I didn't quite understand it, and it was kind of directed mean towards me, I had to sit back from it and not attack but take it in. I had to try and understand where they're coming from and why they would say this because I'm not from their part of the world.

"The only bad thing was the way the show stopped for us. When it started, they said, 'You got the job, here's your key, bring your bags.' They didn't tell us anything else, and then the last day, you're flooded with press, and all of a sudden you turn into this superstar with no guidance, no help at all. And what happens if you're somebody that doesn't even understand business?

"You know what's funny? My manager says, 'He's the Michael Jordan of <u>The Real World</u>.' The reason he says that is it's been four years now where I've had to, on my own, learn about this business and learn every nook and cranny about it to protect myself. Because where I come from, if you don't protect yourself, someone's going to get over on you, and they're going to sh*t on you. And they're going to take everything you've got. And now because I see what's been going on, and because I have a total grasp of the entertainment business, I'm going to turn it around. And not only am I going to be the Michael Jordan of <u>The Real World</u>, I'm going to be the Superman of the entertainment business."

"He's a complex person. He needs to operate basically off his look, so his intelligence and capacity to learn are not developed. It's a limitation, but it's also a choice." —Norman

"Eric has charisma to burn. And it was surprising that, as a 20 year old, he was willing to open himself up to the camera, to be made so vulnerable. But Eric took risks that scared us. He'd hook up men behind Julie, rollerblade in town, or get a drink and hang out on the window ledge. We were always worried about him. He had a nice relationship with Julie. They were the youngest in the cast. He had a contentious relationship with Heather, and with Becky, and had some great discussions and fights with Kevin. He was never boring."
—Mary-Ellis Bunim, executive producer

"He was just a big baby. I'd be like, 'Eric, for real, put your shirt back on.' I didn't have time for that."
—Heather

Heather

With brothers and Dad

Heather meeting her idol, Larry Johnson

Age 18

Age 4

18

"Before I did The Real World, I wasn't really doin' nothin', you know? I had an album deal, but it was taking too long, they had other people in the studio. My manager sent another client down to audition for the show, and I went with them, and I wound up getting it. I mean, I was just wastin' time before, hangin' out, so I figured I'd do it. • I didn't really have no first opinion of the show. I mean, I heard free food, free rent, and I thought, I'm just gonna stay here. It was fine by me, it didn't matter if they had cameras in our face. When I saw what was going on in the loft, I thought, how they gonna make a TV show outta this? We was livin' in this nice apartment, but that ain't no kinda show. I was surprised by the reaction from the public. I mean, there's nothing wrong with it, I was just surprised. • I thought they did a good job overall. Only one thing gets me. My father is my best friend, and he wasn't on the show at all. You saw everybody else with their mothers and fathers, but nobody gave me a family background. It's like people assumed I was from New York, but I'm from Jersey City, where my family is. I'm real close with my family, and I thought that was wrong not to show that, especially with the whole thing of African-American fathers not being around their kids. Other than that, I thought they did a good job with the show. • I'm still in touch with Julie. I met a lot of people, but she's a really good friend. They probably didn't expect that. I said to myself, I'm gonna make it my business to get to know her, to show her how it is where I'm from. She cool. And Norman, that's my boy, too. I didn't have too many problems with people, I didn't have any arguments, like they all was having. I'd see that and think, why these people trippin'? But Eric, he was just too bitchy, he was just a little too much. He was always whinin', like a mama's boy. We'd be sittin' around havin' these conversations and he'd be like, 'I wanna go home!' Then leave! What I thought was we had to deal with these people. He was a big fat crybaby. I'm doin' exactly what I want right now–how long will his image last? I don't have to worry if I gain 10 pounds, or I'm wearin' jeans or whatever, but how long will his thing last? He's doing what he did before. I'm makin' steady progress. **Dealing with MTV and The Real World didn't f**k up my life, it only helped.** • Everyday people recognize me. They're cool, though. I just tell them, 'Don't make a big deal.' It embarrasses me a little bit. People really feel like they know us. I sign autographs when I'm eating, while I'm on the train. It's cool, I can't knock it."

"Heather is the best. We talk all the time. If we don't speak for several weeks, we panic. We stand up for each other, watch each other's back. I really think we balanced each other out. To me, the biggest advantage of the show was getting to be friends with her." —Julie

"Heather is very cool, sure of who she is, and never afraid to let you know exactly what's on her mind." —Mary-Ellis Bunim, executive producer

"I love Heather. I think she's an incredible individual. I think she's a beautiful girl. I think she has a huge heart. I think she's got a lot of drive, a lot of dedication to what she's doing. We had a little bit of a problem in the middle, but then we worked it out. I think it's evident because we still talk now." —Eric

"Heather's not afraid of anything." —Becky

Birmingham, Alabama • April 1995

"I decided to audition for *The Real World* because I've always done dance and theater, and I audition for anything. I was driving home from Memphis when I popped a tape out and heard an ad for the audition in Birmingham. So I went down with my sister, and it was a bunch of goons up there going, 'I hate my life, I have no ambition and no drive, I want to be on TV.' I was like, 'No way,' but my sister said, 'Look at these idiots, you'll get it!' And **I thought it'd be a great opportunity to get to NY.**

I was the first one cast.

"I didn't know what this show was going to be about, but they did say, 'Oh, it'll be seven people from all different parts of the country.' When I got to the loft, I felt kind of set up; I was the only one who didn't know New York. I think the reason the cameras followed me around so much was because I didn't know anybody else in the city. I only had the camera crew to hang out with.

"That time I went out with that guy, I almost started crying. The only reason I went out with him is because I knew the producers really wanted me to have a date. So one night me and Heather are at Gonzalez y Gonzalez, this Mexican restaurant down the street from the loft, and this guy comes up to me and says, 'I think you're very attractive–do you want to come to this party?' Me and Heather go, and the guy asks if I want to go out sometime, and I say okay, but there's a catch, there will be all these cameras around, and he says that's fine, and we think, well, this is the guy I can go on a date with. But it was so awful. We're sitting in Lox Around the Clock with all the cameras, and he says, 'I'm used to being around a lot of cameras,' and it's a leading statement if ever there was one, so I ask why and he says, 'Because I used to do a talk show. I was voted one of the best looking guys in Boston.' And it only gets worse, like when he says, 'You've got a great hip structure' and then gets up because he has a cramp. Russell Fine, the best camera guy in the world, is just looking at me saying, 'I am so sorry. Please know that I feel for you.' But my dates lately are no better. I went out with a guy a couple of months ago, and we're driving home, and he pulls out a travel size bottle of Scope and gargles and swallows it. **I could write a book on bad dates.**

julie

"I'll always remember something Norman said to me. It's really hokey, but he was sincere. He said, 'You're just a butterfly. If they're forced out of their cocoons too soon, they die. Don't worry about what others want— go when you're ready.'"

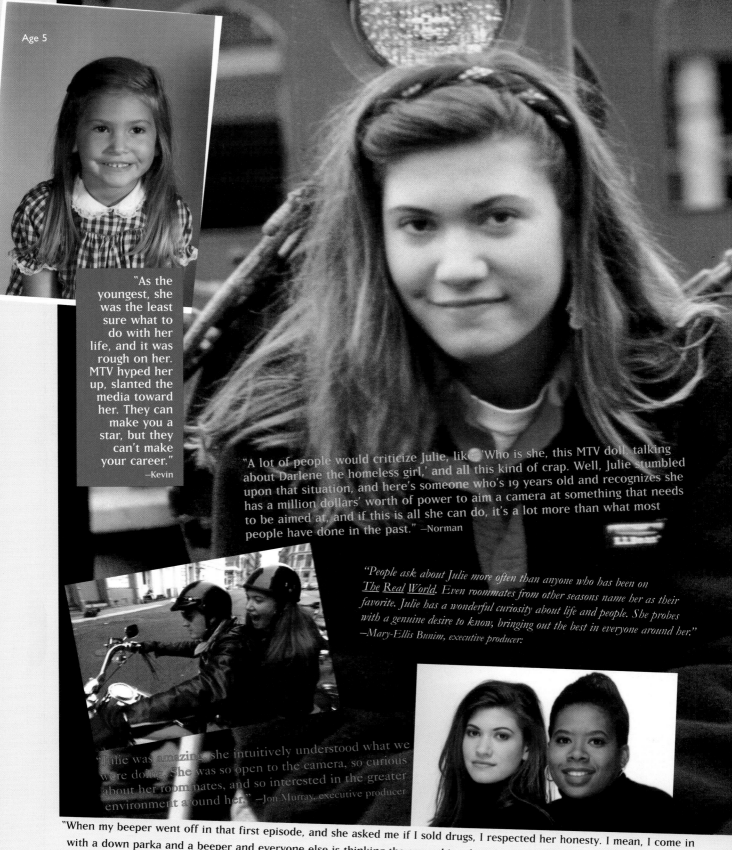

Age 5

"As the youngest, she was the least sure what to do with her life, and it was rough on her. MTV hyped her up, slanted the media toward her. They can make you a star, but they can't make your career." —Kevin

"A lot of people would criticize Julie, like, 'Who is she, this MTV doll, talking about Darlene the homeless girl,' and all this kind of crap. Well, Julie stumbled upon that situation, and here's someone who's 19 years old and recognizes she has a million dollars' worth of power to aim a camera at something that needs to be aimed at, and if this is all she can do, it's a lot more than what most people have done in the past." —Norman

"People ask about Julie more often than anyone who has been on The Real World. Even roommates from other seasons name her as their favorite. Julie has a wonderful curiosity about life and people. She probes with a genuine desire to know, bringing out the best in everyone around her." —Mary-Ellis Bunim, executive producer

"Julie was amazing, she intuitively understood what we were doing. She was so open to the camera, so curious about her roommates, and so interested in the greater environment around her." —Jon Murray, executive producer

"When my beeper went off in that first episode, and she asked me if I sold drugs, I respected her honesty. I mean, I come in with a down parka and a beeper and everyone else is thinking the same thing, but she said it. She cool." —Heather

"Kevin had a lot of anger that surprised us, but it came out in interesting, provocative dialogues with Julie, Eric and Becky. It would have been a much less interesting series without Kevin." —Mary-Ellis Bunim, executive producer

NYU faculty I.D.

KEVIN

Reading his poetry at the Schaumberg Center, Harlem, New York

22

"I got onto the show in a weird way. I was eating in the Stardust café on 57th & 6th in New York City when this woman comes in with her friends and tells me, 'I like your look.' She gives me a card that says 'MTV-<u>The Real World</u>.' I wasn't real keen about being on TV, but I was freelancing at the time, and I thought, if I do this, I can blow up, so I did see it as a career move.

"When I first walked into the loft, I felt like, wow, I won the grand prize on <u>The Price Is Right</u>. I was tripping, but it was hard, too. I think I had a lot in common with Heather. Going through <u>The Real World</u> was real therapeutic for both of us. I still see her- I just wrote her bio for Pendulum Records. You know, when she did <u>The Real World</u>, she had a record deal with Elektra. When that fell through, she started a beauty supply store, and it did really well. She's a fighter, and she's grown a lot, really taken control of her own life. I have a lot of respect for her.

"Maybe <u>The Real World</u> put us all out there in a way some of us weren't ready for. Like Julie. I think it was tough on her...and it was really hard to go into MTV and see her working there as a receptionist, which is the job she took after the show ended. I remember a couple of years ago she was still negative. But

three years gives you a chance to reflect, and I'm sure she's cool with it now. Which is good, because she's really a very giving person, very concerned about other people. She calls every once in a while and will leave a message like, 'I'm just callin' y'all to say hey!' but she doesn't leave her number.

"Even though we had our problems, I thought our season was the best. We were really a slice of what's going on in our generation, except we're all artistic. The other casts, it seemed like they were playing up to the camera.

"I had <u>no</u> clue <u>The Real World</u> would become as big as it did. If I'd have known, I would have negotiated a better deal. I mean, we were making like $100 a week, and at the time none of us had steady jobs. After the show, I'd see people on the subway, and they'd say, 'How come you're riding the IRT?' Everyone recognizes you and thinks you're living high, but we were all broke. Norman had lost his company, and the rest of us were struggling. I think the

only one of us who got a gig was Eric, on MTV. I read recently that he thinks the rest of us were jealous of him. Well, I wish homeboy the best of luck. I'm all about positive karma.

"I'm a TV fanatic—so I was just tripping when we got inducted into the Museum of Broadcasting. I mean, I used to go there when I was a kid. That's when it hit me how significant <u>The Real World</u> is."

Age 14, "during my John Travolta phase"

23

Norman

"Norman is the nicest guy. He generated so much energy on the show that you never saw. I think the producers were a little disappointed that he wasn't a gay activist. I think they wanted someone who was like, 'Here I am and I'm gay, by God!' but Norman was just everyday people." —Julie

"The whole experience was very Star Trekian—we'd go encounter aliens and work with them."

> "I have a lot of respect for Norman, too. That guy is so damn talented—he's a poet, an artist, a businessman. On *The Real World*, they made him look like the quirky gay guy. I thought he got shafted." —Kevin

With Charles Perez at the march for Reproductive Rights in Washington, D.C.

Posing as a "hippie kleptomaniac" to play a joke on Kevin

"How I wound up on the show is that an ex-partner of mine and I had this tremendous loft in Brooklyn, and we had rented it out to like video companies, so we were on the registry of locations. So several people from MTV came up, but they were on the secretive side of things, like, 'We want to do this Biosphere kind of project, where we put people in a space and then we're going to videotape it and put it on MTV.' They were very excited. I like to see when people are passionate about something, and it seemed like it could possibly have a really good impact, and I was like, "That sounds like the kind of project I would like to do," though it's questionable when you put something onto, like, MTV because it isn't PBS, it's a totally different mental sphere. Anyway, we talked, but about a week later we found out they didn't want to use our space. And then, I don't know, another month passed, and someone called and said, 'You know, you were kind of like really interesting. Would you want to submit a tape?' And I'm thinking, what does this mean, television and all this crap? Here's a person who's gone to Interlochen Arts Academy, Cooper Union, Yale, and now this MTV project, and I'm like, okay, I can play that Warholian game of being on TV.

"So I did send a tape, saying all this—and got a rejection letter that said, 'Sorry, MTV can't use you and whatever you know, thanks for trying—and watch this *Real World* show!' I didn't think anything of it. Then they started to find out more about me and were like,

'Dating men, are you? Hmmmm—we need to talk with you again tomorrow.'

And I was thinking, whatever, maybe they won't ask me back, but they were like, 'We need to know what your parents think about this type of situation and do they know anything?' And I'm like, 'Well, no, they don't know anything that no one else knows,' because there's no need for me to make an excuse anymore. I don't see my world where I make excuses, otherwise I feel I'm a lesser person—I feel handicapped.

"After three years, there's like this bizarre amnesia that's going on. It's like, 'Did we go to high school? Where did you go? I know I've worked with you, you look really familiar and I can't stand it!' There was a time I signed 200 autographs at my cousin's basketball game. It's endless, it's beyond endless. I went to a party at Warner Bros., and the cast of *Friends* were there, and I was more recognized than they were."

"One thing I didn't like about our season was what they chose not to show. The day after the LA riots was the day Eric and I had our party, the one where Heather got arrested. It was really tense that whole night. At 6:00 in the morning, we started having this really heavy discussion on race relations. This was also right before I got into the argument with Julie. Not to include the stuff about the riot made the show very apolitical, I thought." —Kevin

RACE RELA

Los Angeles riots, April 1992

"This was right when the riots were breaking out in L.A., and there were threats of riots in New York. So I race back to the house and start shooting this altercation, or whatever you want to call it. • These two cameramen are on the street in front of our loft on Prince and Broadway, filming this argument. Accusations are being made about what exactly happened, and none of us really know because no one was there. It was extremely intense, and I didn't know at what point I should step in because nothing had ever gotten this fierce. There were 40 or 50 people that had stopped on the sidewalk, and cabs were stopping, listening to this argument. They didn't know anything about <u>The</u> <u>Real</u> <u>World</u>, they just saw two people, a white person and a black person, screaming at the top of their lungs with two camera crews around them. They thought it was in relation to the riots. There were black people and white people in the crowd, and Julie and Kevin were turning around, trying to solicit their participation in this, and it seemed like it was going to escalate and get really ugly. We were scared to death. Fortunately, the crowd got so big that Julie and Kevin both agreed that maybe we should take it inside." —George Verschoor, producer/director

"I think they got around a lot of stuff with Kevin. Like when we'd play pool, he'd say, 'Don't you see the symbolism in using the <u>white</u> ball to knock all the other balls around?' He'd play pool and use the eight-ball as a cue ball. It was ridiculous. They didn't show a lot of this because they wanted to keep him a likable character. • When we had that argument, the cameras weren't there. I grabbed the phone and called the production office, but Kevin yanked it out of my hand and threw it across the room. It's very interesting for me, vis-à-vis Kevin. I mean, I grew up in the South, I went to public school all my life, where the kids are mostly black. My friends I grew up with are infuriated by that incident. It's not like I don't know black people. That's what Kevin wanted it to look like, like I didn't understand what was going on." —Julie

World gets to... Jamaica

NEW YO

THREE female cast members of M' "Real World" got a fright-filled Third World experience when they ventured to Negril, Jamaica for some footage about a month ago.

Sources close to the experimental documentary series — which is tracking the daily lives of seven hipsters living in a SoHo loft à la that PBS series on the Loud family — say the trouble unfolded at a reggae concert.

The three "Real World" women, Julie Oliver, a rapper named Heather B. and Becky Blasband, a singer in a rock band called Enfants Terribles, were being filmed frolicking at the Rastafarian fest when a local band promoter, mistakenly thinking that MTV was shooting footage of his group to take back to America, demanded money for the privilege.

The photogenic females, who were in the process of buying jerk chicken, were hurried into the back of the production crew's pickup truck.

Sources say the promoter and a angry mob of about 15 then tried to overturn the vehicle.

"The chicken people also freaked out be-

...ey thought they hadn't been paid," says our source. "The money had to be handed out the window to them."

The mob finally let the truck pass, but, says a source, some of its more mobile members then chased the production crew and the "Real World" stars — at speeds of over 100 mph — back to their resort.

Nothing came of the high-sp... source says that members tion returned the following o... invite the TV trio to a Trench...

The thrill of danger in... stimulated the hormones o... mer waitress at the nightclu... "Real World" director name... Sources say a mutual attra... into full-blown lust in the trop...

Problem is, when the torrid... covered on the island, Richm... as director because, says o... couldn't maintain his objectivit... Sources say there may also ha...

ulation in contracts signed by "Real World" cast and crew members that they may not interact in a personal or physical fashion.

When we reached Blasband, 24, she told u... she and Richmond "didn't reali... [backlash would...

Sklaash to...

"In Jamaica we had probably one of the most hair-raising situations we've ever had. It really got life-threatening for a moment there. It was the result of some random guy who got angry, saying, 'I don't want you to film my band!' I said, 'Fine, we won't film your band.' Later on he found out it was MTV and said, 'I want you to film my band!' So I said, 'Fine, I'll film your band.' I was just trying to keep everybody happy. Two hours later, we're out in front after the concert, and the guy and his henchmen came up saying, 'I want $20,000 for those tapes you shot of my band.' He and his henchmen started making some threats about small holes in my head and I said, 'Wow, wow, wow!' When these guys knocked the camera out of the cameraman's hands, I said, 'Get in the truck and lock yourselves in there.' It was like The Year Of Living Dangerously. I thought I'd never get off that island alive. They blocked the road and surrounded us and started digging in my pockets for money. The roommates were scared out of their wits—with the exception of Heather, who was just laughing hysterically through the whole thing. Later she said, 'George, that was nothing! I've been in worse sh*t in Jersey City! At least there were no guns, dude.'

"We got away and took off, and then there we were in a high speed chase, going 80 miles an hour with this car right at our bumper. We thought if we made it to the hotel we'd be fine, but they chased us right through the lobby. Heather was laughing the entire way. Julie was in tears, and Becky was in tears. Fortunately, the police are very good in Jamaica, and they mean business when they show up with their automatic weapons. They put those guys in their place."
—George Verschoor, producer/director

"Julie, Heather, and I were standing across the street eating jerk chicken, when we hear our guys yelling, 'Get in the van!' We looked over, and there was this whole angry crowd gathered, and George was just standing there handing out money, completely scared out of his socks. We jumped in the van, and the crowd surrounded it. Julie and I were crouched in the truck, clutching these chicken bones. The look on her face—her eyes were huge, and she had these two thin little bones clutched in each fist. Of course Heather's not afraid of anything."
—Becky

JAMAICA

"Then there's the famous affair [with Bill, one of the directors]. He was terrified. I felt horrible. If I'd had any idea they were going to fire him, I wouldn't have done it. I went to the producers and tried to talk them out of it, but they said, 'It's a moral issue.' Finally I thought, if that's what they want, then I'll be the slutty bitch. My ex-boyfriend said, 'My friends saw this show, and they can't believe I went out with a tart like you.'" —Becky

BECKY AND BILL
AFFAIR

"I was in Jamaica and happened to witness the affair. It was really heart wrenching for me because it was the ultimate breach of a contract that we had behind the scenes. You cannot take it that far, you can't go there. And then to try to explain to the roommates was excruciating. They didn't understand. They were ready to mutiny, saying, 'That's real, too.' It was, but there's also a loss of objectivity. Bill, to his credit, said, 'Look, I understand, I made a mistake and I'm going to resign.'" —George Verschoor, producer/director

GLUED TO THE TUBE

Living in the 'Real World'

HO'D EXPECT MTV to be the place for a taste of "The Real World"?

Yet there it is, in all its interpersonal incompre- Don't believe the hype types: This new 13-epi- (debuting Thursday y past the channel's cele- upation with image, tak- side the heads and hearts ts trying to get it togeth- ong in this confounding

o take seven totally dif- rs from seven different

New York,

10012

MTV: When it comes to 'The Real World,' life is soap opera

ued from Page A12

rray and Bunim — she's a n soap producer, he has a and documentary back- d — proposed this "reality " instead.

hen you get six or seven esting personalities togeth- hings will happen," said n Corrao, MTV's vice pres- for development, an in- enthusiast. "You don't to write it."

with other forms of reality ramming, an increasingly lar way to fill air time, the gs show up on the bottom "The Real World" costs be- n $100,000 and $110,000 episode, which makes it the expensive half-hour of regular programming on MTV but still cheaper than a traditional scripted drama.

Once the network gave the go-ahead in November, the producers launched their search for the project's two central elements: the people and the place.

After visiting and rejecting several dozen locations, the producers found this building downtown and broke through the walls of two adjacent apartments to form a single, vast four-bedroom loft — one that few artistic young wannabes could actually afford to rent, even en masse.

Both home and set, the plac has been bugged, with 14 mik set into ceilings and night table in addition to the wireless on the participants wear. The phones have been tapped so that viewers can hear both sides of conversations. In an adjacent work space with a separate entrance, a crew of up to 13 people at a time puts in 10-hour shifts surrounded by dubbing racks, a sound-mixing console and swags of cable.

The residents of Loftland are a deliberately diverse collection: three women, four men. Five whites and two African Americans. Six people already living in or around New York and, at 19 the baby of the bunch, Alabamian Julie Oliver. Three musicians,

Of the 500 people the produ ers auditioned, 15 made the fin cut and were subjected to half dozen on-camera interviews.

"They were asked the most i timate questions we could thi of, to see if they were willing share their lives," Murray said

Sharing lives will not be pa ticularly lucrative, at least n directly. MTV pays for the lo and for food. Each member the "cast" receives $100 a we for walking-around money and $1,300 check at the end of t 13-week experiment, $2,600 tal.

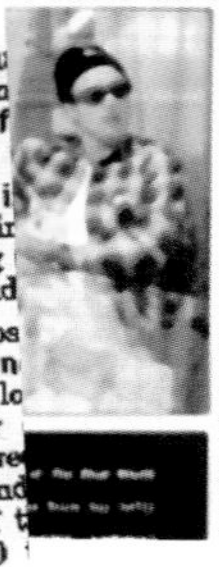

CABLE

Real life, real strangers at the center of 'The Real World'

By DIANE JOY MOCA
Daily News Staff Writer

They didn't need actors or writers. They didn't even need scripts.

All Mary-Ellis Bunim and John Murray needed when they set out to create a hip version of a soap opera were a few cameras and seven willing young adults.

After three months of taping, "The Real World" emerged — a weekly reality series full of humorous moments, dramatic tensions and contemporary attitudes.

Combining the techniques of documentary filmmaking and a rock 'n' roll score, the new half-hour program follows the adventures of seven real-life strangers ages 19 to 25 who agree to move into a Manhattan loft together and have a camera record their every move. The original series infuses the fast-paced style of MTV with the traditional elements of a soap opera — ongoing stories, interesting characters, dynamic relationships and intriguing cliffhangers.

Among the seven strangers in "The Real World" is Becky the singer.

rest of their life," said Lauren Corrao, vice president of series development at MTV. "It's all you ever think of when you are in college — What am I going to do when I get out in the real world? All of them are in a sort of transitional period that is completely identifiable to our audience."

If MTV decides to continue "The Real World" after its initial

MTV GETS REA

Stars of rock channel's new soap opera aren't actin

6394D

BY MIKE DUFFY
Free Press TV Writer

Eric is geeked. He can't believe it.

And no wonder. When "The Real World" begins, a stunned and bedazzled Eric Nies has just encountered the rambling, 4,000-square-foot duplex loft that will be his home for the next 13 weeks.

It's in the heart of Manhattan's artsy downtown SoHo district, your basic adventurous person's life fantasy come true. F there are a few con tions. Six to be exac will be sharing this urban space with a m ages 19 to 25. Four they'll cry, they'll ge

13 weeks in a rambling

Relationships will op. Feelings will be There may even be love in the air.

For "The Real you see, is a soap real life. No actors, n al scripts, no g make-believe. This people who hav brought together b and who agreed to eras follow them ar record their everyd

"I kind of expect kind of crazy and o trol, and it was," sa

UPDATE ANOTHER REALITY

Perfectly mismatched on *Real World,* Julie Oli and Heather Gardner have true roomie chemis

▲ From left, Kevin Powell, Andre Comeau, Oliver, Eric Nies, Gardner, Norm Korpi and Becky Blasband groove in their new *World.*

➤ Julie (left, with Heather in members her TV fears: "It w Good, bad, ugly. Be gentle, t

DOES MTV'S COOLER-THAN-COOL, louder-than-Louds documentary, *The Real World,* have you nervously biting your remote control waiting for the next of the 13 weekly installments (concluding Aug. 13)? Are you ravenous to know if Julie and Eric's coy flirtation will ever, like, *get real?* Or if racial tensions between Eric and Kevin will explode? Or if any of the loft's incongruous inhabitants, the seven twentysomething roommates recruited by producers, then tossed together, will ever do the dishes?

Fast-forward to now. The show's in the can. The reekingly trendy SoHo space was dismantled last month. The four men and three women have departed for life without cameras and, mostly, without each other. But check out Julie and Heather. They're TV perfect in contrast: Wide-eyed Julie Oliver, 19, is a native of Birmingham, Ala., the youngest of seven children ... er a retired lighting-company executive, mo... housewife). She was an unambitious student at racially mixed Shades Valley High School but has been an eager dancer since she was 9. And big-mouthed Heather Gardner, 21, is from Jersey City, N.J., the oldest of three kids of divorced parents (father manages a frozen-food warehous mother is a nurse). She was Lincoln High School senior-class president but dropped out of St. Peter's College in Jersey City to be a rap singer. Practically *The Patty Duke Show!* Heather and Julie—who started off rockily but found they shared a subversive sense of humor—are living toget er again. Call it *The Real Real World.*

Exterior: Town house in Jersey City (across the Hudson from Manhattan)
Interior: A clothes-strewn one-bedroom apartment ($725 a month)
(Subject: TRUTH)
Heather: You're a liar. She is

MTV gets in touch with reality

There's a lo under this sc comfortable w

Throughout cast members tails about th other during views. The ac rally as viewe ing to pursue Big Apple, an folds spontane mates discuss a to mind, from reer goals.

"They are all what they're go

Heather: Nothin *Julie:* Yeah. We We don't eat the eat Chinese food *Heather:* I don't *Julie:* [During th be sittin' there wi

THE REAL WORLD: MTV's REAL HIT

Hey, you take what you can get.

When MTV's real-life soap *The Real World* debuted in May, it was criticized for only featuring kids in the arts—designer Norman, dancer Julie, singer/songwriter Becky, writer Kevin, model Eric, rapper Heather and guitarist Andre.

"Frankly, we didn't have a lot of young brokers from Wall Street come forward," quips Cocreator/Producer Mary Ellis Bunim. "Maybe in the next round."

Yes, *The Real World* is more than a one-hit wonder: Bunim and partner Jon Murray are talking with MTV about a second series, she says, possibly set in California ... and possibly using some of this series's "stars."

"I've been told it's the highest-rated show on MTV," she notes proudly. But MTV's not only hot for the show because of ratings: Bunim relates that it has turned MTV fans from zappers to "appointment viewers."

And the music channel hypes it further with *The Real World* marathon weekend, airing episodes one through seven back-to-back 11 a.m.-2:30 p.m. Saturday and 1:30-5 p.m. Sunday.

But it's not only fans who are smitten with the show. According to Julie Oliver, "The experience was so great, I would definitely do this again.

"It's like I have a family up here [in New York] now," says the Alabama native. "Eric and I are extremely close, and Heather and I are incredible friends. I've moved in with her in Jersey."

So what can we expect in the next six episodes? After the girls take a weekend romp in Jamaica in episode eight, Bunim promises the depth that critics complained was lacking in the opening shows.

"These kids let their hair down and they're really quite frank about their differences," she notes, from Norman talking about his gay life to Kevin sharing his experiences as a young black man.

"I can guarantee you that the networks are going to watch and see what happens with this show," she adds. "A lot of attention is being paid to how this evolves and whether it forges new ground on how to create drama." ■

By Karen Condor

Julie, why'd you do it? "I just wanted to be able to say, 'This is how I am—the good, the bad and the ugly.'"

Seven loft dwellers in search of reality

6394D

By PAULA SPAN
WASHINGTON POST

NEW YORK

footage is ... llory re- ... lches and ... f "Whose ... s half a ... g.

people ... s rather ... ks. The ... en cam- ... cording ... s, mu- ... ly col- ... sound- ... Roses, ... called ... le hy- ... opera, ... that ... de 2

...ray, ... deo ... uilt ... y'll

genic, although a squad of carpe cleaners was required the next day.

All of which reassures Murray an co-executive producer Mary Ell Bunim, who's in Los Angeles editin the resulting tide of videotape, tha their concept, "a group of young peo ple living in a loft together in New York City pursuing their dreams," is viable genre.

Originally, MTV was interested in an actual soap opera, the kind requiring scripts and actors, aimed at its core audience of 18- to 24-year-olds. But writers and actors cost money.

Murray and Bunim — she's a veteran soap producer, he has a news and documentary background — proposed this "reality serial" instead. "When you get six or seven interesting personalities together, things will happen," explains Lauren Corrao, MTV's vice president for development, an instant enthusiast. "You don't have to write it."

The residents of Loftland are a deliberately diverse collection: three women, four men. Five whites and two blacks. Six people who were already living in or around New York and — after auditions in Austin, Texas, and Birmingham — Alabamian Julie Oliver, at 19 the baby of the bunch. Three musicians, various other fledgling performers and artists.

Of the 500 people the producers auditioned, 15 made the final cut and were subjected to half a dozen on-camera interviews before filming

To be young, gifted and taped by MTV

Twentysomethings live life on-camera

By Tim Goodman
Staff writer

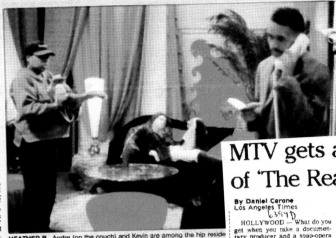
HEATHER B., Andre (on the couch) and Kevin are among the hip residents...

Consider it life with a really cool soundtrack.

MTV keeps on the cutting edge by delivering "The Real World," 13 weeks in the life of seven young men and women sharing a SoHo loft in New York. The docudrama unfolds tonight with two half-hour segments shown back-to-back.

MTV originally wanted to air a drama in the "Beverly Hills 90210" mold, but "The Real World" creators pitched this idea: Take four males and three females (two black, five white), ages 19-25, who don't know each other from Adam or Eve, and put them in an ultra-hip four-bedroom loft in New York.

The cameras rolled 60 hours each week. Every conversation, every argument and every kiss was filmed.

"Yes it's contrived," said Mary-Ellis Bunim, executive producer and one of the show's creators. "We're not saying this is a documentary or pure verite." Bunim and co-creator Jonathan Murray did it because it was "a fascinating look at a group of twentysomethings." Bunim said. "And to create a hybrid drama. It was extremely experimental. You don't see kids scripted this way in dramas."

The group includes a female rapper, a poet/writer, a couple of musicians, a male model and enough hipness to fill Madison Square Garden. "I think each one of these kids is unique," Bunim said. The seven were chosen from 500 who either responded to MTV's East Coast search or were rounded up in dance clubs, health clubs or record stores, Bu...

in New York — because someone "who would re... the typical urban kid" S...

TV PREVIEW

What: "The Real World"
When: Tonight, 10 p.m.
Where: MTV

Getting Real

MTV puts its own demographic in a fishbowl

by Wes Eichenwald

...zzy aquarium ...postmodern ...ety of snazzy ...sidence. It's ...rium that we ... loft for the ...exclaims, jaw ...sion of par... ...him and six ...uths.

...exactly the ...'s take on ...isodes pre... ...at on Sat... ...half-hour ...7:30 p.m., ...undays at ...urdly the ...n MTV... ...d dream ...personal ... cool to ...free for ...r demo-

...twentysomethings. But they figured that they might as well go for as much reality as possible. Thus, producers Mary Ellis Bunim and Jon Murray (with backgrounds in daytime soaps and in news and documentaries respectively) set about capturing this reality through hundreds of hours of filming. Although the result may not be high art, it's worthwhile as a glimpse of how 1990s young adults relate to one other and to the outside world. With the pressure of paying the rent (or living with the folks)

DREAM WORLD: what kind of reality is a rent-free loft in SoHo?

temporarily the freedom wanted to be

The Real three wome said fully f them for 13 stipend. In ... erywhere e streets to th to clubs. The are involved media-relate sampling of th erage MTV grow on you.

The Real W home-movie camera angles background moments rather unmistakable ductors, to be boring is a gre When you g appropriate...

are ... ter... scrib but thre dorm orde male chai suppo com Kevi nove Mar recor rock desig very But Julie, 'baby

---

MTV gets a dose of 'The Real World'

By Daniel Cerone
Los Angeles Times

HOLLYWOOD — What do you get when you take a documentary producer and a soap-opera ...ducer and ask them to de...

"We set up the situation purposefully so there would be conflict and sexual tension," said Jon Murray, 38, a veteran news and documentary producer. "The loft was a real pressure cooker. I mean, there

---

MTV's 'Real' cr...

By Phil Kloer
TELEVISION CRITIC

MTV continues to move away from being just video wallpaper with an attitude. From political reporting to AIDS awareness, MTV is getting real. And real interesting.

In one of the stranger ideas ever tried for TV, the cable network recruited seven young adults, strangers to one ...her and stuck them in a lavish New...

Juli... has le... Heather long-ha... hunky sexual ... singer/ writer.

Th... race a charac... new h... ...tle, is essen... opera. Although... ray says that the television ca... edges that it's as entertainm...

To that en... real-life to p... viewing. Mur... to ask one of... example, and... roommates t... chance to h...

Despite... the action... ray says, "... cameras ... to score o...

Committed to video: some heavy-duty flirting, a falling-out that almost leads to a fistfight, political disputes during New York's Democratic Presidential primary and one guy admitting that he's bisexual.

How do these storylines play out? All Murray will say is that "we have a couple of episodes that remind me of the second season of thirtysomething."

—David Lieberman

A Slice of Reel Life

...ith The Real World, MTV has ...eated a new program genre: ...soap opera rooted in reality. ...hat a concept!

...ake seven young, attractive artistes, ...put them up for three months in a lo-...for loft in New York's trendy SoHo dis-...t, throw in a camera crew to chronicle ...ir every move, edit the footage with the ...ck-cut pacing of a music video, add a ...k soundtrack, and what do you get? A ...w weekly MTV series called The Real ...rld (Thursdays at 10 P.M. [ET]).

The show's premise is somewhat simi-...to PBS's An American Family, the ...dmark 1973 documentary series in ...ich a TV production crew took up res-...nce with the Loud family to capture ...ir everyday lives on film. The differ-...e is that The Real World, despite its ti-

Real World is Jamaica: free of the SoHo ...n (in creases) enjoy an MTV-arranged ...aribbean vacation.

> "The morning after *The Real World* premiered the MTV switchboard was inundated with calls from kids who wanted to be on the show. Then letters began to pour in from kids who identified with particular cast members. Julie got the most mail, some actual proposals of marriage.
>
> "When we announced casting for the second season, 10,000 applications poured in. By season three we were up to 30,000. The ratings were doing the same thing too...up, up, up.
>
> "The press coverage was intense and we finally realized that *The Real World* had achieved a mainstream acceptance when we were parodied by *Saturday Night Live*, and the first season's episodes were installed in the Museum of Broadcasting."
>
> —Mary-Ellis Bunim and Jonathan Murray, executive producers

Love and the Loft Dwe...

The producers of MTV's bal-lyhooed new series "The Real World," — a documentary about life in a SoHo loft — have finally filmed some romantic footage. But it was not what they expected.

The producers had been hoping for some romantic involvement among the loft's residents — seven men and women ages 19 to 26 who agreed to live together and be filmed for 12 weeks. Alas, no sparks ignited among the inhabitants.

But no one had factored in the presence of the crew.

During the filming, the Jamaica for away. "They guys that we said Bill Ric... show's dire... smitten with Rebecca Bla... and I had be... other, so in s of months. W the weekend Unfortun bers were no to the cast, le with them on land.

Now Mr. R asked to leav have a camera "Becky and T night," he sai shot of us kiss good terms. W little bit on ca "It's a funny

---

It's a real young world at MTV

GET 'REAL'

New MTV program blurs boundaries between real life and soap operas

By James Ryan

LOS ANGELES — Its title is "The Real World," but MTV's stab at a reali-ty-based soap opera is anything but.

The youth-oriented music-video network paid seven non-actors between the ages of 19 and 25 $200 a week to move into an ultra-hip, giant-sized loft — equipped with 60-gallon aquarium, pool table and sleek furniture — in New York's trendy SoHo district to allow "The Real World" cameras to capture their every trial and tribula-tion.

The first of 13 24-minute installa-tions (each culled from 50 or so hours of weekly taping) airs tonight at 9.

A number of national media critics have taken "The Real World" to task for its lack of reality, many drawing unfavorable comparisons to the famous

1973 PBS documentary series "An American Family," which chronicled the daily life of the Loud family and its tumble into dysfunction.

Yet MTV and the producers of "The Real World" maintain that documenta-ry-like veracity was never their inten-tion, and the comparison is unfair.

"We were approaching this as a hy-brid between documentary and...

musician, a dancer, a writer, a graphic artist and a singer/songwriter. Not banker, lawyer, accountant or garbage collector in the bunch.

Bunim says it wasn't their intention to cast a purely artistic group; that's just the way it turned out. "When we started this search we were after diversity," she explains. "It just sort of came out this way...

MTV, Making Its Own Reality

In a SoHo Loft, a Cast of Roommates in a Round-the-Clock Soap

By Paula Span
Washington Post Staff Writer

NEW YORK — Dinner is a dud, footage-wise. A lot of desultory requests for napkins, a few belches and conversation on the order of "Whose Gato-... feeds half a loaf of Italian bread to

voltage gathering tonight, the young and the list-less.

Executive producer Jon Murray, watching the proceedings on video monitors from the control room built into the rear of the loft, isn't worried. It's only 9 p.m., for one thing. "They'll loosen up," he says. "Their prime hours are between midnight

...be the fi... ...e narra... ...mix. Jul... ...g dance ...droppe... ...ity to b... ...a simila... York ...rd," h

Heather

"After the show, I signed a talent-development deal with MTV, to form my own thing, like Eric (host of *The Grind*). Nothin' ever happened with it, but I used the money to open my own beauty salon, Nubian Nails & Hair, in Jersey City. Then me and my producer, Kenny, decided to press up a record. We mailed it to different DJs, and a label called. So I got a deal with Pendulum Records. The new album's called *All Glocks Down*. I feel better these days, my mind is not so scattered. I mean, I have money, I'm not afraid of my phone being turned off, my lights. I got a place by myself in Jersey City. I love my hometown, I want to live here the rest of my life."

Heather's recently released CD single, *All Glocks Down*

where

Julie

"I'm living in Alabama, with my parents, teaching jazz and ballet at a private school. There're only two teachers—me, and my old dance teacher, so we're really busy. I'm also working with handicapped children, trying to help them get out into the world. I'm staying at home with my folks. My dad got sick last year. He's doing well now, but I'm glad to be at home, to be around my family."

Kevin

"Right now, I'm doing 20 different things. I'm a staff writer at *Vibe*, which is a music magazine. I've done five cover stories, the latest one on Tupac Shakur. I get so much mail from these stories! I think *The Real World* helped me a lot. It gave me visibility, more than the average twenty-something has. It's really hectic. I had to change all my numbers.

"I'm still livin' in Brooklyn, working for *Vibe*, and hosting an HBO show called *Vibe/Five*, doing interviews with people like Laurence Fishburne and John Singleton. I really got bit by the camera bug after *The Real World*. I hosted MTV's *Straight from the 'Hood* right after the show, which I loved. Then *Vibe* called, and I needed a steady check. It's been an outlet onto TV. I'm doing HBO *E-news*, and I'm working on a script. *The Real World* is responsible for this—it got me to see the power of the visual medium. I studied political science at Rutgers, now I'm doing music videos. I

are they now?

want to write, direct, and produce feature films, and I still continue to write. I edited an anthology this year called *In the Tradition, An Anthology Of Young Black Writers*. I've also been on the lecture circuit for about two years, talking about Generation X and *The Real World*."

VIBe

This is my last interview. If I get killed, I want people to have the real story.

TUPAC SHAKUR

JAILHOUSE EXCLUSIVE
THE VIBE Q BY KEVIN POWELL
Jimmy Jam & Terry Lewis
Naughty by Nature
Inside the New
South Africa
Malik Yoba

MTV NETWORK

FREELANCE

MTV Staff I.D.

SIGNATURE

recognize

poems by
Kevin Powell

Kevin's recently published collection of poetry

33

Becky "I'm living in Denver now with my boyfriend, John, who used to be the lead singer with the band The Fluid. I met him at a concert in Los Angeles. I'd never seen a performer like that since Jagger when I was 16. They were part of the grunge thing coming out of Seattle then, and they were going to be really big. Iggy Pop was smitten with them. Then they signed with Hollywood Records, and it all fell apart. Now he's having some success with modeling. We're moving to New York in July or August."

Norman

"I still keep a room in New York, but I live in LA—I came here to exploit the resources. LA embodies everything America wants to be, what it can be—it's America's ultimate city. It's always evolving. I'm making art now, using architecture and landscape. In Michigan, where I grew up, there's nothing mentally challenging—the lack of stimuli motivated me to start painting. I have a studio—my landlord is this recluse that is like 80 years old who dresses up in a hedgehog outfit and a different hat every day. I also take my easel up into the hills. Why do I paint? I'm making something for humanity, for posterity. It's a constant struggle to find the ultimate voice. I've always maintained that I will not grow old, only continue to grow grander. Life is a big adventure."

Andre

"Since leaving the loft, he has been living with the members of his band, Reigndance, in their communal house in New Jersey. 'The band's been getting better gigs and bigger audiences...But other than that, everything's exactly the same.'" –*ENTERTAINMENT WEEKLY*, August 7, 1992

Eric

"I have tremendous plans. They're huge. My plans and stuff for the rest of my future are really, really big, and I mean they're underway, and they're in motion right now, but I'm not at liberty to speak about 'em. I love doing *The Grind*. It's a lot of fun for me. I love the kids on *The Grind*. They got big hearts. They're all working hard. Everybody's smiling, having a good time. And that's what's important to me. I don't enjoy being in uncomfortable situations where people aren't having a good time. That's what I'm all about—having a good time. Keep a smile on your face. And be happy. I'm even considering changing my last name to Nice. It's already started. We have a clothing line coming out. We're going to have Nice jeans."

From Eric's new workout video, *MTV's The Grind Workout*

Name: Aaron
Born: 2/20/71
Hometown: Orange County, California
Education: BA economics, UCLA
Career Goal: Certified public accountant with "Big Six" accounting firm
Job: Accountant
Living Situation: Newport Beach, California
Favorite Group: Jane's Addiction, Public Enemy, Indigo Girls, Blind Melon, Cypress Hill

AARON

Name: Beth A.
Born: 8/7/70
Hometown: Eugene, Oregon
Education: Aviation maintenance, Lane Community College
Career Goal: "To join Los Angeles Police Department, Juvenile Correction division"
Job: Craft services
Living Situation: Hollywood
Favorite Song: "In–A–Gadda–Da–Vida," Iron Butterfly
Favorite TV Show: *Beverly Hills, 90210*
Favorite Snack: Sugar
Romantic Involvement: "Married!" to Becky
Car: Toyota Celica

BETH

Name: Beth S.
Born: 2/14/69, "Valentine's Day"
Hometown: Garfield Heights, Ohio
Education: BFA, acting/BBS TV, film and radio, Ohio University
Career Goal: "Well-fed starving actress"
Job: Starving actress
Living Situation: "Less complicated"
Favorite Song: "I Will Survive," "To Be Real," "Upside Down," "I'm Coming Out"
Favorite Group: "Cleveland Society of Poles and, of course, The Cleveland Indians
Favorite TV Show: *Melrose Place, Friends, Mad About You*
Favorite Snack: Weight Watchers Chocolate Mousse bars, Ben and Jerry's Chocolate Fudge Brownie yogurt with M&M's on top
Romantic Involvement: "In love"
Car: Black 1993 Toyota Celica GT

BETH

GEORGE

Name: David
Born: 4/23/71
Hometown: Washington, D.C.
Education: Duke Ellington School of the Arts, National Conservancy of Dramatic Arts
Career Goal: "To become a good stand-up comedian"
Job: Stand-up comedy, film, and TV
Living Situation: Shares a Los Angeles condo with wife Jeanette
Favorite Song: "Can You Stand the Rain?" New Edition
Favorite Group: Miles Davis, A Tribe Called Quest
Favorite TV Show: *Cops*
Favorite Snack: Cashew nuts
Romantic Involvement: Married to Jeanette
Car: 1980 280Z Classic

DAVID

Name: Dominic
Born: 11/12/68
Hometown: Dublin, Ireland
Education: "Catholic education"
Career Goal: "Hat model"
Job: "Hack"
Living Situation: Pasadena, California
Favorite Song: "Anything by Ringo Starr"
Favorite Group: Beatles, The Rolling Stones
Favorite TV Show: *The Larry Sanders Show*
Favorite Snack: Marlboros
Romantic Involvement: "Apparently single"
Car: A Mazda and a Harley

Name: Glen
Born: 4/20/70
Hometown: Roslyn, Pennsylvania
Education: BA in communications, La Salle University
Career Goal: "To make music and movies"
Job: Working at temp agencies between touring with Perch
Living Situation: Apartments in San Francisco and LA, and parents home in Pennsylvania
Favorite Song: The Tigger song from *Winnie the Pooh*
Favorite Group: Perch, Delilah
Favorite TV Show: Anything on PBS
Favorite Snack: Rice Krispie treats
Romantic Involvement: Has a girlfriend
Car: Ford conversion van and a Nissan Sentra

Name: Irene
Born: 8/14/67
Hometown: Covina, California
Education: Two years studying fashion merchandising, Mt. San Antonio
Career Goal: "To stay a deputy sheriff for 10 to 15 years and then retire"
Job: Deputy Sheriff
Living Situation: House in Covina with husband Tim and son Corey Alexander
Favorite Song: "The one my husband wrote and sang for me at our wedding"
Favorite Group: Jon Brennan
Favorite TV Show: *Friends*
Favorite Snack: Rocky Road ice cream
Romantic Involvement: Married to Tim
Car: Nissan Quest

Name: Jon
Born: 7/30/74
Hometown: Owensboro, Kentucky
Education: Davies County High School
Career Goal: "To be a successful recording artist"
Job: "Being a traveling singer"
Living Situation: Owensboro, with parents; Nashville, with manager
Favorite Song: "It changes every day. Right now, it's 'Pick-Up Man,' by Joe Diffie"
Favorite Group: Alabama
Favorite TV Show: *Seinfeld*
Favorite Snack: Hot Tamales and Kool-Aid
Romantic Involvement: "No, unfortunately"

Name: Tami
Born: 4/17/70
Hometown: White Plains, New York
Education: AA speech, Santa Monica College
Career Goal: To have her own talk show
Job: Singing
Living Situation: Home in New Jersey, with husband Kenny and daughter Lyric Chanel
Favorite Song: "Save the Best for Last," Vanessa Williams
Favorite Group: Female
Favorite TV Show: *New York Undercover*
Favorite Snack: Salt and vinegar potato chips
Romantic Involvement: Married to Kenny Anderson of the New Jersey Nets
Car: BMW M3

REUNION EPISODES 1 & 2: One year later, the NY roommates reunite at the loft. They catch up, they eat, they dance. They discuss where they are—Eric's hosting <u>The Grind</u>, Julie's still dancing, Norman is pursuing his career as an artist, Becky is singing and tending bar, Kevin is writing, Heather has opened a hair salon, and Andre's still pushing Reigndance. They talk about the struggles the new cast is in for... Across town, Dublin-native Dominic, a journalist, meets Tami, a singer. They drive an RV to Kentucky, to pick up Jon, a young, Christian, country-western singer. They watch him sing and sign autographs at Goldie's, where he is a big fish in a small pond. They hit the road,

Jon, Dom, + Tami get to know each other on the road to Los Angeles (episode 2)

detouring at Graceland. EPISODE 3: En route to Los Angeles, the trio eat bull's testicles for dinner and debate religion over breakfast. They stop in Vegas before hitting Venice, where they meet Aaron, a surfer/accounting major at UCLA; Beth S., a production assistant; Irene, a cop; and David, a comic. Beth's cat and Dom's dog do not get along. EPISODE 4: The animals fight, the roommates fight. David doesn't like Jon's Confederate flag, Jon doesn't like David's taste in music. They almost come to blows. Beth S. takes everyone to a party where they are not welcome, and Dom is pissed. Animosity runs rampant in the house. EPISODE 5: David is attracted to Tami; they get tattoos together. Tami goes on <u>Studs</u>, but loses, despite trying to rig

Tami on <u>Studs</u> (episode 5)

the outcome. A house bowling outing ends badly when David loses his temper. They call a house meeting, but nothing is settled. EPISODE 6: Aaron takes Dom to UCLA. Beth S. decides she

Bowling night turns bad (episode 5)

wants to be an actress and goes on casting calls. Jon sleeps till noon every day, then hangs out with Irene (whom he calls Mom) and her fiancé, Tim. Jon sings well at the Western Connection. EPISODE 7: The guys gang up on the girls, the girls have major attitude, and everyone's tense. David's game of pulling off covers turns nasty when Tami is exposed in just her underwear. She reacts, saying she might press charges. EPISODE 8: The incident divides the roommates: the guys don't understand what's going on, and the girls want David out. He confronts them, but they won't back down. He's asked to leave. He does so, going on tour with his comedy routine. EPISODE 9: The house needs a new roommate, and they choose Glen, a singer in a rock band. He shares a room with Jon; they play basketball; they go see a band called The Inspiral Carpets. EPISODE 10: The roommates take a trip to Joshua Tree. They are all unhappy and exhausted; Dom thinks the

The gang after an Outward Bound course in Joshua Tree National Park (episode 10)

trip's "pointless and dangerous." Working together, however, proves unifying. Tami announces she is pregnant. EPISODE 11: Tami's mom admonishes her: Tami works in an HIV clinic and should know better than to have unprotected sex. Still, her mom is supportive and goes with Tami for the abortion.

Aaron's girlfriend, Erin, visits (episode 11)

Tami opens up about the months she and her mom were homeless; how they always have and always will take care of one another. Aaron's girlfriend Erin visits. EPISODE 12: Irene has a picture-perfect wedding, with all of her housemates

Irene's wedding (episode 12)

in attendance. Beth finds a "Men of Westwood" calendar featuring a beefcake shot of Aaron-with-surfboard and plasters copies all over the house. Aaron is displeased. EPISODE 13: With Irene's departure the house gets a new roommate, Beth A., who does catering for films. She and Jon get on very well, even when she wears her "I'm Not a Lesbian but My Girlfriend Is" T-shirt. Though Jon's never met a lesbian, he's comfortable with Beth A. Tami is not. EPISODE 14: Dom goes home to Ireland to visit his family. He spends time with his parents and pub-crawls with his siblings. Back in LA, Jon enters a country-music contest and wins the semifinals. EPISODE 15: Beth S. gets headshots to boost her acting career, in vain. Tami goes into the recording studio with a tough producer. She goes to a psychic. She goes to technical school. She (briefly) has her mouth wired in order to lose weight. She quits her job at the HIV clinic. EPISODE 16: Jon is offered a film role, but he's not comfortable with the idea. He goes home and sings at Goldie's, before family and friends. It's hard for him to leave. EPISODE 17: Glen's band, Perch, descends upon the house. They laze around all day, throw parties, and put on a baffling slideshow. The house is not pleased. Jon competes in the finals of the music contest and wins. EPISODE 18: Beth S.'s old boyfriend visits; it's awkward. Her new boyfriend visits with more success; Beth S. denies the rumor that she had oral sex in the closet. Tami and Tootie go out and break

Perch in the house— Where's Tami? Hide the knives! (episode 17)

up. Dom and Tracey drive around on his motorcycle. Jon goes to the rodeo; Beth A. goes to a gay square dance. The house throws a party. EPISODE 19: The house takes a trip to Cozumel, Mexico. Glen and Beth A. share a room, as do Dom and Aaron. Tami, Beth S., and Jon hang out by default and are angry at the cliques that seem to be forming. The boys dress in drag at a pool party, Dom passes out in the sand, and Beth S. crashes her moped. EPISODE 20: Beth S's mom, a radio personality known as The Polish Voice of Cleveland, comes for a visit. She cleans, she cooks, she shakes her head. Beth A. teaches Beth S. to box. The house plays Paint-Ball, a survival game, where

The gang goes horseback riding in Cozumel (episode 19)

they shoot one another with paint pellets. EPISODE 21: The house puts on a showcase at the club, Night Winds. Dom acts as MC, Jon sings, as do Tami and her group Reality. Glen and Perch take the stage, chastising Tami's group for lip-synching. EPISODE 22: The housemates get ready to move out. It's especially hard for Aaron, who has to study for finals and graduate from UCLA. The group nitpicks to the very end. A few tears, but not much emotion. Jon leaves the house as he came, with a "Yee-ha!"

Aaron has to finish up classes amidst the chaos of moving out (episode 22)

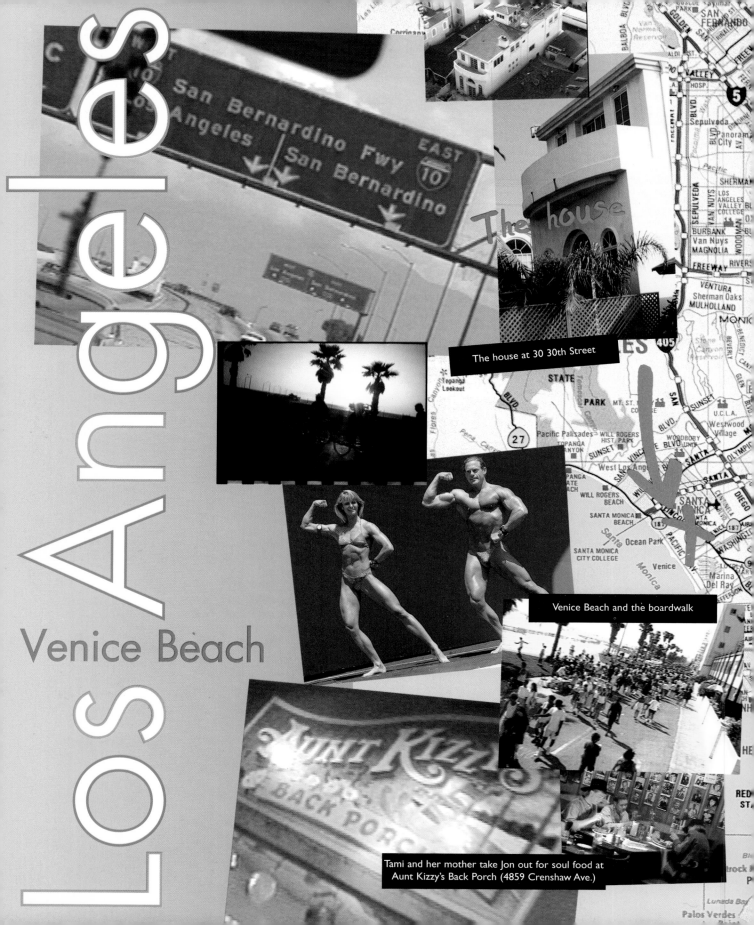

Los Angeles

Venice Beach

The house at 30 30th Street

Venice Beach and the boardwalk

Tami and her mother take Jon out for soul food at
Aunt Kizzy's Back Porch (4859 Crenshaw Ave.)

Troubadour

One of Dom's hangouts for seeing new bands
(9081 Santa Monica Blvd.)

David performed stand up at Laugh
(8001 Sunset Blvd.)

Aaron takes Dom on a tour of the
UCLA campus in Westwood

Tami and her Studs date, Kenya

A favorite watering hole of
Aaron and Dom's

NightWinds

Western Connection

The house put on a showcase at Night Winds
(1026 Wilshire Blvd., Santa Monica)

Jon's country home in the big city of Los Angeles
(715 East Eighth Street)

Aaron decided not to
take part in this book.

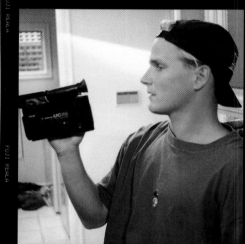

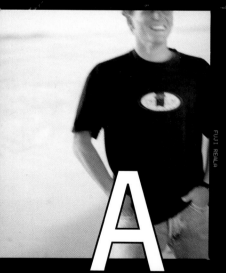

Aaron

"He's a very educated, intelligent,

fun person. He's right on, he's the

"You can never be right with Aaron—he's always right." —Irene

sh*t, he's really neat. I'd call him a

"Aaron may be afraid his new 'business' image isn't compatible with what he thinks is his
'surfer/hunk/frat boy/*Real World*' image. But while everyone enjoyed watching him surf, they also
responded to his strong values and conviction. He got trainloads of mail from interested women, most
of whom wanted to marry him." –Mary-Ellis Bunim, executive producer

liberal Republican—though he'd

"Aaron had nothing to gain by doing The Real World. But he did it, and had a great time.
Now he's in the tie-and-jacket world where rising talents aren't supposed to be on MTV."
—JON MURRAY, EXECUTIVE PRODUCER

probably be offended that I said

"Aaron's more conservative than I am. I understand his views on why welfare and
affirmative action shouldn't exist, even though I don't agree with them. He's a Ronald
Reagan/George Bush kind of guy, and I'm a Jimmy Carter/Bill Clinton person." –Dave

that. But he has really good views." —Beth A.

"She was very attractive on camera, and it was always a pleasure to photograph her because she had a great face and moved quite well and carried herself well, and it's really fun when that happens."
—Van Carlson,
Director of Photography

Beth A. and her dad

KODAK TMX 5052   KODAK TMX 5052

37A   38   38A   E   39

I'M NOT GAY, BUT MY GIRLFRIEND IS

NUCLEAR FREE ZONE

"I learned a lot about women from her, even though she's a lesbian." —Glen

"I did not like Beth A. I thought she was insincere. I think the only reason they put her on the show was because she was a lesbian, and because they knew that would piss me off. I have nothing against lesbians, but I used to go around saying 'God, don't bring a lesbian in this house.' It was like a pet peeve. So they bring in Beth A., and she has absolutely no other facets besides being a lesbian. It's her claim to fame, that and the whole gay rights thing. She's not the only lesbian in the world."
—Tami

10 AM CITY HALL MAY 1st

46

Firefighting 1978

"The only kind of picture you can get is how people bounce off madness."

Beth A.

West Hollywood, California
April 1995

KODAK TMX 5052

"I went to the memorial for Pedro here in Los Angeles. That was the first time I really felt proud to be a part of this. I felt honored that I got to be there. Judd and Pam, those are beautiful people. Norman came rushing from the airport, but he was late, and he ended up standing outside and couldn't get in. He'd established a relationship with Pedro.

"I'm excited about the all-cast reunion. I didn't think I'd be that excited, but I've changed my attitude after the memorial.

"I was happy with the way I was portrayed in the show. I felt I was portrayed as a positive lesbian role model. I didn't have an old lurid paperback title pinned to me. It wasn't sensationalized in that way.

"Tami was the only person I didn't get. She was an aggressive, rude person. I'm an adult, I'm thinking my grandmother is going to watch this show, I can't knock her head off. We had one friendly conversation the whole time she was there. When there's one rotten egg, the whole batch is spoiled. When the show aired, I couldn't believe she looked so nice. The first thing everyone said when they met me was, 'Watch out for Tami.' Everyone was afraid of her. She was very physically aggressive. That time she confronted me about leaving my things on the bathroom counter, what you didn't see was that I'd just spent an hour scrubbing that bathroom.

"I liked Beth S. I understood where she was coming from. You can choose to understand someone, if you have any heart at all. She never had anyone telling her she was okay.

"Beth remains an enigma— a beautiful, elusive woman who chose the moments she shared with our cameras." –Mary-Ellis Bunim, executive producer

"In the afterbirth I look at it as a positive experience. I'm glad I did it."

Beth S. and her mom

Venice, California April 1995

Beth S.

In college

Her sister's wedding

"When we had the paint-ball battle, everyone got into their fatigues, got their guns, and said, 'Let's get Beth S.!' I thought, 'Watch out. You're dealing with a woman who has been oppressed and enraged.' And she kicked their butts!" —Beth A.

"The Rolonda Show called me and said, 'Would you like to be on Rolonda, for a show about roommates?' I asked who was going to be on, and they said, it's supposed to be you and Jon Brennan. I called Jon and he called me back and left a message saying, 'Beth, I think this is a setup, because I've never heard anything about it. Watch out.' But I had already left.

"I would have refused, but by the time I heard that it was David who was going to be on, I was feeling trapped. The Rolonda Show had messed up our reservations, so my boyfriend had paid for our hotel. I felt like I had to do the show.

"That was my first and last talk show. David acted like the perfect performer/comedian. He had a lot of people in the audience, and they were the ones who stood up and asked questions. I just tried to give them nothing.

"We had a lot of problems. Maybe it's because we were all performers. I have no idea, really, what it was. We wouldn't have lasted one night together if it weren't for the show. Nobody respected anybody else. Where can you go from there?

"After the show ended, I got this call on my birthday from a friend, saying, 'Beth, you're in a skin magazine.' Yes. So I ran down to the newsstand and find this magazine. Dominic had written all this really nasty stuff about me. Who does he think he is? Dom and I never hung out. He doesn't know who I am, I don't know who he is."

THIS AREA IS BEING USED BY BUNIM-MURRAY PRODUCTIONS FOR TAPING OF A TELEVISION PROGRAM. BY YOUR ENTRANCE INTO THIS AREA AND YOUR PRESENCE, YOU GIVE UNQUALIFIED CONSENT TO BUNIM-MURRAY TO RECORD, USE AND PUBLICIZE YOUR VOICE, ACTIONS, LIKENESS AND APPEARANCE IN ANY MANNER IN CONNECTION WITH THE PROGRAM. IF YOU DO NOT WISH TO BE TAPED AS PART OF THE PROGRAM, PLEASE EXIT THE AREA UNTIL ALL TAPING HAS BEEN COMPLETED.

"The whole dating thing is very weird. If I were interested in 17- or 18-year-olds, I'd be set. The guy I'm seeing said he was apprehensive at first about dating me because of some things he saw on the show. Of course, when he got to know me, he saw I was different. When people meet me, they end up liking me."

Age 4

"She was selfish and self-centered." —Glen

"Beth S. may have gone too far on the night of the Tami–David incident, but generally I thought the rest of the cast didn't give her a break. She might have relaxed if they had tried to get to know her."

-Mary-Ellis Bunim, executive producer

DAVE

North Hollywood, California
March 1995

"Was the show fun? Who would put up with that kind of hell for 'fun'? The worst thing about being on-camera was adjusting to <u>not</u> being on-camera. It makes you paranoid, but then you miss it. But it helped me with other projects. The on-camera experience was wonderful.

"At first, I didn't even really want to be on the show. I've had an amazing journey out of D.C. I left home at 14; I had problems with my mom. I was in foster homes, then I lived with my neighbor. I went to a theater conservatory to study comedy for two years, then to Chicago for two years and began working. When I came out to Hollywood, I lived in the YMCA. My best friend, Dave Chappell, took me to a <u>Real</u> <u>World</u> audition. I took the personality test, and that was cool, and they offered me the show. I was like, 'What I got to do?' and they told me I'd be getting free rent, visibility, and some money. Hey, it got me out of the YMCA. I'd been in LA two months, and it really seemed like God was talking to me. He was. I had a great time.

"I have no resentment—not anymore. That blanket incident didn't blow over immediately because the girls decided to position themselves like they did. When I was asked to leave, I was terrified, heartbroken. What would happen to my credibility? I had so much animosity at the time, all I could do was concentrate on my career. I knew I had three months before the show aired. I changed managers, prayed a lot, moved to a tiny Hollywood apartment with no radio and no TV, and began to work my butt off. I auditioned for <u>House</u> <u>Party</u> <u>3</u>, and gave it everything I had. I got the part. I also did <u>Def</u> <u>Comedy</u> <u>Jam</u>, The Apollo, I was just pushin' to the max before any bad press hit. When it did, I was on the set of <u>House</u> <u>Party</u> <u>3</u>, and everyone was like, 'Man, you got a raw deal.' Hell, I could of told them that! So I had to make a change again, I had to really be on my toes. I didn't do any press, I didn't talk about it, I didn't whine, I just focused on my career.

"I HAVE NO ANIMOSITY ANYMORE, BUT DO HAVE A LOVE-HATE RELATIONSHIP WITH THAT SHOW.

I loved the crew. I used to do silly sh*t, like walk them into walls or come out of the room naked. I was just bein' myself, bein' controversial."

"Dave knew exactly where the camera was. When the camera showed up, Dave was on, and when it went away, Dave shut up. Early on, I really enjoyed his humor and especially the guys he hung around with—they kept us going as a crew. It was just a riot to follow them around. We spent an afternoon on Melrose with Dave, when he got his tattoo, and that was just a blast. Because of his style of humor, Dave was able to push everyone's buttons—he could push our buttons, as well. His problem was, he just didn't know when to stop."
—Van Carlson, director of photography

"I'm not sure that Dave ever understood that the living situation was real; that it was not a fictional show where the producers could do a quick rewrite if a character got in trouble."

—JON MURRAY, executive producer

"Dom was the Bad Boy." —Tami

"A very wise person for his age—very wise about life." —IRENE

"Dominic was the first person cast in the second season. Everyone instantly recognized his charisma, his verbal acuity, his wonderful sense of humor, and how funny his hair was." —Mary-Ellis Bunim, executive producer

"Dominic always likes to tell me that it wasn't *The Real World* that made him bitter—he was always bitter. It'll be interesting to see how he changes when he gets the fame and recognition his talents will eventually bring him." —Jon Murray, executive producer

"He has a real flair for life. He's a great person, very outgoing, an intelligent, nice person. He's hysterical, he's a fun person—not American!" —Beth A.

"No comment."

—DOMINIC

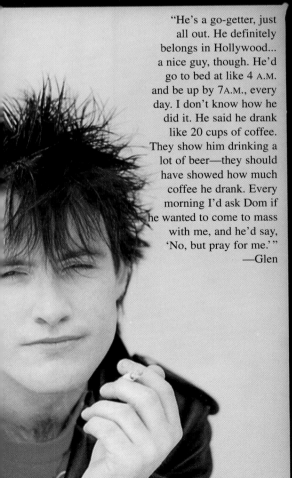

"He's a go-getter, just all out. He definitely belongs in Hollywood... a nice guy, though. He'd go to bed at like 4 A.M. and be up by 7A.M., every day. I don't know how he did it. He said he drank like 20 cups of coffee. They show him drinking a lot of beer—they should have showed how much coffee he drank. Every morning I'd ask Dom if he wanted to come to mass with me, and he'd say, 'No, but pray for me.'"
—Glen

REALA ▶ 10

Dominic decided not to take part in this book.

FUJI REALA

REALA ▶ 11

"I felt Glen was very false, that he did things only for the show. When he first came for the interview, I felt he'd been prepped; that he had all the right answers. I felt like they told him 'get in good with Tami and you'll get in with the others,' so he started making me breakfast every day, kissing my ass...until he got in good. Then the breakfasts stopped." —Tami

High school graduation

GLEN

"Glen sent in an application tape where he let his two young nieces make him up for the audition. They smeared eye shadow, lipstick, and rouge from ear to ear, and he wasn't at all self-conscious, he was very funny. We thought Glen could be a possible replacement for Dave, after Dave was asked to leave. The cast obviously agreed; they chose him from the three guys we sent in." —Mary-Ellis Bunim, executive producer

RECYCLE RECICLE

KEEP OUR BEACHES

ROSLYN, PENNSYLVANIA / MARCH 1995   "The person I really love the most from the show is Beth A. She's a great, great person. When I came on the show as a replacement, I felt a lot of pressure. When Beth A. came on, I felt more comfortable. I could hang out with her and her friends and feel relaxed because there was no sexual stuff. I also really like Dominic, he's a go-getter. I have respect for what he's managed to do. He's an honest family person. And we're both Irish. And we're all the youngest brothers in our family: me, Dom, Jon, and Aaron. I thought that was kind of meaningful, all of us being the youngest boys. Aaron's a great guy, too. We've stayed in touch—he feels like a brother to me. He's really honest and funny and sarcastic, not arrogant at all. But being on the show didn't help him, in terms of his career.   ·   I was really hurt when Jon turned against me because I became friends with Dom and Aaron. I'm a very God-centered person; I go to mass three times a week, but they were already portraying Jon as 'the Christian,' so he started looking at me like I was the partyer. But last time I spoke to him, he was much more open. Beth S. annoyed me at times. She was too showy. I'd get disappointed in her and Tami for making the show glamorous. Why? They didn't give themselves the time to really grow. Irene came off tough, but she is actually very sweet, and she found a good man to marry; Tim is a very nice guy. One-on-one, everyone was cool. The only person I didn't get that from was Beth S. When I first got to the house, I made an effort to talk with everyone, and I spent about two weeks hanging with her, but we just didn't get along. I had just the opposite experience with Dom and Aaron. I got close with them only after fighting.   ·   I liked the crew better than I liked my roommates. I'm convinced this show can only be done with the crew they have. They're all amazing. The only thing is that the show does wear on you. I thought everyone would forget about us, but they didn't, and that's helped and hurt the band. Nobody takes us seriously because of the show, the industry holds back. Another thing is being under the microscope. If you're having a bad day, word gets out and you're labeled a jerk. I vowed to my friends and family that if I got on the show, I'd be as honest as I could; that if my hair looked awful some morning, I was just going to leave it looking awful and be myself. But it's tough, being away from friends and family, not having those people to turn to. **It's like *1984*, being on-camera all the time. If you even dare think it's going to be shown around the world, you just become paralyzed.** "

"Glen and I hung out together. We're still friends. In Cozumel, we shared a room. [The crew] would unlock the door in the morning and sneak in with the camera, hoping to catch us at something. We'd just say, 'Sorry.'" —Beth A.

Age 9

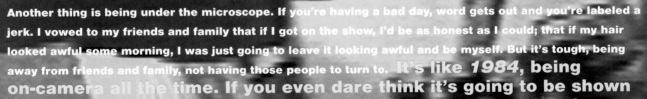

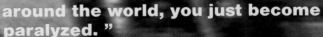

Irene

"We always felt like she was the mom because she was the oldest and because she was getting married." –Tami

Covina, California
March 1995

"It was actually really funny that I wound up on *The Real World*. I'd never heard of it before. The producers wanted someone in law enforcement and put flyers at work. I didn't know what I was getting into when I started the interview process. It all happened within three weeks. I slid right in. I asked Tim if it was okay, and he was more excited about it than I was! And I thought it would be fun. I wanted my wedding to be on TV, like Princess Di. But MTV didn't pay for the wedding or anything; that wouldn't have been ethical.

"I'm not really in touch with anyone from the show but Jon. We talk all the time. People say he was mooning over me, but that's not true. I was the only other one close to being normal in that house, so we attached to each other. We both come from tight families with church associations, and because of that we felt comfortable around each other.

You can't get to know someone in 22 minutes, and then you're only on for five of those minutes.

"For me, *The Real World* was living with a bunch of kids. Only me and Tami had regular jobs; all our schedules clashed. It got to where I had to sleep in the closet—it was the only room that had a door! Lucky I was only there three months.

I think I would've shot somebody if I had to stay longer– just kidding!

"People didn't really get a chance to have sex—they had to do it out of the house. There was lots of alcohol, but no drugs. They really background you and choose people that haven't done that. One thing that did change, however, was that Jon cusses a lot now. He came into the house this straight country boy and left with a whole new vocabulary."

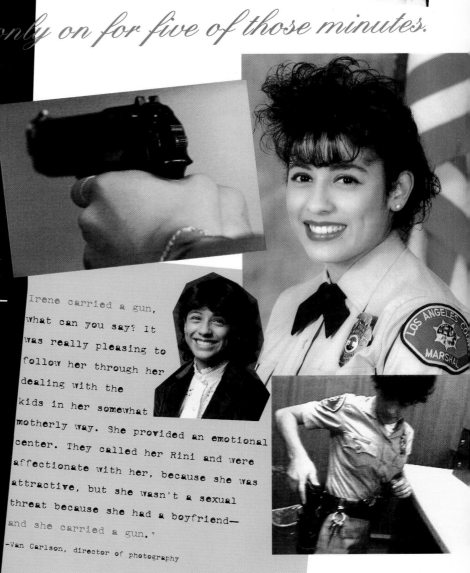

Irene carried a gun, what can you say? It was really pleasing to follow her through her dealing with the kids in her somewhat motherly way. She provided an emotional center. They called her Rini and were affectionate with her, because she was attractive, but she wasn't a sexual threat because she had a boyfriend— and she carried a gun."
—Van Carlson, director of photography

JON

**Owensboro, Kentucky
March 1995**

The Owensboro Bar-B-Q is one of the places where Jon performs for his hometown fans

Garth Brooks and Jon in Jon's favorite photo

"The show made me out to look judgmental, but I had a relationship with everyone. Not like the rest of them. If the purpose of the show was to get to know all the other cast members, then I was one of the only people who succeeded. It's a shame. 'Was it real?' is what everyone always asks me. Well, they edit it to make sense. For instance, you didn't see what led up to the Tami and David thing. Still, I'd say it was a pretty fair representation. So it is 'the real story of seven people...' living with 20 cameramen. You're supposed to have zero contact with them, but these are human beings, and it's hard not to say, 'how ya doin'?' What bugged me most about being on-camera all the time were my zits. I look at myself on TV and say, 'Am I that ugly?' Then again, it helped me be loose in front of the camera.

"In a lot of ways, I really felt alone in that house. Beth A. had an apartment, so did Dom, a lot of the others had boyfriends or families or whatever. Sometimes they wouldn't come home. Me, I was always there, kind of like the watchdog. I knew everything that went on in that house.

There was a lot of stuff I had seen before, but I don't think the experience really changed me. It opened my eyes and basically reinforced my morals.

"We had a joke: one of the surveillance cameras was trained on the couch in the pool room, which was in position to look at the TV set. Our joke was that the surveillance camera just had a burned-in shot of Jon asleep on that couch. Days would go by and that's what he would do. He'd watch that country music station."
—VAN CARLSON, DIRECTOR OF PHOTOGRAPHY

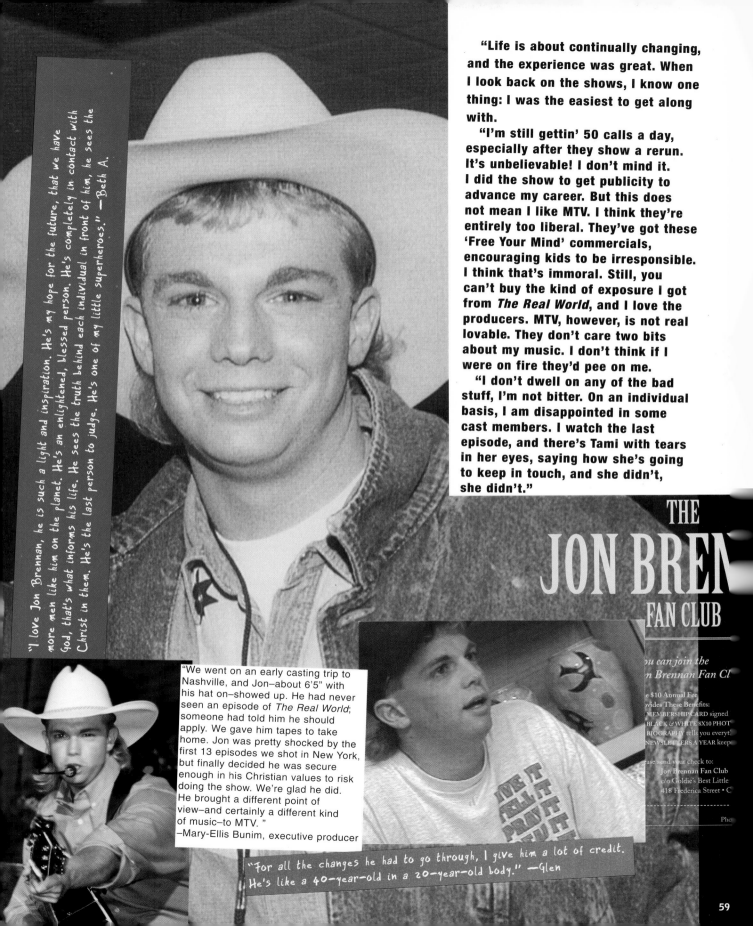

"I love Jon Brennan, he is such a light and inspiration. He's my hope for the future, that we have more men like him on the planet. He's an enlightened, blessed person. He's completely in contact with God, that's what informs his life. He sees the truth behind each individual in front of him, he sees the Christ in them. He's the last person to judge. He's one of my little superheroes." —Beth A.

"Life is about continually changing, and the experience was great. When I look back on the shows, I know one thing: I was the easiest to get along with.

"I'm still gettin' 50 calls a day, especially after they show a rerun. It's unbelievable! I don't mind it. I did the show to get publicity to advance my career. But this does not mean I like MTV. I think they're entirely too liberal. They've got these 'Free Your Mind' commercials, encouraging kids to be irresponsible. I think that's immoral. Still, you can't buy the kind of exposure I got from *The Real World*, and I love the producers. MTV, however, is not real lovable. They don't care two bits about my music. I don't think if I were on fire they'd pee on me.

"I don't dwell on any of the bad stuff, I'm not bitter. On an individual basis, I am disappointed in some cast members. I watch the last episode, and there's Tami with tears in her eyes, saying how she's going to keep in touch, and she didn't, she didn't."

THE
JON BREN
FAN CLUB

...ou can join the
...n Brennan Fan Cl

...e $10 Annual Fee
...vides These Benefits:
...MEMBERSHIP CARD signed
...BLACK & WHITE 8X10 PHOT
...BIOGRAPHY tells you everyt...
...NEWSLETTERS A YEAR keep...

...ase send your check to:
...Jon Brennan Fan Club
...c/o Goldie's Best Little
...418 Frederica Street • C

Pho...

"We went on an early casting trip to Nashville, and Jon—about 6'5" with his hat on—showed up. He had never seen an episode of *The Real World*; someone had told him he should apply. We gave him tapes to take home. Jon was pretty shocked by the first 13 episodes we shot in New York, but finally decided he was secure enough in his Christian values to risk doing the show. We're glad he did. He brought a different point of view—and certainly a different kind of music—to MTV. "
—Mary-Ellis Bunim, executive producer

"For all the changes he had to go through, I give him a lot of credit. He's like a 40-year-old in a 20-year-old body." —Glen

59

"I give her credit for being tough. I think she's got a big heart but is afraid to show it. I also think she was using the fame to become a star. She wasn't very honest around the cameras, but I guess you could say the same about me." —Glen

KODAK 5115 PPA
KODAK 5115 PPA
KODAK 5115 PPA

Female
(Tami re-named band)

"When Tami got her jaw wired, I thought, how disgusting that a beautiful young woman would do that, and on television. I lost all hope for her. She had the chance to be a role model, and she had a responsibility she didn't take. —Beth A.

Climbing at Joshua Tree

TAMI

Washington, D.C. April 1995

60

'Why did I do <u>The Real World</u>? Hmmm, why did I? I had watched the first series, in New York, and thought it would be cool to live with a whole new batch of people. Most people I knew already would consider me cold or arrogant or the b-word, so I thought it would be good to start fresh. And I did learn a lot about myself, not so much from being on the show but from watching. I saw I could be brash or mean and realized I had to curb that, be a little nicer. Still, I stand behind everything I did on the show. I mean, it was me.

'I think <u>The Real World</u> was stressful at times—it had its goods and bads. You have to get used to a camera following you all the time, you have no private time. You're forced to interact when you don't want to. Then again, you come away with something you remember for the rest of your life. When we all left, I really felt in my heart we'd all created a bond. I kept in touch and sent cards and things of that nature. But then people go back to their own lives, and you don't keep up. I know some people are bothered that I haven't been.

'I do like Jon, I really do. We've kept in touch so much at first, but now he's been on the road, and I've been doing the album, but he's great— a great entertainer. We hung out a lot with Beth S., especially toward the end, but that was basically because the house had formed cliques: Dom and Aaron, and Glen and Beth A., so that left me and Jon and Beth S., but she was really irritating actually. I used to look at her and think, how did you get on this show? She was everything they said they were not looking for: an actress, and real crabby at it, she didn't have a job. And she pissed me off with that damn cat. I'm allergic, and she just shows up with it.

'I have a lot of facets to me, but they want each person to be a character, so I had to be the bitch... at least I'm good at it.

'It's been two years since our season aired. At first, I was like, 'Why show this and not this?' but I'm not angry. I understand they have to make it good TV, and what they showed <u>was</u> me. I wasn't being false when I did it. I think anyone who's not real to begin with will start acting fake once they get on the show. They turn into someone else. I felt like I stuck out like a sore thumb because I was myself. I had some good moments, but I also felt I came off as really shallow, like when I did <u>Studs</u> and I tried to set it up. Now that's pretty bad, but the way they put it together on <u>The Real World</u>, it made it seem like I was a major jerk, that I ditched the guy immediately after we lost. And that's not true... we dated for quite a while after that.

So I guess that comes back to haunt me a little. That, and the incident with David. What I also hear about a lot is the abortion, and my quote on the show saying I was not about to get married. Well, all that's changed. And something else: when I was talking about those butt pads, I don't need those anymore; I got instant baby butt.'

Jon Murray, executive producer: "We never anticipated the roommates kicking someone out of the house. We tried to be fair to everyone involved. We gave David some money to help him get an apartment. We tried to show the incident and its aftermath without drawing conclusions for the viewer–we wanted everyone to draw their own conclusions."

Dave: "I'm cool now, my life goes on, but what hurts me is the word *rape*. I mean, some people didn't see all the episodes, and they hear that about me, and they think I did that. That really hurts. What's really bad is, if you listen to the tape, you can hear Irene say, even before Tami's getting all upset, 'I'll call the cops and say it was rape!' I mean, what is that? Still, the controversy fueled my edge."

Mary-Ellis Bunim, executive producer: "Tension had been building in the house for weeks between Beth S., Dave and Tami. But they all went too far that night. They lost perspective and control of the situation."

Irene: "What people didn't realize is I could see the hallway—I knew what was going on. And I could see David's side of things, to a point. But you have to take into consideration Tami's position. Her choice was to laugh, because everybody's watching—TV cameras, the people in the control room. But afterwards, she was pissed. It was really embarrassing. A lot of girls don't come forward, they don't say anything. David should have stopped when she asked him to, but he was raised a different way, and he just didn't understand. In my work, they can come down on people just for hugging—someone might be offended. There's just not a lot of ways to interpret it. And I was offended. I would've kicked his ass right there. Tami was going to, too, and I wouldn't have stopped her. I couldn't if I wanted to, she's so much bigger than me. But I didn't like what Beth S. did; shouting 'Kick his ass!' only added gas to the fire. She should've taken Tami aside instead of screaming. Tami left that night—she was gone two days.

"I can't compare it to when Beth S. pulled the covers off Dom. It's apples and oranges. Dom was drunk, and he really didn't care. And I heard David talk about Tami and how he wanted her...and he wanted her bad. The only way he was ever going to see her half-naked was to pull those covers off her, so he had an ulterior motive. If you look on one of the tapes, David is saying, 'I'm gonna get you, Tami,' and he meant it. I saw it happening, but the audience didn't, not day to day."

Tami: "I got a lot of flak for that, especially from black people, saying, 'Why'd you kick him out? He's a brother!' But it wasn't just that incident. He started fights with Beth S. all the time, he tried to choke Jon. And that was something that always bothered me: when he was trying to choke Jon, all the guys ran in and pulled him away. Why didn't they do that for me? After saying no 60 times, you'd think they would've pulled him off of me, but they didn't."

Beth S.: "When I got mail about the David incident, really slamming me for it, I was so upset that I wrote everybody back, and I actually got apology letters. • You have to understand, David was in the house for two and a half weeks. You get the impression, watching the show, that it was months. Every day something was happening with him. It was every day. He choked Jon on the third day we were in the house, for God's sake! I'm sorry, I just don't want to live with someone who's pulling his pants down all the time. He had too many chances, as far as I'm concerned. • That first fight was four hours long. A lot of things were said. I said, at one point, in context, 'You have the mentality of a rapist if you don't believe that when a girl says no it means no.' Then he took off with, 'She just called me a rapist!' • I had the flu. I had a fever of 103. That's why I was sniffling, I wasn't crying about him. And that thing about me seeing Dominic in his boxer shorts, that was totally different. He used to walk around in his shorts all the time. He couldn't even get up the stairs that night, we had to take his clothing off and put him in bed. That's what had just happened."

HOW FAR IS TOO FAR?

Irene's Wedding

Irene & Tim
March 27, 1993

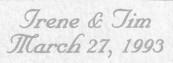

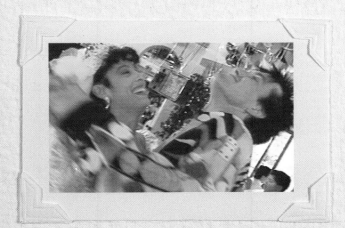

Dave

"I'm on the road, doing stand-up. I married Jeanette this spring, and we're livin' in the Valley. I'm not in contact with anyone from *The Real World*, though I did meet Beth S. on *Rolonda*, the roommates-from-hell show. The audience abused her, but they loved me. Hey, I'm livin' my life, it's cool. But the show does have legs. I had to move three times because people kept calling. It's really cultish. Every time I turn on the computer, we're on-line. It's weird."

Performing at The Comedy Store in Los Angeles, May 1995

David with his new wife, Jeanette

where

Beth S.

"What am I doing now? I lost my cat. Somebody swiped him in Santa Monica last October, so I'm frantically looking for my cat. I'm still doing freelance production work, mostly on music videos and commercials. And I'm acting. It hasn't helped as far as acting because people know me as Beth S. from *The Real World*. I'll be in a shopping mall and these young girls will follow me from store to store, whispering, 'Go on, say something to her!' My friends get really annoyed. When I go back to Cleveland, oh my God! Sometimes there are crowds. Everyone is nice. I try to talk to them. Sometimes it's a little much. Let's talk about you, or me, not about whether or not I masturbate!"

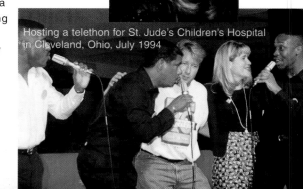

Hosting a telethon for St. Jude's Children's Hospital in Cleveland, Ohio, July 1994

66

Dominic

Dominic is working as a freelance writer. He is an editor at *Film Threat* magazine and a movie reviewer for *Sassy*. He also writes screenplays.

...ting cameras in their home for several months.
...wer, **Dominic Griffin**, is one of seven roommates
...zed in the ground-breaking 1993 MTV documen-
...show called *The Real World* that chronicled the
...enice, California, roommates by putting cameras
...me for several months.

...career began in 1974 with a stint as
...ic columnist. For a brief period, Loud
........led ....years
.... Records
.... D. Not
........................) sales,
.... is work
...ared in *Details*, *Entertainment Weekly*,
...cate and *Vanity Fair*.
...n, a writer prior to his *The Real World*
...me to the United States from Dublin
...at age 17 in search of a suntan yet still
sports a Casper-the-ghost-like complexion. A student of Shakespeare, Yates and Joyce, Griffin
never dreamed he could make a living as a writer
but is trying real hard; he's the senior editor of
Film Threat and has written for *Us*, *Daily Variety*,
...azine, *Hits*, *Album Network* and *Hypno*.

Irene

"I'm still working in the courts. My aunt takes care of our son Corey Alexander, five days a week. I like being at work, but I miss the baby. When he was first born, I thought I wanted to stay home. I found out I can't be a mom all day long—I need to keep busy. [Husband] Tim works at the courthouse also, but not where I work. We're very happy."

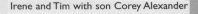

Irene and Tim with son Corey Alexander

are they now?

Glen

"I've been preparing two months to go on my first tour with Perch. We're going everywhere but the Midwest, in a van. And Jon Brennan gets to travel by bus! But we're very excited. Kim Adams from the Whiskey (in LA) is doing the booking. She doesn't have very much experience on the East Coast, but I'm putting everything in God's hands.

"Did you know you can get beat up for being on *The Real World*? I was at The Gate, a club in L.A., and these guys came up and took my drinks and then said they were going to kill me because I had been on *The Real World*."

Beth A.'s wedding, Lincoln City, Oregon—June 24, 1995

"Getting married was the most amazing thing I've done in my whole life. It was also the most frightening—like being on top of a rollercoaster and looking down and just going swoosh! I had to keep reminding myself that it was my day, to slow down and enjoy it.

"It was a really small wedding, 13 guests. We put everyone up in a cabin in the woods in Oregon. We were surrounded by trails with 10 waterfalls all around. We took our vows in front of Silver Creek Falls. It was so beautiful.

"Being a newlywed feels incredible. We made such a strong commitment; we were able to let go of any expectations we had and go deeper. It's like, 'Alright girlfriend, this is fun!'

"Otherwise, my best friend Nikko and I have a craft service business. We provide holistic food on sets. We do a lot of music videos. We spend so much time together that we tend to pick up conversations out of nowhere, things we started days before. It confuses people.

"I'm getting involved working with people in prison, getting them nondenominational literature. It came out of my anger at the system we have. Locking people up in prison makes them worse, not better. It's time for conscious change. It's really important to start seeing the whole person. I'm involved in this through my church, it's called the Prayer Ministry for Incarcerated Persons. That's what's really moving through me right now.

"I have a good life. I have a nice home, lots of animals, enough money, and a wonderful wife."

Beth A.

Beth A. and wife Becky

69

Performing at this year's Owensboro Bar-B-Q festival

Jon

"I'm livin' with my family right now. It's cheaper. I got no girlfriend and no car. I'm drivin' my brother's pickup, but I'm gonna have to give that back.

"I been workin'. I opened for Shenandoah, Tim McGraw, Blackhawk. They don't expect much from me because I don't have an album out yet, but the audience loves us. I am about to sign with a major label. The Nashville Network calls me the 'MTV Cowboy.' Most big producers in the country music business don't know *The Real World*, but they know who I am. They say things like, 'Ain't you the guy with the hat who lived with all those people?'"

Aaron

Aaron is currently working as a certified public accountant with a "Big 6" accounting firm in Orange County, California.

Tami's Mom

Tami's Baby

At Tami's wedding, August 26, 1994

Tami, Kenny, and daughter Lyric

Tami

"I'm working with my group, Female, which are the same girls you saw on the show. We've got a record coming out on Mercury Records. We're doing the video and photo shoots and everything right now, and it's taking all my time. I've been in D.C. five days a week for three months—I only get to go home to New Jersey on the weekends. I do really miss my daughter [Lyric, born September 30, 1994]—sometimes I feel I'm missing the most valuable bonding time with her, and it's kind of depressing. My mom takes care of her while I'm away. My husband, Kenny Andersen, is there. We got married last August. A mutual friend of ours set us up, and we just, well, we dated three months and got engaged. He's a point guard for the New Jersey Nets. Before I met him, I didn't follow any basketball. Now, I'm the biggest basketball freak in the world. We're both busy people, but our home life's pretty private."

70

San Francisco
1994

Name: Cory
Born: 8/28/73
Hometown: Fresno, California
Education: Studying communications, UC San Diego
Career Goal: To teach high school English, photography and video production
Job: Student loans and Dad
Living Situation: Shares house in Del Mar with two guys and one girl
Favorite Song: "Good Enough," Sarah McLachlan
Favorite Group: Indigo Girls, Sarah McLachlan
Favorite TV Show: *My So-Called Life, Party of Five*
Favorite Snack: Healthy: apples and cottage cheese. Unhealthy: chocolate
Romantic Involvement: None
Car: 1987 Mazda 626, four-door. "It's inconspicuous—I speed and I don't get tickets"

Name: Judd
Born: 2/12/70
Hometown: Long Island, New York
Education: BFA, University of Michigan School of Art
Career Goal: "World domination and/or cartoon characters who will outlive me"
Job: Cartoonist
Living Situation: San Francisco
Favorite Song: "Mr. Tanner," Harry Chapin ("one of 30 favorites")
Favorite Group: They Might Be Giants
Favorite TV Show: *M*A*S*H, Law And Order, The Simpsons, St. Elsewhere, Hill Street Blues*
Favorite Snack: Snapple iced tea
Romantic Involvement: A special woman
Car: "Boxy, simple, safe, white Mazda Protege 323"

Name: Jo
Born: 7/8/71
Hometown: London, England
Education: Studying geology at Santa Barbara City College
Career Goal: Marine geology
Job: Marine Technology Department, Santa Barbara City College
Living Situation: Santa Barbara, California
Favorite Song: "Bodhisattva Vow," Beastie Boys
Favorite Group: Beastie Boys
Favorite TV Show: "I don't watch TV"
Favorite Snack: Carob raisins
Romantic Involvement: "Always"
Car: Skateboard

Name: Mohammed
Born: 3/28/70
Hometown: Washington, D.C.
Education: English major, UC Berkeley
Career Goal: "Music is already a career." Wants to write more, and write and direct films
Job: "Mostly music, some writing" Also on the lecture circuit, speaking on African-Americans in the media, African-Americans and AIDS, and spoken word
Living Situation: In San Francisco, with best friend Will
Favorite Song: "Adore," Prince
Favorite Group: George Clinton and Parliament, Steely Dan
Favorite TV Show: Doesn't watch TV ["I don't even have cable, only primitive TV"]
Favorite Snack: Pancakes
Romantic Involvement: On and off with Stephanie
Car: No car. Rides a mountain bike

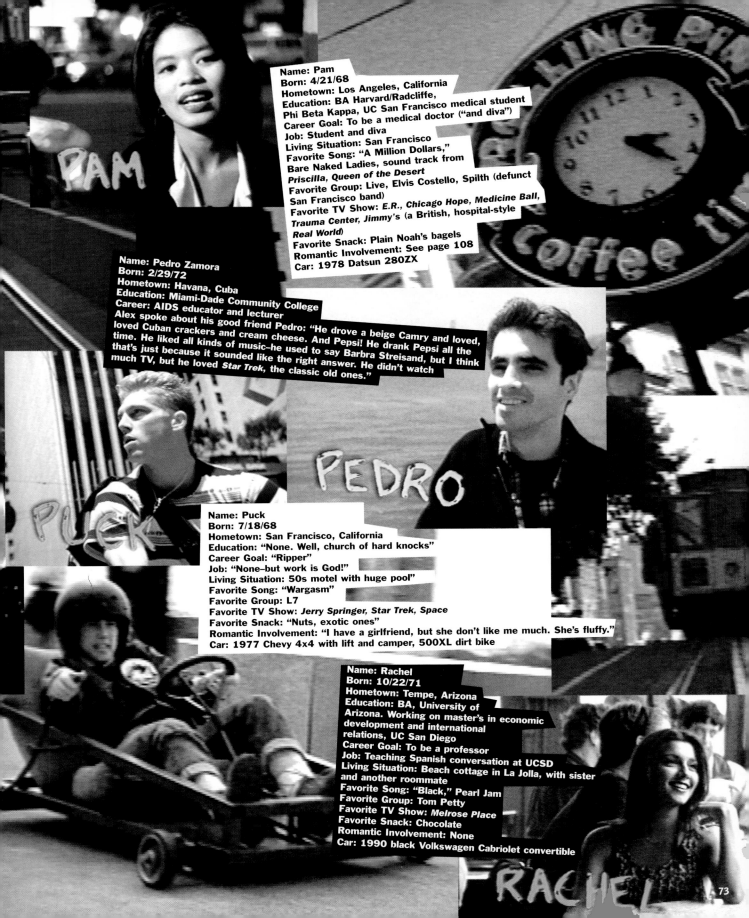

Name: Pam
Born: 4/21/68
Hometown: Los Angeles, California
Education: BA Harvard/Radcliffe, Phi Beta Kappa, UC San Francisco medical student
Career Goal: To be a medical doctor ("and diva")
Job: Student and diva
Living Situation: San Francisco
Favorite Song: "A Million Dollars," Bare Naked Ladies, sound track from *Priscilla, Queen of the Desert*
Favorite Group: Live, Elvis Costello, Spilth (defunct San Francisco band)
Favorite TV Show: *E.R., Chicago Hope, Medicine Ball, Trauma Center, Jimmy's* (a British, hospital-style *Real World*)
Favorite Snack: Plain Noah's bagels
Romantic Involvement: See page 108
Car: 1978 Datsun 280ZX

Name: Pedro Zamora
Born: 2/29/72
Hometown: Havana, Cuba
Education: Miami-Dade Community College
Career: AIDS educator and lecturer
Alex spoke about his good friend Pedro: "He drove a beige Camry and loved Cuban crackers and cream cheese. And Pepsi! He drank Pepsi all the time. He liked all kinds of music–he used to say Barbra Streisand, but I think that's just because it sounded like the right answer. He didn't watch much TV, but he loved *Star Trek*, the classic old ones."

Name: Puck
Born: 7/18/68
Hometown: San Francisco, California
Education: "None. Well, church of hard knocks"
Career Goal: "Ripper"
Job: "None–but work is God!"
Living Situation: 50s motel with huge pool"
Favorite Song: "Wargasm"
Favorite Group: L7
Favorite TV Show: *Jerry Springer, Star Trek, Space*
Favorite Snack: "Nuts, exotic ones"
Romantic Involvement: "I have a girlfriend, but she don't like me much. She's fluffy."
Car: 1977 Chevy 4x4 with lift and camper, 500XL dirt bike

Name: Rachel
Born: 10/22/71
Hometown: Tempe, Arizona
Education: BA, University of Arizona. Working on master's in economic development and international relations, UC San Diego
Career Goal: To be a professor
Job: Teaching Spanish conversation at UCSD
Living Situation: Beach cottage in La Jolla, with sister and another roommate
Favorite Song: "Black," Pearl Jam
Favorite Group: Tom Petty
Favorite TV Show: *Melrose Place*
Favorite Snack: Chocolate
Romantic Involvement: None
Car: 1990 black Volkswagen Cabriolet convertible

EPISODE 1: Cory, a college student, rides the train from LA to San Francisco with Pedro, a Cuban AIDS educator; bike messenger Puck bombs through the streets of San Francisco—and is arrested before he can reach the house; Judd, a cartoonist from Long Island, is already there, as is Rachel, a Republican applying to grad school; Pam, a medical student; and Mohammed, a musician and writer. When Pedro announces he is HIV+, everyone except Rachel is cool with it.

The Puck at house night (episode 9)

Cory looks for work in a coffeehouse (episode 7)

EPISODE 2: Puck blows "snot rockets" and refuses to shower. Pedro is disgusted; Rachel is enamored. She and Puck flirt, buy wigs, and tool around San Francisco. On Valentine's Day, the house forms a Lonely Hearts Club and eat a garlic-laced meal at the Stinking Rose. EPISODE 3: Rachel goes to an "Empower America" benefit and meets her idol, Jack Kemp. Mohammed reads poetry at his dad's club. Pedro meets Sean, another HIV+ AIDS educator. The house has a group poetry writing session, explaining who they are. EPISODE 4: The house hangs out together, all except Puck, who feels like everyone's picking on him. He invites the house to his soapbox derby, but only Rachel attends. Pedro has a birthday breakfast. EPISODE 5: Judd is dogged about finding work as a cartoonist and gets a gig at the San Francisco Examiner. He also makes the rounds in Hollywood with ideas for an animated series. Mohammed performs with his band, Midnight Voices. Pam discusses her eight-year, long-distance relationship with Chris. EPISODE 6: Rachel and Puck flirt and engage in petty jealousies. Rachel has two girlfriends visit; Puck hits on one, Judd on the other. Pedro and Sean fall in love. Puck makes gay jokes at Pedro's expense. EPISODE 7: Cory looks for work in a coffeehouse, but settles for one in retail. Pam keeps long hours at med school. Cory dates Geoff, a friend of Puck's. Puck finds a lost puppy, posts flyers, and finds its owner. EPISODE 8: Pedro has a checkup—his T-cell count is down. He continues his speaking engagements, including one at Stanford. Puck and Rachel and Cory go beachcombing at Inverness. Judd, Pedro, and Pam and her boyfriend, Chris, spend the day in the park. EPISODE 9: The tension between Pedro and Puck mounts. The house begins to take sides. Pedro and Sean become engaged. EPISODE 10: Rachel and Puck kiss and fight. Puck meets Toni, they date, they decide to get married. He further alienates himself from the house by not caring about anyone else's needs. At Mohammed's birthday dinner, the topic of conversation is Puck and his insensitivity to others. EPISODE 11: The house confronts

Puck and Rachel riding around town in the Critical Mass bike ride (episode 6)

The soap box derby (episode 4)

The gang's out for Mohammed's birthday, but end up discussing Puck (episode 9)

The final showdown—Puck gets the boot (episode 11)

Puck, but he won't listen. Pedro's had it; if Puck stays, he goes. The house is reluctant to throw Puck out and tries to speak with him. He will not compromise, nor will he discuss the issue. Though it grieves them to do

Pam's boyfriend makes a surprise visit for her birthday party (episode 12)

so, the house kicks Puck out via speakerphone. EPISODE 12: Without Puck, the house is peaceful. Rachel and Pedro visit her family in Arizona. It's a straitlaced Republican Catholic house. Pedro speaks about AIDS awareness at the local school. Judd throws a "This Is Your Life!" birthday surprise for Pam, the last surprise being her boyfriend, Chris. The house goes skiing at Tahoe. Rachel gets her navel pierced. EPISODE 13: Pedro visits his family in Miami, but doesn't feel well. Cory resists the guilt trip Puck tries to lay on her for his eviction. Pedro returns to San Francisco, feeling better and overjoyed to see Sean. EPISODE 14: Puck continues to berate Cory. Rachel and Judd take Puck out for a drink, but it ends badly. Mohammed's girlfriend, Stephanie, tells Rachel and Cory that Puck cannot bother them if they don't let him. Rachel tries, but Puck is exhausting. The house picks a new roommate, Jo, a rock climber from London. She takes Rachel and Cory climbing. EPISODE 15: Jo secures a restraining order from her ex-husband. Judd and Rachel pretend to be a couple in order

A drink with Puck turns into a fight in the bathroom of a bar for Judd and Rachel (episode 14)

to attract others. It works: Judd meets a girl...who calls off their date because she's getting married. EPISODE 16: Pedro pushes himself at work, winding up in the hospital with pneumonia. The house feels helpless in the face of Pedro's illness. Mohammed and Stephanie are on the rocks; he has a brief fling with Sadie. The house goes horseback riding. EPISODE 17: The house goes to Hawaii. The girls surf and snorkel while the guys grouse. Pedro goes para-sailing. They all go on a bike trip in the rain forest in Waianapanapa Park. The women are gung ho, and the guys are not. EPISODE 18: Rachel gets a tattoo. Jo fends off the attentions of Steve, who wants to be more than a friend. Rachel and Jo become best friends, excluding everyone else in the house.

Pedro's friend Alex speaks at the commitment ceremony (episode 19)

EPISODE 19: Sean and Pedro plan their wedding. The whole house pitches in. Pedro's best friend, Alex, flies in from Miami. He has mixed feelings about the wedding because he wants Pedro to come home to Miami, whereas Pedro and Sean are planning a future in San Francisco. Alex ultimately supports the union and

speaks at the ceremony, which is held at the house. Puck and Toni are in love. She cheers him on during his soapbox derby race. EPISODE 20: Pedro, Judd, Cory, and Pam play in the tide pools off Monterey. The four have become extremely close. Mo is deep into his music, and Rachel and Jo are peas in a pod. On moving day, they are the last ones in the house, fielding one last phone call from Puck.

Puck leaves a final annoying message for the gang (episode 22)

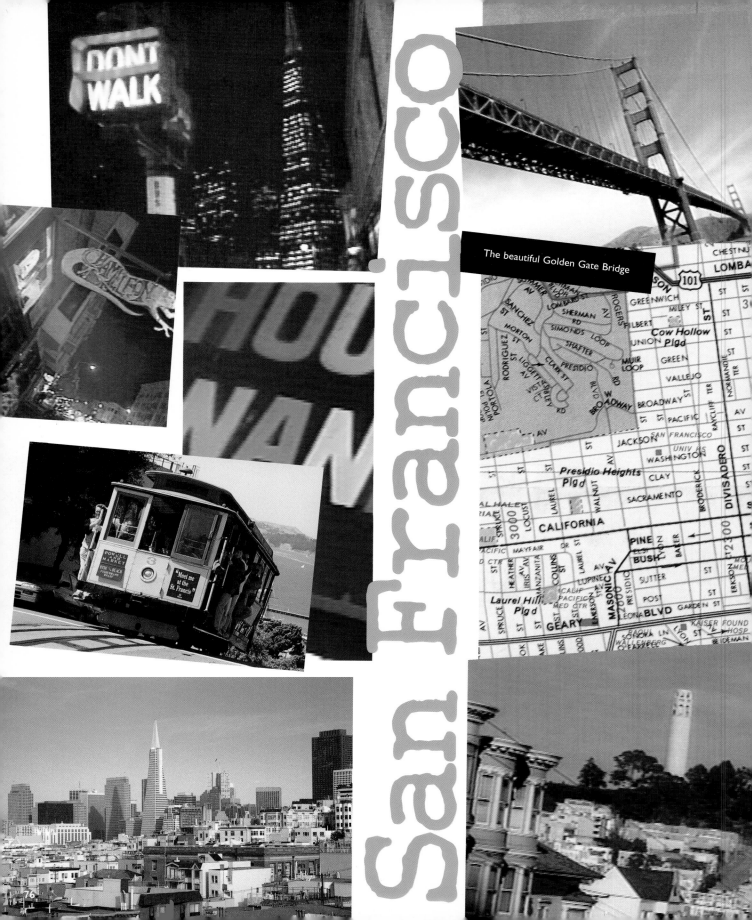

The beautiful Golden Gate Bridge

San Francisco

View down Lombard Street—the crookedest street in the world

Judd and Pam spent many an evening sipping cappucino at Café Trieste in North Beach (601 Vallejo)

The flat

"Home Sweet Home"
The house at 953 Lombard Street

For Mohammed's birthday, the gang goes out to dinner at Khan Toke Thai House (5937 Geary Street)

Pedro and Rachel have one of their final dinners here at House of Nanking (919 Kearny Street)

Want to get a tattoo? Here's where Rachel got hers, Ed Hardy's Tattoo City (722 Columbus Avenue)

fishbowl

by JUDD WINICK

I'VE SEEN A BIG OL' FISH BOWL
ITS FULL OF DIFFERENT FISH.
THEY TALK, THEY FIGHT,
THEY LAUGH, THEY CRY
BUT THEY NEVER CLEAN A DISH.

THEY SWIM IN DIFFERENT DIRECTIONS.
SOME SWIM LEFT, SOME SWIM RIGHT,
SOME JUST SWIM DOWN THE MIDDLE,
NEVER LOOKING FOR A FIGHT.

THE FISH ARE DIFFERENT COLORS
AND THEY THINK ABOUT IT A LOT.
IT WORRIES SOME TO NO END,
OTHERS JUST SMELL FUNKY
AND BLOW SNOT.

SOMETIMES WE HAVE NEW FISH
WHERE OLD FISH JUST COULDN'T STAY.
SOME FISH MAKE THE WATER COLD.
SOME FISH FIGHT INSTEAD OF PLAY.

I WONDER ABOUT THIS BOWL.
I WONDER IF ITS BIG ENOUGH.
I WONDER IF THEY'LL NIP AT EACH OTHER
IF THE SEA GETS A BIT TOO ROUGH.

I HOPE THAT THESE FISH KNOW
HOW MANY WISH THEY COULD BE WITH THEM,

AND I HOPE WHEN THEY ARE DOWN,

THEY'LL RELAX... SMILE... AND SWIM...

CORY

Del Mar, California April 1995

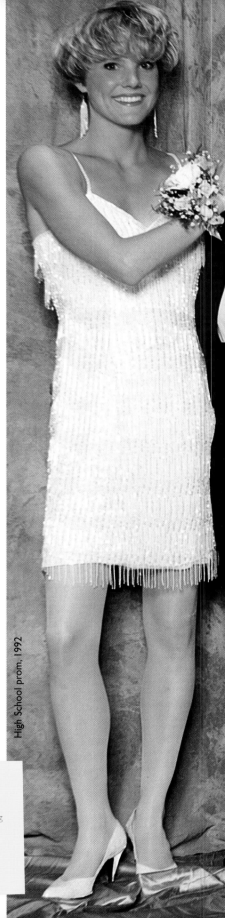

High School prom, 1992

"The last interview was too probing, putting me in imaginary situations to see how I'd respond. I called my mom and cried and told her I didn't want to do it. It's kind of like when you're born. In The Real World, you have to establish a new way of living. It's very intense—the people I lived with were very strong and assertive, which is good, but you realize there is a camera around, and everyone has their agendas.

"The Real World was definitely the weirdest experience of my life. I knew it would be hard, and challenging, but you never foresee it. You can't. I had never watched the first two seasons, I didn't really know what it was about. But they had an open casting call at the school, which I heard about on the radio. I thought it would be interesting to see a casting session; I was going to view it critically, maybe write a paper on it for class. I had no intention of being on the show. This was like two weeks before they started shooting. I went in and was clueless and that's what they wanted. Within two weeks, I'd done the interviews and the video, and they asked me to come to LA. I was kind of pissed, because I had midterms. But when I got on, I dropped out of school and got ready to go to San Francisco. My parents were skeptical. I guess they were afraid it would be sleazy or seedy, but my dad asked around at work, and some other people told him their kids watched it.

"I never felt such a struggle in my life for definition over every tiny little situation. We'd talk about things for hours, because people would have to have control. It's a commendable environment in which to establish friendships, but it's also very competitive. I regret I didn't have more of an agenda, because everyone else knew theirs. I felt like I had to figure out what my motives were, or I'd be crushed. I was a little bit too willing to compromise, to not be aware what the results of that compromising would be.

"I've tried to pay attention to my experience, not to the shows. I only saw them once, because I don't want them to have power over my memories. I do not want to see them again, not now. If I see it on MTV, I turn it off. I ask my friends not to watch it. I just want my little life."

"Although Cory emerged from the series with very strong friendships (Judd, Pam, and Pedro), she didn't always enjoy the daily process. Being on The Real World is psychologically taxing. Cory's a wonderful girl. I hope that years from now she'll look back with some pride and find memories of the experience." —Mary-Ellis Bunim, executive producer

It actually makes it harder to meet people. The school paper ran this 'Win a Date with a <u>Real</u> <u>World</u> Girl' ad and they didn't even ask us! I'm just glad I had good friends here from before I left.

"Afterwards, it was a real relief to be away from the camera. I could close my door and be alone and do absolutely nothing. But as soon as I began doing that, the series started airing. I didn't expect the celebrity attention. People ask you questions and tell you what they think of you, which is hard for me because I take everything so personally. I think this affects people to different extents. It was overload for me. It's just now that I'm starting to love my life, to love being where I am, to think of myself as intelligent."

Age 4 1/2

With Steve in Tahoe

Rock climbing at Stinson Beach

"I remember talking to Cory before her final interview, about some volunteer work she'd done in Mexico. She impressed me with her understanding of thier culture and her ability to get things done within its machismo boundaries. She had an intuitiveness about people, she was smart, and very open. I was surprised she had so much trouble adapting to the living situation in San Francisco."
—Jon Murray, executive producer

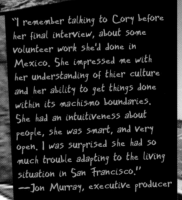

"<u>The</u> <u>Real</u> <u>World</u> was definitely the weirdest experience of my life."

JC

Jo

Mammoth Lake, California April 1995

"I didn't go through the same process for being on the show. I was working in Tahoe, and the group came skiing. They were looking for a roommate at the time. I was working at Bennigan's, and the producers came in. They were asking me a lot of questions, and I'd had a really good day climbing, so I was very up. They told me about the show, but I'd never heard of it. They asked if I'd like to live with the group, and I said, 'Great—I'd love to!' They gave me their card, but I never thought I'd hear from them. But then I went for the interviews, and they filmed me on the beach. It all happened within two weeks.

With Steve

Beach baby

I thought, this is going to be really fun, all this attention and the cameras and the people.

"Then they told me, 'Now your roommates have to decide, so bring enough stuff in case they want you to stay.' I didn't really think about it, I just went to San Francisco.

"I did feel a little left out at first. They'd just gotten over the Puck thing, and they really weren't prepared to have another roommate. I was walking on eggshells for a while. But it was really easy to talk to Rachel, and Cory, too. Even so, sometimes everyone in the house would be talking about things I didn't understand. I felt kind of left out. That carried over to when Pedro died. I didn't go to the funeral because I didn't feel I belonged there. It was really difficult, actually, but I felt in a lot of ways that he was Pam and Judd's friend. When he was sick and in the hospital, I'd call, but I still felt like the outsider. I didn't want to be there and feel that way, so I just didn't go to the funeral.

"I really did like Pedro, though. We never really spent a lot of time together, but I admired and respected him for everything he was going through and how he dealt with it. He never really had time for me, and I can totally understand why. We did things together, as a group, but one-on-one we didn't really have that rapport. I never spent too much time with Pam, either. She was very busy with school; she's very knowledgeable. I didn't get very close to Judd, either, because he is a workaholic! He's a very sweet person, but he never had time for me. I was constantly asking him to go get a coffee at Freddie's, which was right on the corner, but he was always too busy working.

"Cory and I really hit it off. We both love the outdoors, though I'm a little more extreme. I'll put my life in danger, whereas she likes little picnics; but still, she's very sweet. She just needs to stand up for herself more. And I love Mo. He is the mellowest, nicest person you could ever meet. We never had a problem, he's a really spiritual guy. And his dad's incredible—he gave Mo a lot

of wisdom. And Rachel, what can I say? She's great. When we're together, we're really bad, we're always into trouble, and it's so much fun. When I saw her at the benefit for Pedro, we just hugged and swung each other round, like some kind of advertisement. I love her to death. That leaves Puck. I did meet him after the shows aired; we'd go cruising. I was expecting this monster, but he was okay. You've just got to be really firm, tell him how you want to be treated. He's an exaggerator, but that's Puck. I just tell him to shut up.

"If there's anything about the show I would change, it's to tell everyone I'm a really good student! I have a GPA of 4.0."

With Rachel and scuba instructors in Hawaii

"Not everyone on the crew knew that Jo was married and in the process of getting divorced, so it wasn't just the cast that got the surprise when Jo made her announcement." —Mary-Ellis Bunim, executive producer

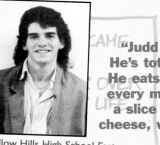

Half Hollow Hills High School East,
Class President, 1988

"Judd is Papa Judd. He's totally disciplined. He eats the same thing every morning: a bagel, a slice of tomato, and cheese, which he melts. " –Rachel

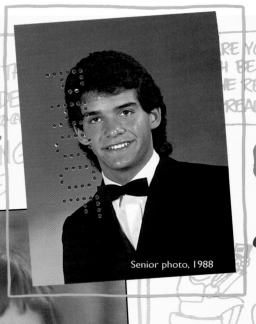

Senior photo, 1988

J U D D

ON FEB 12T A MEMBER THE REAL 70 HOURS WAS VIDE

RE YOU GOING TO H BEING FAMOUS E REAL WORLD REAL?

MEETING THE

SO, IS IT REAL? IS IT REALLY REALLY REAL? I MEAN REALLY REAL... Y'KNOW REALLY?

Age 10

ON FEB 12TH 1994 I BECAME A MEMBER OF MTV'S THE REAL WORLD™ FOR OVER 70 HOURS A WEEK MY LIFE WAS VIDEO TAPED. HERE ARE SOME PERSONAL MOMENTS IN HELL...

THE REAL WORLD

YOU GOTTA HOOK ME UP WITH THOSE BABES YOU LIVE WITH, JUDD

YOU GUYS SUCK!! YOU KNOW THAT !!? SUCK!!

ARE YOU THAT IN REAL LIFE?

"He was always telling me, 'Buck up little camper!' " –Cory

Los Angeles, California • March 1995

"I applied to be on <u>The</u> <u>Real</u> <u>World</u> because I'm a TV bug. I'm probably the biggest fan of the show of any cast member of any season. People sheepishly admit they watch it. It's a guilty pleasure: "The roof caved in on me, the remote was pinned to my chest, and <u>The</u> <u>Real</u> <u>World</u> was on. I had to watch it!

"The fan mail—it was like <u>Sleepless</u> <u>in</u> <u>Seattle</u>. Pam gives me a hard time, she doesn't get it, but basically I put out a big personal ad when I was on the show. It's simple and sweet, most of it, from nice, normal women with jobs, and kids. I feel bad but I've had to hire someone to go through it. I took a tip from Henry Rollins, and now I ask people to include a self-addressed postcard if they want a reply.

"It rewrites your life. You start looking to the screen for validation. We're all pigs. We all did this for the attention—except Cory. Cory's the little sister I never had. Everyone asks, did Cory change? Well, yes and no. It wasn't so much that Cory grew, as that we got to know her better.

"Puck and I used to be tight. We hung out a lot, went to bars. He and I had it out a couple of weeks after he left the house. He was saying horrible things around town about Pedro: 'I hope he dies,' like that. It was sickening.

"You don't forget about the cameras, but after a week or so you drop your guard. The worst thing is, what made me crazy is wondering what the crew was saying and thinking about us. They'll be snickering. You look at them and say, 'What?' They say, 'Nothing, I'm not even here.' Yeah, sure.

"I had major hair anxiety"

"But I got along really well with the crew. Rachel got along, too, but it irritated everyone because she kind of broke the rules about not interacting with them. With me, I was in the house seven hours a day drawing, alone, and they'd come out and talk to me because they were bored."

"Judd is a dork. He can chew on his shoe till the end of time." –Puck

Mo & Stephanie

Francisco's squalid
Tenderloin district, but
there's a certain sense of
serenity that sets in as
one passes through the
grove St. Located just off the
Hayes intersection above a
g is the Upper Room, which, for
years, has developed a repu-
to spiritual stomping grounds
ent of Bay Area African

lub, which strictly enforces a no
smoking policy, has soared on
h of its eclectic, organic hap-
earheading the movement is
ner, Rafiq Bilal, and his fam-
ncludes son (and MTV *The Real*
mil) Mohammed, whose band,
oices, provides a musical foun-
the venue.
heart of our progress is this
f artists that are up here, in
light Voices is the central
friends and associates spin
orbit of," says Rafiq.
ive percent of the performers
Americans, and that creates a
e in and of itself—a progressive

place for recovering drug addicts and
alcoholics. Through natural evolution and
some well-planned events, the club meta-
morphosed into a social spot for hip-hop
shows, dances, and poetry readings, to
the point where things became, in
Mohammed's words, "hella crazy."
"All the sudden the place was getting packed," he says. "There was still a
lot of beautiful energy, but because of
some knuckleheads, we had to stop doing
the hip-hop. But by that time we had
become a *place*, and the energy went out

hear that. That's a real strong
character, and I think you pic
the record."
"Dancing here is like th
Mohammed adds, "people lett
lot of their frustrations and s
a cure, but it's a necessity. Pt
I gotta go to the Upper Room
"I have to say, from the
of an insider generation, I witn
nights of dancing and it almo
chill through me," Rafiq says.
way of dancing is a different a

SING CONSCIOUSNESS
IN THE UPPER ROOM
BY AIDAN

its own rhythm.
Upper Room's sort of become a
lot of young performers," says
ie, who's also in Midnight

from there to the dance nights, the poetry... one can walk in here

"Mohammed came across as less articulate
and philosophical than he is. They took all
these dopey quotes, very simplistic, rather than
showing him as the intelligent man he is." –Judd

Age 6

With Will Power, of Midnight Voices

Comic strip:

Panel 1: I JUST DON'T GET THIS WHOLE "DEFINING A GENERATION" THING.
ME NEITHER.

Panel 2: WE'RE THE MTV GENERATION, THE BABY BUSTERS, GENERATION X. NONE OF THEM REALLY GIVE THE OVER ALL PICTURE.
NOPE.
munch munch

Panel 3: I DON'T THINK WE CAN BE SO EASILY CATEGORIZED. WE'RE TOO DIVERSE IN SO MANY WAYS.

Panel 4: WE'RE SEPARATED BY GENDER, RACE, SEXUAL PREFERENCE, ECONOMICS, NOT TO MENTION AGE. WHEN DOES A GENERATION START AND END?
YEP.

Panel 5: I MEAN, WHO ARE WE REALLY?

Panel 6: (no dialogue)

Panel 7: WELL, WE'RE THE GENERATION THAT CAN EAT CEREAL AT ANY TIME OF THE DAY.
BEATS DISCO.

"Mohammed is a great shopper. He's one of the best shopping guys I've ever
met. He does really good fashion stuff for himself and
finding stuff for you, which is really
thing, too. He actually knows a lot of places where to get
the secondhand clothing
nice. He does
at the stores." –Pam

Stephanie dancing

Easy-E and NWA created an imag-
nd lifestyle that dominates contemporar
outh culture. It's upsetting but positiv
ow that boys in the hood are dying fror
AIDS instead of crack or bullets, the
American and rap communities are standi
p and taking notice. **Please remember**
ou're going to have sex, wear
ondom. If you're sexually active, g
ested every six months.

I can still see that boyish grin, thos
cs, and that Jheri curl peeking from u
aseball cap. He's not dead yet, but the th

86

MOHAMMED San Francisco, California • March 1995

"I think I went on *The Real World* for a lot of reasons. One was my music. The other was the fact that I grew up in a communal home, and I wanted to take it to the next step, living with other people. That was cool. As far as my music, I don't know if it helped my career. It did open a window, got me more recognition, but *not* on MTV. That's a separate thing. • **The show takes strands of your personality and strings them together and makes that into a character. I'm the guy who eats cereal and smiles a lot–they did not get a lot of me vocalizing.** • I'm still in touch with Judd and Cory and Rachel, but not really with anybody else. Not with Puck. The thing about him was, he was always on, and the show lost realism. I think everyone else was pretty genuine. Puck would act cool, then he'd decide to be an a**hole for the camera. It's pretty sad. And the thing about him, he can be cool if he wants to, but he just doesn't want to. After a while of him sayin' stuff like 'Your daddy's bald, your mama's got saggy t*ts,' you have to tell him 'That's just not cool,' and he says 'But I was cool at such and such a time,' and you're like 'So what?' After he left the house, we all had a chance to become friends. • I had people who knew me from San Francisco ask me, 'How come we didn't see you more?' I don't know why. At one point, the producers told a reporter who was doing a story on me that they just didn't have enough footage of me. Pedro and I would stay up late at night, discussing politics in Cuba versus politics in America and black-Latino relationships. I don't think they made a conscious decision not to show these things, they didn't see them. I was kind of like Ralph Ellison's *Invisible Man*, they just didn't see me. Then again, I wasn't all that interested in stepping into the spotlight."

"He's really deep." –Rachel

"He's very intellectual and spiritual. His reality is <u>definitely</u> very balanced between the internal and the external. We're a lot alike in that way, but I don't think he acknowledged that." –Cory

PAM

San Francisco, California   April 1995

Senior photo, 1986

1992

Pam & Chris

"Music for me has always been my release, my escape from academics, and trying to do this musician thing, it became my work, so that I was applying the regimentation I used for school to what used to be my fun thing. I decided, you can be a doctor and play music on the side, but it's hard to be a musician and practice medicine on the side. I decided I could have both if I went to medical school. I'm very perfectionistic, that's why I didn't do anything in the house. That was sort of weird, but I just couldn't do it. I played in the house, but mostly through my headphones.

"I used to be that girl with the really long hair down to my knees, then I cut it off. When I was singing, it was always black, but I had a long tail. Then I started getting into streaks of color that got brighter through med school. I've gotten comments from supervising physicians for having wild hair. I'm going to dye it back before I start again. It wouldn't be good to stress my patients out any more. It's this crazy color that washes out so it's different every week. There's red and purple; I look like sherbet and Rockin' Pops, and all those things that are fun. I have a good time with my hair.

"I've always been lucky with my wardrobe. I went through a stage in med school when I wore all black because I lived in an artsy house. Then I rediscovered color. They missed a lot of good outfits on the show! I had 50 pairs of shoes I moved into the house. Every couple of weeks I'd bring more clothes in just to mix things up a bit. I think it's always been a combination of sort of contemporary stuff along with a lot of thriftstore shopping."

"She's one of the most intelligent people I know. She's good at 100 things, and not just good, but incredible. She's very motivated, and too self-critical. She's awesome. She's become one of my best friends." –Cory

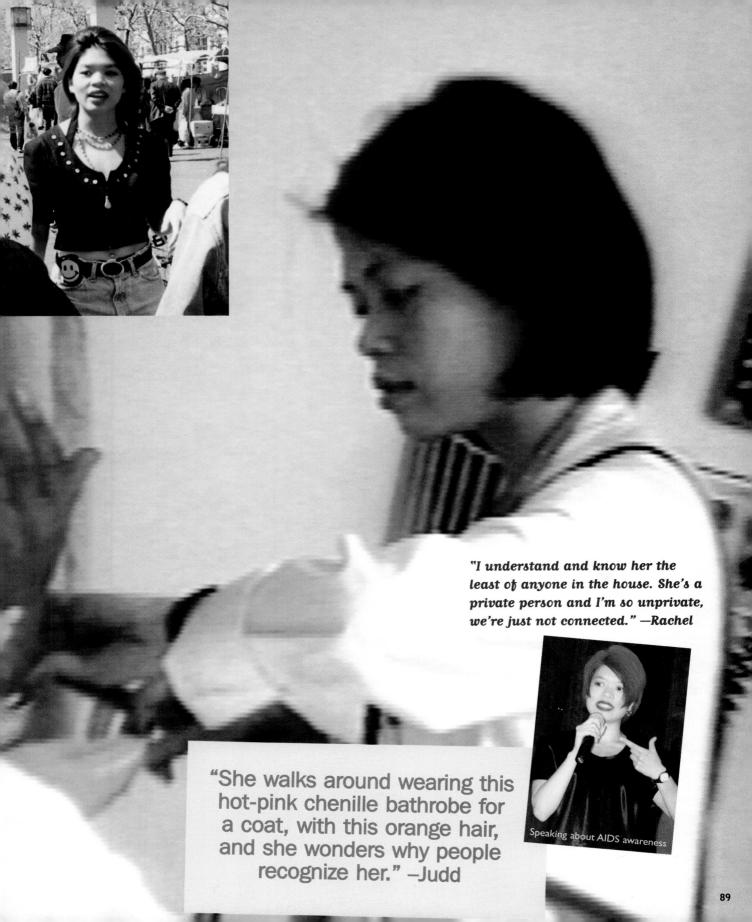

"I understand and know her the least of anyone in the house. She's a private person and I'm so unprivate, we're just not connected." —Rachel

Speaking about AIDS awareness

"She walks around wearing this hot-pink chenille bathrobe for a coat, with this orange hair, and she wonders why people recognize her." —Judd

89

With Grandma

At Bay Area AIDS Walk

Pedro & Dad

Pedro

"I'll never forget the afternoon that Jon (Murray) opened Pedro's letter and read it aloud to me. Pedro asked us for the opportunity to share his story. The irony is that we all felt incredibly lucky to have the opportunity to share the remainder of his life. We learned so much from him."
–Mary-Ellis Bunim, executive producer

"Pedro and I met a year before *The Real World* thing. We met at the gay and lesbian March on Washington in D.C. We hung out a little bit while we were there, and we actually spoke to each other on the phone a couple of times, but other than that we didn't really speak at all between Washington and San Francisco.

"I had a crush on him, but I had no idea he felt the same way about me. He told me that he felt the same way from our meeting in Washington, but we were both involved in things at that point, so it wasn't really viable. When he came to the city, it was like, we'll see what happens. And it worked out.

"Pedro and I were pretty open to the whole idea of putting our relationship on the air. We had no idea that they would make us such a central part of the whole thing. But it was part of the territory. We didn't talk that much about it, but I know that he was very concerned about how I felt about the cameras. The crew gave us plenty of time without cameras. They were very respectful and very concerned about what they were doing.

"The idea that this could possibly turn out the way it actually did was of interest to both of us. I was pretty happy with the portrayal of Pedro and our relationship.

"One of the things people tend to forget, just because of how charismatic and outspoken and assertive he was, is that Pedro was 22. There were a lot of aspects about him that were sort of young, though he didn't display them very much in public. He was very up for experience and educating himself. I don't mean academically, but in life, period.

"One of his big issues was the whole thing of being gay. Being gay in Miami and being gay in San Francisco are two totally different things. When he came to San Francisco, he was introduced to an incredibly wonderful world that was open about sexual identity and public displays of affection. It's a completely different thing in Miami, even in South Beach, the gay part of the city. He loved it. That was one of the reasons he was convinced that he wanted to live here, because he was tired of that. Rounding out his person, once again, a lot of the emotional aspects of his life, what he was feeling, what had been his thoughts and ambitions, he was finally going to be able to deal with that stuff, too, in San Francisco, being away from the nurturing environment of his family. It was definitely going to give him an opportunity to do some exploration. He was craving it, and he wanted it.

"It comes off that Pedro was this very solid individual who knew what he wanted, who had already made life's decisions about what was going to happen, and that's just not true. He was just like the rest of us, still searching for that truth, that feeling of fitting into something and discovering yourself. He was really concerned about, 'What am I going to do after MTV? Should I go back to school? What should I do? I don't want to do AIDS work all my life. I want to do what I want for myself, it's time for me to focus on me.'" –Sean Sasser

"I didn't like Pedro, we didn't connect. He wouldn't eat with my grandfather, he didn't come to my soapbox derby, he didn't come to any of my stuff. Why should I care about him? Also, he let his life be ruled by his sexuality. It was too much. —Puck

Pedro and Sean

"The one thing I feel best about in this show is what Pedro enabled us to present to the rest of the country, and not just about AIDS, but about who he was as a person, things that networks can't get away with. You think of the problems networks have portraying gay relationships, interracial relationships, and he was all of those." —Gordon Cassidy, story editor

Age 10

Pedro and Judd, Hawaii

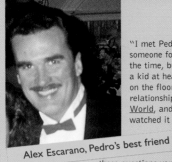

Alex Escarano, Pedro's best friend

"I met Pedro in 1990. He was 19, and had been in a relationship with someone for several years. We became the Three Musketeers. I was 33 at the time, but I always felt younger than Pedro—he was so wise, but he was a kid at heart. I mean, he'd testify before Congress, then come home and sit on the floor and play Scrabble. The duality was wonderful. When Pedro's relationship ended, he was incredibly depressed. I was watching The Real World, and I thought it might be the thing that would cheer him up. So we watched it one day, and we wrote a letter to the producers, saying that Pedro was an educator, that he was from Cuba, that he was HIV+. They called back and asked if he'd submit a video. I interviewed him on the roof of our apartment, just asking all these questions very casually. It was a game at first, but then it became a possibility, and I did have concerns. I never would have encouraged him to apply if I knew he'd get sick that quickly. • You have to understand—Pedro's life was dictated by two major events: his mother's passing, when he was 15, and finding out he was HIV+, when he was 17. After his mother died, Pedro went out searching for affection. He led this kind of dual life: perfect student, perfect son, and then the other part, which was promiscuous and reckless. When he found out he was HIV+, he reacted with denial, like most people do, just saying, 'No.' But then he turned it around. At 17, he sat his family down and told them. His father didn't know what HIV+ meant, so Pedro explained it was a virus that causes AIDS. His father says he just saw a corpse in front of him. It was really amazing, though. Pedro's family supported him the whole way. I mean, his family, they're very Cuban, very machista, some of them are not very educated, and yet they stood by him 100%. I credit Pedro with some of this; with educating them. • Being on The Real World was a way to not just talk about AIDS but to show what it's like. Some days are great, party party, and some days are terrible, you're sick in bed. He could also show that being with others is not a threat. I credit his roommates with this, too; with being willing to make the effort. • When I got to the house in San Francisco, it was really strange. The camera was on you the whole time—it was very awkward. But everyone else seemed okay with it, and that helped me get used to it. I did feel bad for the crew, though, because they had to lug all this equipment around so much. It was always really hectic, and the lack of privacy was very strange. Pedro and I would be having a conversation about nothing, and as soon as we started to talk about anything private, you'd hear the cameras, clump clump, and the lights would go on. • I had mixed feelings about the ring ceremony. I was glad Pedro had found somebody, which is what he wanted most of all, but it was going to keep him in San Francisco, and I just didn't believe that. But it was a beautiful, beautiful day, absolutely wonderful. Pedro was like a little kid, getting rings and cakes. He was not the Pedro I knew. In Florida, he was always very proud to be who he was, but he was not very out. But being in San Francisco, it's what you do, you're in the majority. Still, it's very gutsy, and I supported him the whole way. What a role model he was. He showed so many people that love is love, no matter what. If he'd lived, just think what more he could have done." –Alex

"Pedro...Pedro is very powerful, very articulate, brilliant, beautiful. Killer smile, killer laugh. Although his life was short, the presence of death in his life made him stand out—charisma that very few people have. He was less afraid to push for change. He's also funny and so much fun. He's fun to hang out with and play with and be silly with. A very committed friend to people that he can trust. He taught me to pick and choose my friends and stand by them. But he won't fool around with people who are lukewarm. He taught me that. 'Make up your mind,' he'd say, 'Don't waste time—time is valuable.' There was an immediacy, rather than waiting until later. Small things, big ideas, all were more urgent. With Pedro, you had the sense that talk will become action as he verbalizes it. Of all the people in the house, I learned the most from Pedro. I learned so much from Pam and Judd, but there was something about Pedro that leaves a lasting impression." –Cory

"He was just like the rest of us, still searching for that truth..." –Sean

"When Pedro became sick on the show, the other roomates were concerned about the crew filming him, exploiting his illness. It was Pedro who eased their concerns, explaining to them that it was important for the viewers to see both his good days and his bad days." –Jon Murray, executive producer

Mom, Pedro and sister Mily

"Pedro's family lived in a two room house with a dirt floor. They had the only refrigerator in town, and everyone would put their things in it. Once for some reason his mother had this cake, and she put it in the fridge and said to the kids, 'Now don't you touch this cake.' Well, she left, and the kids lasted about five minutes. They ate the back half of the cake, thinking she wouldn't notice. Another woman in the town had the only TV set, and she'd put it in the window, and all of the kids would sit on the front lawn to watch it. Pedro had never seen a paved road till he got off the boat." –Judd (Talking about Pedro's childhood in Cuba)

"Me and Pedro had this relationship that we'd talk about looks and boys, and he would always show me these articles that came out about him in gay magazines and straight ones. He'd read me the parts where it said how attractive he was, how his eyelashes were a mile long and his eyebrows were so strong. He'd really emphasize how handsome he was, and he'd bat his eyelashes. I love it when people say I look like Shannon Doherty, and Pedro loved it when people told him he looked like Jason Priestly. We'd do this Brandon and Brenda thing, putting our heads together and smiling for everyone." –Rachel

"His whole life is a piece of performance art. We'd watch the dailies and wait for the time of day to come when he would stop, and it never came. He was always, at all times, "The Puck." That's how he engages with life—he sees himself as a character." —Gordon Cassidy, story editor

"I never had to live with him, but I think he's really a brilliant guy. Very over the top and very fun, but he does tend to get abusive." —Jo

Hollywood, California / March 1995 "MTV has offered me three different shows: Headbanger's Ball, Sandblast, and Super Rock. But that's not for me. I want the Gong Show. I would kill the Gong Show. Can you see me in a ruffled shirt and one of those 70's suits?

"Sometimes Puck thinks he's been offered something when he's only auditioned for it..." —Jonathan Murray, executive producer

"I'm designing snowboards. One says, "Haloes, 59 cents." I'm going to superimpose pictures of my scabs.

"I did a TV commercial for Elizabeth Arden cosmetics—it's me speaking about love. Bruce Weber wants to take my picture. I've been meeting with Quentin Tarantino, Renny Harlin. They send limos to pick me up. When I got to Hollywood, I went to parties and jumped cars off cliffs, I did that kind of stuff.

"I want to be that guy in the van—Charles Kuralt—he's my idol. I'm the Shaquille O'Neal of TV. You can't script me, I'm going to slam-dunk you all day long.

"I had 15 motorcycles in a garage down the street. I had a house, a dog, good dates. I had a life like that, and now I have this.

"My parents were creative folks. We lived in our van for a long time. Canoed like crazy. I didn't have to go to school all the time. I did graduate from Fremont High School.

"MTV knew about me beforehand. I was known in San Francisco for party stunts. I was notorious. We call them party fouls, like splashing the condiment table. We'd get backstage at some concert, and I'd toss the condiment table, get all the yuppies covered in food. MTV called me. I knew a little about the show because I'd dated Eric's sister, Tara.

"I went in for an interview, and they had on their wall a picture of this other messenger. I shot him down. The director, George, was way into me. And I liked doing the show. I could have cruised like that for five or six years and be totally content. It also means good dating opportunities. I went out on a date with Traci Lords."

"He can be cool if he wants to, but he just doesn't want to. One day we were all hanging out in Rachel's room. My friend Anthony was joking and capping 24/7 on Puck, and he just didn't have any comeback. Everyone was laughing at him, so he left. Five minutes later, he sticks his butt through Rachel's window and lets out a fart. He did some of the most asinine things, but they didn't make it onto the show. If they had, we would've had women's groups, antidefamation groups, everyone coming down on us. Instead, they would show Puck doing something, then leaving the house and walking alone, feeling alienated." —MOHAMMED

"A liar and a manipulator. A vulture. I don't think he's inherently bad, just very disrespectful. Puck is the representation of what democracy would be if no one had any morals: complete anarchy." —Cory

Puck and Joker

I'm the Puck!

Was Puck Ever A Bike Messenger?

The Covered Wagon Saloon, 5th and Folsom, San Francisco 1/14/95, 7:20 P.M.

92

PUCK

Puck's Pearls Of Wisdom

Friends and Enemies: "It's funny. I'm such an a**hole, but I have all the friends, huh?" * "I miss a lot of those people." * "They're all a bunch of pu**ies." B.O. "I'm humming! Can't you see the stink coming off me?" * "The dirt is in my body. It comes from inside my body out." Food: "I like any soda that's blue, because it looks like Windex." * "I'm buying my own peanut butter and everyone else can kiss my butt!" Wheels: "The car is my enemy." * "I have a collection of scab photos." * "The State of California—suckers! They gave me my license back!" God: "Why judge people? It's in the Bible—you don't do that!" * "Full on! I love Jesus, I'm ready!" * "I feel spiritually close to God, that you can talk to Jesus Christ and all that stuff." * "Jesus is my hot rod." Dating: "My heart just pumps romance." * "I'm too intense for one girl. I'm just too scabbed and gnarly." * "Sex should be, what, 5 percent of your life?" Me, Myself, and I "I'm separate and phat and going like a jet!" * "I'm going to write a book that every kid in America is gonna want to read, to see what they can do to be famous." * "Nothing is my fault."

..a
ght alo

..the absolute best movie

"If Puck had conceived this persona as a role, I'd say it was a brilliant career move. The problem is, it isn't a role and he can't turn it off."
—Mary-Ellis Bunim, executive producer

"People don't realize he repeats stories about five million times—he was edited very well to make him look cool."
—Rachel

Thräsh
Live To Skate • Sk

Mike D.

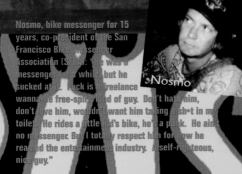

Nosmo, bike messenger for 15 years, co-president of the San Francisco Bike Messenger Association (SFBMA): "He was a messenger for a while, but he sucked at it. Puck is a freelance wanna-be free-spirit kind of guy. Don't hate him, don't love him, wouldn't want him taking a sh*t in my toilet. He rides a little kid's bike, he's a punk. He ain't no messenger. But I totally respect him for how he reamed the entertainment industry. A self-righteous, nice guy."

Nosmo

Mike D., former bike messenger of five years: "Was Puck ever a bike messenger? For a couple of days, maybe. I've never seen a messenger with a BMX. You can't cover the ground you have to on a BMX. He's just a f**king a**hole. He's not his own person and he doesn't have his own ideas. There's 10 punks you could interview that are just like him. He's just a testosterone, adolescent a**hole."

gah Boy

Rachel: "Puck blamed us for destroying his business. He said, 'That's it, I'm not gonna even try anymore.' But it was such a lie. He was a bike messenger, but he wasn't delivering packages."

93

Getting a tattoo

"She's conservative in politics and that's it." —Cory

TATTOO CARE

1. Remove bandage in 2 hours. Gently wash ne

Rachel

"They made this thing about Rachel, but I really liked her. She's a **rebellious Catholic bad girl**, very cute, very flirtatious, and when she spoke this perfect Castilian Spanish, I just melted." —Alex

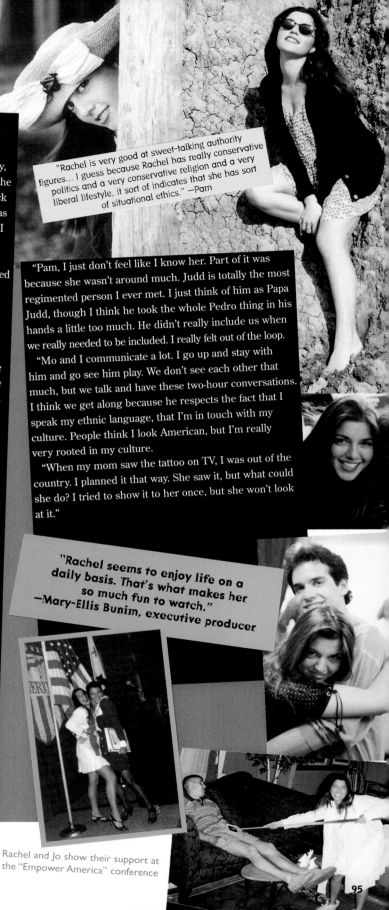

La Jolla, California • April 1995

"I enjoyed being on the show. People look at me now and say, 'You're so mellow.' They don't understand that the show puts the most aggro moments on. Besides the month leading up to Puck leaving, the show was a blast. He made life miserable, and I was really torn about that whole thing, and I knew he felt bad. But I felt like sh*t, too. My body was going to hell, I wasn't working out, my skin was bad. As soon as he left, I felt great—and even greater when Jo moved in. I didn't mind the cameras, and I loved the crew. I was just a full-on flirt with the crew. They hated me and Jo—they could really get in trouble if they hung out with us—but we loved to tease them.

"I love Jo like a sister, we're perfect together. She'll do anything to flirt and just to be stupid. I'd never want to be her boyfriend, but I love being her girlfriend. And Puck, I really like Puck, but I'd never want to live with him again. I think you have to get a break from him. Our relationship was totally one-sided. I think he was so proud to show me his city, and that was cool, but I find myself to be an interesting woman, not just a Puck observer. Maybe he was intimidated because I'd been to school, but he'd never listen to me. All he'd say was, 'You're boring, you got nothing going on.' But he was also very sweet. He'd go across the street and pick flowers or find me these terrible earrings or a button that said 'Have an Erotic Day.' He'd leave all these things on my pillow. Then again, he was talking all this sh*t about me on Kennedy's show, about how I should've stopped the rest of them from kicking him out, and then saying, 'She pirated me in the middle of the night.' That's just bullsh*t. Everybody knew Puck was always trying to kiss me. Finally he came in my room, and Cory was asleep, and we kissed, so how did I pirate him? He talks sh*t when he's Puck, but when he's David, he can be all sweet to me.

"I'm a bad judge of character initially, I trust too easily. Pedro is like my sister Leah: they pick it up right away, they'll say, 'That person's full of sh*t.' Months later, after I've been totally screwed over, I'll see it.

"People think our lives stopped after the show. I went to Venezuela after the show, when I was working for the embassy, and I talked to Pedro. He was in New York, and it was all so normal, just chatting. People don't get that; people leave us at House of Nanking, where they saw us having that discussion on the last episode. It wasn't like that at all. But people did make him St. Pedro. I mean, he could be selfish, and he was mean to Cory sometimes. She gave up having fun to organize his ring ceremony with Sean; she and Pam and Judd basically dedicated their lives to that party. And afterward, Pedro took Pam and Judd out to lunch. Cory was really hurt.

"Rachel is a virgin, and I'm just the Punisher, y'know? So we didn't really do anything. Even so, I just slammed her on Kennedy's show." —Puck

"Rachel is very good at sweet-talking authority figures... I guess because Rachel has really conservative politics and a very conservative religion and a very liberal lifestyle, it sort of indicates that she has sort of situational ethics." —Pam

"Pam, I just don't feel like I know her. Part of it was because she wasn't around much. Judd is totally the most regimented person I ever met. I just think of him as Papa Judd, though I think he took the whole Pedro thing in his hands a little too much. He didn't really include us when we really needed to be included. I really felt out of the loop.

"Mo and I communicate a lot. I go up and stay with him and go see him play. We don't see each other that much, but we talk and have these two-hour conversations. I think we get along because he respects the fact that I speak my ethnic language, that I'm in touch with my culture. People think I look American, but I'm really very rooted in my culture.

"When my mom saw the tattoo on TV, I was out of the country. I planned it that way. She saw it, but what could she do? I tried to show it to her once, but she won't look at it."

"Rachel seems to enjoy life on a daily basis. That's what makes her so much fun to watch." —Mary-Ellis Bunim, executive producer

Rachel and Jo show their support at the "Empower America" conference

"I gave everyone the opportunity to talk—they wouldn't listen. Rachel could've stood up for me when they were trying to kick me out, but she didn't. No one did. All a bunch of p**sies." —Puck

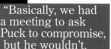

"One thing that really pissed me off was something that happened that they didn't film. The way they showed it, we asked Puck to come back to the house so we could tell him we wanted him to leave, and he's on the speakerphone, saying no, and then we kick him out and they show him riding off into the sunset like, 'So what?' That's not how it happened at all. Puck did come back, screaming his head off outside the house. Our neighbors were yelling, 'Shut the f*ck up!' and Puck was just off. He looked scary; I really thought he was going to kill one of us. And the crew asked us, 'On- or off-camera?' It's the only time they ever gave us a choice. I said I off-camera. The others agreed, and the crew sent Puck upstairs to talk to us. This was the most gnarly thing. His face was totally red, he was livid, I was really afraid he'd kill one of us. He was shaking and crying. He picked up an apple and tried to bite it and wound up screaming and spraying the apple everywhere. It was all really freaky." –Rachel

"I lecture at schools, and kids look up to Puck as a role model. That hurts me because I'd never want a child of mine to idolize him. They ask me, 'Why'd you kick Puck out?' and I turn it around and ask them, 'Why did we ask him to leave?' And they start suggesting things like he wasn't a good listener, and he was mean to Pedro, and he was rude. So I ask them again, 'Why did we ask Puck to leave?' and they get it. I try to make them understand what the media can do." –Mohammed

"Basically, we had a meeting to ask Puck to compromise, but he wouldn't. Pedro decided he didn't want to live like that anymore, with someone disrespecting him, putting him down every day, feeling poked and prodded and challenged. Pedro was the one who stood up and said, 'I don't like myself anymore. I'm angry, and frustrated. I've never felt this mad. Just because I'm on TV, I don't have to stay. It's real for me. I'm sick, it's not healthy for me, I don't feel at home in my own house.' At that point, we were like, 'Whoa, Pedro's not the problem—Puck is.' We all realized we didn't like who we were, being constantly put down and disrespected in our own house, tiptoeing around Puck.

"Pedro left. He took a cab to Sean's and was not coming back until we made a decision. Obviously, the problem was Puck, not Pedro. We had to say, 'You know what? If Pedro leaves, we're gonna get a new roommate, and we won't have Pedro, but we'll still have the problem!' So we asked Puck to compromise, but he wouldn't do it. He said, 'I'm the Puck. It's my way or no way.' There was just no way you could be yourself with him there, no way we could share our lives. There had to be mutual respect, and there just wasn't. We're living in a house with no doors! So we said, 'Puck, you gotta leave.'

"Pedro and Puck are both strong people, and we couldn't live with both. We wanted to believe we were bigger than the problem, that we were seven committed people who could overcome this, but Puck made the choice. We told him a ton of times, 'You're really making us struggle,' but he doesn't understand. He doesn't care and doesn't try to. It took Pedro to verbalize it, and he was exactly right." –CORY

"I think for the reality of how Puck was, he came off looking great. When we saw the show, we were like, 'Wow, they're really bending over backwards to make him seem likable.' It came down to being a matter of we wanted to bargain it out with him somehow, but when someone won't even come to the table to sit down and talk, it sort of leaves us with no alternative. That's very much the way it happened. Puck would just blow up if you dissed him at all or criticized him a little bit. Any small thing against him would just cause him to explode, which is classic for narcissists. • When we came back from Hawaii, 10 of the 40 messages on the machine were from Puck. One of the things he did was call us and leave jokes on the machine, like, 'What do you get when you cross Pedro and Elvis?' and he says, 'Pelvis.' That was the cutesy joke. The other joke he told was, 'What do you get when you cross Pedro and a Chinese woman?' and the answer was, 'Someone who sucks your laundry dry,' or something like that. And he left a couple that were very racist and very homophobic, which MTV then chose not to show. MTV shows the one that's sort of cutesy and makes it seem like, 'Oh, Puck, that crazy guy. He's calling up and it's sort of like no big deal.' And the fact is that Puck, on the one hand, can be funny and say these things, and on the other hand, in the next breath he's very racist and very homophobic and very threatening."
—Pam

CORY: "One night, me and Rachel and Pam dressed up in wigs and went to the Tonga Room in the Fairmont Hotel. It's the cheesiest place where they have a fake thunderstorm and the singers come out in this boat and get all wet. It's so bad and so funny. So we get there, and we get really drunk and start dancing with these exchange students. Then we crash this Asian fraternity/sorority bash, and Rachel is so drunk, she gets on stage with the DJ and starts talking into the mike, saying, "I always wanted to be in a sorority". THEY'RE ALL IN FORMALS, AND WE'RE IN WIGS, AND WE'RE GOING WILD. Rachel was on the ground doing I don't know what, and we are just laughing hysterically. They finally asked us to leave. So we call Judd and tell him he's got to come meet us. He comes out, and we drag him to a grocery store because at this point we're convinced we need more booze and food, but by the time we get out of the store, we're collapsing, and we can't find a cab, and Judd is basically carrying Rachel and all these bags of groceries wondering, 'What the hell am I doing?'" RACHEL: "I remember I was stealing candy by putting it down my dress, and when we got to the check-out Judd said, 'Rachel, put the candy back,' so I took it out and put it back. And Judd says, 'Rachel, put the candy back,' and I pulled out another piece, and we kept doing that, on and on...that's all I remember.'" PAM: "We played a lot of dress up, actually. We did that wig thing a lot. Rachel always kept going for the blond wig, and Cory would always go for these long auburn ones. I dressed Cory and Rachel in my clothes and we all wore wigs and went out to the

TONGA ROOM

That is the greatest place because they have the whole Tiki thing. And then they have this band that is like floating on this, like, sort of boat thing that comes out of the middle of the lagoon and plays things like the theme from Hawaii 5-0. Then we went somewhere else in the hotel where there was a sorority that was having a formal, so we crashed the formal. It was an Asian sorority, actually, so there were all these Asian couples—and then there was the three of us. We had no cameras most of the time. That was one of our bonding moments. A LOT OF THE GIRL-BONDING MOMENTS INVOLVED WIGS—WIGS AND MY CLOTHES AND ALCOHOL."

MAKE CHECKS PAYABLE TO: CLERK OF

MARIN COUNTY MUNICIPAL COURT
TRAFFIC DIVISION
P.O. BOX 4988
SAN RAFAEL, CA 94913-4988

CITATION NO.: WH21577
CITATION DATE: 04/04/94
DOCKET NO.: 0837445   VLN

YOU HAVE BEEN CITED FOR THE FOLLOWING VIOLATION(

SH 27174.2

COURTE

IMPOR

IF YOU APPEAR IN PERSON, YO
IF YOU MAIL IN BAIL, YOU M

you are here

'HANDS UP

100

SEE REVERSE

"Pam and I did have one bonding experience, when we got arrested for climbing the Golden Gate Bridge. This is right after Puck got kicked out, and I was really bored. I have this rebel side, and there were just no partyers in the house. My friends came down from ASU and said they were gonna climb the bridge. I asked Pam, and she agreed to come along; I don't know why. The crew wouldn't come—it was like a felony or something, so there were no cameras. It's not really scary climbing at all, until we saw these flashlights. It was the cops. We had to decide whether to go up or down, so we went down, and me and my friend starting crawling, figuring we could make it to the walkway and just start jogging, like we were runners, then get the car and pick up the others. But as soon as we start jogging, we hear,

AGAINST THE WALL!'

and I'm trying to see if the others are going to get away, when Pam comes walking out with her hands on her head. It was so funny. So they put the girls in one car and start asking us these questions, like what ethnicity we are. And I wanted to really push it, so I said, 'Look into these eyes,' and they start laughing with us. They wound up taking pictures of us and just giving us a ticket." –Rachel

Alcatraz
3 miles

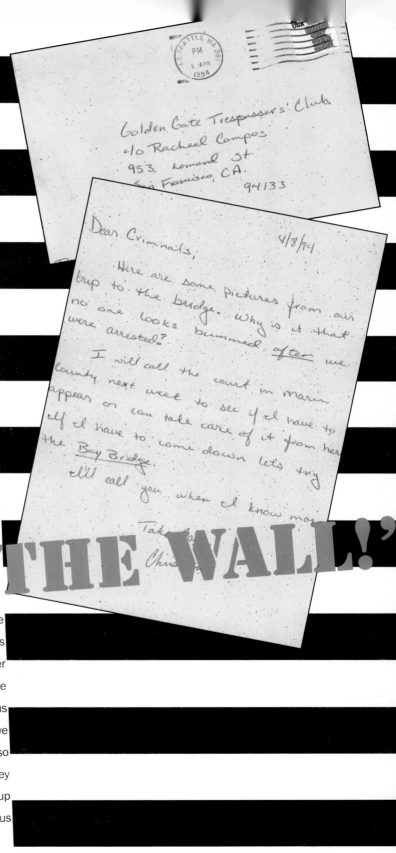

Golden Gate Trespassers' Club
c/o Racheal Campos
953 Lomand St.
San Francisco, CA.
94133

Dear Criminals,   4/8/94.

Here are some pictures from our trip to the bridge. Why is it that no one looks bummed after we were arrested?

I will call the court in marin county next week to see if I have to appear or can take care of it from here. If I have to come down let's try the Bay Bridge.

I'll call you when I know mor

Take
Chris

"I think Judd said it best—that the two of them [Rachel and Jo] are sharing the same brain.

"We went drinking with our snuba—it's between snorkling and scuba—instructors that night, and they were telling us all about these jokes they play. They lift someone's camera on board, shoot a moon—you know, pull down their pants—then put the camera back, so when the people get home, there's this moon on their roll. Later, they went to the bathroom together, and Cory noticed her camera was missing. We went running into the bathroom with the camera crew—and there were these two macho guys in the bathroom stall. They didn't have their pants down or anything, but we caught them together in the bathroom with Cory's camera." –Pam

"The minute we got to the rain forest, it rained. Cameramen were getting drenched, everyone was pissed. It was chaos. The guy who was leading the trip, Cruiser Bob, was running around in the rain, tripping everywhere, shouting, 'Don't trip over the tent stakes!' Judd was such a baby, complaining, 'My feet are wet!' Everyone's feet were wet! I was on the ground laughing, I thought it was so funny. Thank goodness Rockne and Gerard, locals who live close to Waianapanapa, rescued us. They let us use their place and let Judd dry his socks. We took showers and had meals on their patio. Cruiser Bob had been trying to cook inside the van! It was hilarious." -Cory

"A lot of stuff happened in HAWAII, but I can't talk about it. It wouldn't be cool."
—MOHAMMED

and the Merrie Monarch
ern style clothing, the missionaries
ic scale and "singing" to the islands,
g with guitar and ukelele from
grants had a profound effect on
la. Though the missionaries attempt
of the dance, the Merrie Monarch,
brought Hula back as the national
1882.

hulas which depict the missionary influen
ditional hula honoring King Kalakaua.

Hula Today
costumes have been influenced by steel guitar,
ourism, but Hula is still performed with the
ce of it's tradition.

waiian War Chant greeted many visitors arriving
n Honolulu during the 1930s and 40s. Aawana,
- expresses lively individual style, the music and
ting a time when beachboys serenaded, and lovely
d upon the moonlit shores of Kuhio Beach, Oahu.

"We were camping, and the boys were just like being total wimps. We were making fun of Judd, and he said we were like wimps because we couldn't pee standing up. So me and Jo went into the men's bathroom at the campsite and peed in the urinal. It was an empowerment thing."
—Rachel

Show me your vision.

Shave the love.

Take me with you.

I love you.

Sean.

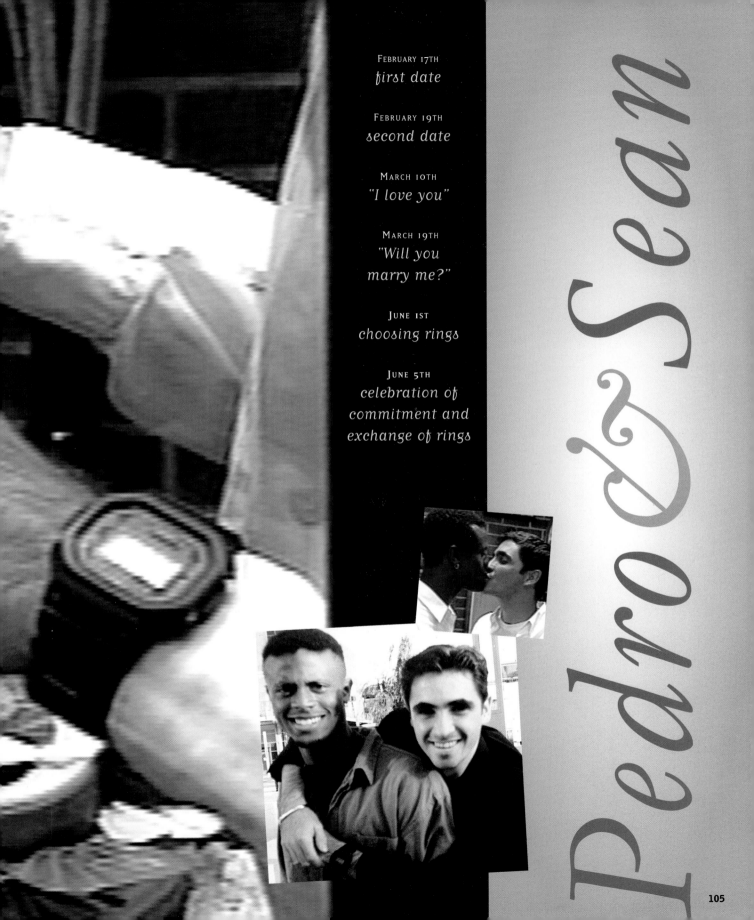

FEBRUARY 17TH
first date

FEBRUARY 19TH
second date

MARCH 10TH
"I love you"

MARCH 19TH
*"Will you
marry me?"*

JUNE 1ST
choosing rings

JUNE 5TH
*celebration of
commitment and
exchange of rings*

Pedro & Sean

Puck vs. Judd

"Judd is a dork. I was at Swingers with Dave Navarro, and Judd and Pam walked in and they're all like, 'Eeew, it's Puck!' I tried to be civil to them, but they were just being dicks. I followed them outside, and Judd was like, 'Can't you just leave us alone?' The guy is such a p**sy! I insisted that one of them get sterilized. I just kept getting in their face, and they couldn't hack it. They got in their car and split. I just laughed and ate their food."

"Navarro was there, but not with Puck. I came in and picked up some menus. Puck pulls up a chair and says, 'Hey, what's going on.' I said, 'Go away, Puck. We don't want to talk to you.' He went off on a diatribe. It was pure, textbook narcissism. He said that if we were a couple, one of us should be sterilized. I just sat there and it made him insane. He needs a reaction. He got so mad he spat on the ground. I thought only people in 1950s movies did that. Under the table my hands were shaking. I was scared, but I also had this macho fantasy brewing where I want to hit and kick him. At first we weren't going to leave, then we said, 'Hell, let's go.' Our food hadn't even come, so I canceled our order and left some money on the table. Puck ran after us shouting 'It's Judd and Pam of <u>The</u> <u>Real</u> <u>World</u>! Sterilize them! Sterilize them!' We drove away, and he came up alongside us on his motorcycle and he spat into the car. It caught me on the shoulder. I just wanted to reach out and grab him and then floor it. I wanted to kill him. A few blocks later we lost him."

"I'm in my third and a half year at UCSD. I graduate this year with a degree in communications. Afterward, I want to go abroad for a year, to Spain or Costa Rica, and teach English. Then I want to come back, get my teaching credentials and teach video, photography, and English at a school with an ESL program because I love teaching."

Mohammed

"I'm living in San Francisco with my best friend, Will, and two ferrets. I'm still singing with Midnight Voices, touring on

where are they now?

the West Coast. We just did show at USC, with Souls of Mischief and Ice Cube. I'm also singing with a new band, Frustration, which is sort of jazz and hip-hop, and hosting a three-hour music video show out of LA that goes to 220 colleges across the country. It's an hour and a half of alternative, an hour and a half rap, and R & B. And my dad's moving his club to Oakland, so I've spent a lot of time doing that. Stephanie and I are still real tight, we hang out all the time."

Jo

"I'm a geology major. I'm not sure what I'll do with it yet, maybe oceanography or avalanche control. That's what I'm doing now. I'm on the ski patrol at Mammoth, and we go out with dynamite and set up avalanches. It's very cool. Whatever I do, it'll have to be outside."

Pam ♡+ Judd

Many a late night latté led to love

At Pedro and Sean's commitment ceremony

"Judd and I got together shortly after I broke up with Christopher. We were in Miami, and we were dating by that time, and people would come up to us and say, 'Oh, we knew, we saw it coming!' I was the last person to notice. People say, 'In episode 12, when Chris comes to surprise you, you look at Judd's face. He looked sad!' I was looking at that one in freeze frame for a long, long time. It turns out that Judd had an attraction going on, I guess while we were living in the house, and I was oblivious. We were very close, but it still came very much as a surprise.

"If anything had happened [during the show], you would have seen it! Whenever Judd and I were together, they were right there filming. That was a big issue, of course, romance in the house. Judd had confided to Cory long beforehand and made her keep it secret. Before Judd talked to me about it, Cory had sat me down and said, 'Judd really likes you and you'd better not hurt him!' She was protecting him. Even before anything happened, people were speculating. I was very focused on my relationship with Christopher, so I kind of didn't see it. I have to say, I really didn't approve of any of his dates. I was just being catty—'Aw, she's no good for him...'

"I took time off from medical school, and I go back in June. When Pedro got sick, I really wanted to spend time with him, so it was a priority decision. I was inspired by Pedro to do more, too, to keep his message out there. We knew as the show aired that Pedro was going to be huge, and that it was going to do wonderful things for young people and AIDS. He got ill so quickly and cut down so fast, both Judd and I feel a wish that Pedro could be out there getting his message out. I've been asked to do things about women's issues, Asian-Americans, but I decided to do talks about AIDS awareness and Pedro.

"I have seven months of classes left. The next step is internship and residency, so I don't know where I'll be. As far as media goes, I don't know. I'm interested in the sociopolitical aspects of medicine—but I'm not sure what that would be. So that's what's going on: med school, speaking, and trying to see a lot of Judd."
–Pam

"I'm doing my weekly column for the <u>San</u> <u>Francisco</u> <u>Examiner</u>, and I'm still working on an animated series, which is looking good now that we're not dealing with NBC anymore—we in the cartooning biz know that little acronym actually stands for Not Buying Cartoons.

"Then I'm doing illustrations for a series of books called *The Complete Idiot's Guide to*...whatever—everything from how to plan a wedding to how to play Wall Street. I'm also on the lecture circuit, going around the country and speaking on 'AIDS in the Real World,' though at this point, I'm becoming more involved with the Pedro Zamora Foundation. I don't know how long I'll keep lecturing. I'm also kicking around the idea of hosting a talk show. Someone approached me. We'll see."

"I think things with Pam turned out all the better because we had this long period of imposed friendship. I knew when we were still in the house that I was in love with her, but she was with Chris, and it wasn't anything even remotely possible. Then when Pedro was sick—we really delayed it a long, long time. I remember being in the hospital with Pedro, Pam, and I sitting in the waiting room watching the episode where it's her birthday, and we do the 'This is Your Life!' act, and at the time, she still didn't know how I felt." –Judd

Pam, Judd and Alex speaking about AIDS awareness

109

Puck

[Via Puck's agent]: "In the past year, Puck has appeared on MTV's *Beachhouse*, *The John Larroquette Show*, *The Jon Stewart Show* and Pauly Shore's *Jury Duty*. He is involved in several commercial endorsements and is currently developing projects with independent television producers. Puck divides his time between San Francisco and New York."

Rachel

"I'll be graduating with a master's degree in economic development, international relations. I don't know what I want to do with it. I'd like to stay in school, get my Ph.D., but I might have to take some time away. I'm a TA for Spanish conversation at UCSD, and I love it. I really like teaching. I'm on a full-ride, Woodrow Wilson scholarship; they give you money for tuition and to live on and a stipend. • It's hard to meet people now—I met more boys before. They're

intimidated or something. I thought *The Real World* would be a plus, but I haven't met that many guys. The longest I've ever had a boyfriend is two months—keeps me focused on school."

Sean

"I'm moving to Atlanta, and I'm going to be working on building a café, hopefully by the end of the year. It'll start out as a little coffee shop. I intend on banking on the fact that coffee culture hasn't hit Atlanta yet. I just decided after returning from Miami last fall that I needed to start doing what I set out to do for myself. I was able to accomplish a lot of what I wanted to do here in San Francisco, which was all about HIV, taking care of myself, spreading awareness, opening some eyes about the infection rates among adolescents, teenagers, and young people. When I tested positive, I thought I was the only one. I was 19, and it was an awful experience, very traumatic, and I wanted to do something about that. To a certain extent, through MTV and with Pedro, I was able to do it, but I'm ready for the next thing—I'm 26."

110

A
TRIBUTE
TO
PEDRO
ZAMORA
1972–1994

REMARKS BY
PATRICIA FLEMING
National AIDS Policy Director
AT PEDRO ZAMORA
MEMORIAL SERVICE
NOVEMBER 20, 1994

Ten days ago, I stood up with President Clinton in the White House as he spoke to the nation about AIDS. The President reminded us that AIDS is no longer the face of a stranger but the face of a friend.

Pedro was one of those friends, one of those educators who taught us all to embrace people with AIDS and to join the fight against this insidious disease. He taught people with AIDS that they can live their lives to the fullest and contribute more to society than they ever thought was possible.

People like Pedro don't come along often in life, but when they do we need to reach out and grab hold and go along for the ride. Because when the ride is over, each of us is a better person.

Today, as we remember a brave young man named Pedro Zamora, each of us needs to reach out and grab hold of another young man or young woman. We need to hug them. We need to teach them and we need to love them. And, for those who are living with HIV, we need to brace them for the fight ahead. We also need to listen to them, because, like Pedro, they can teach all of us so much.

Our nation owes a debt of gratitude to Pedro and his family for their courage and for the beauty of their lives.

A few weeks ago, President Clinton recorded the following message in tribute to Pedro and his work as an AIDS educator. I'd like all of you to hear it too.

Thank you.

Hillary and I are deeply saddened by the news of the death of Pedro Zamora.

In his short life, Pedro educated and enlightened our nation. He taught all of us that AIDS is a disease with a human face and one that affects every American, indeed, every citizen of the world. And he taught people living with AIDS how to fight for their rights and live with dignity.

Pedro was particularly instrumental in reaching out to his own generation, where AIDS is striking hard. Through his work with MTV, he taught young people that "The Real World" includes AIDS and that each of us has the responsibility to protect ourselves and our loved ones.

Today, one in four new HIV infections is among people under the age of 20. For Pedro, and for all Americans infected and affected by HIV, we must intensify our efforts to reduce the rate of HIV infection, provide treatment to those living with AIDS, and ultimately, find a cure for AIDS.

Our hearts are with Pedro's family in this difficult time. In the months ahead, let us rededicate ourselves to continuing Pedro's brave fight.

PRESIDENT BILL CLINTON
NOVEMBER 11, 1994

JUDD: "ITA, the agency who represented Pedro, offered me a tour while Pedro was still lecturing. They wanted me to speak about Generation X and *The Real World* and stuff. When Pedro got sick, they offered me his tour, but I said 'I can't do that—I'd feel parasitic. It would be like Greg Brady talking about *The Brady Bunch*.' And they tell me, 'We represent him, too.' Anyway, before I could start doing any of that, Pedro got really sick. When he couldn't fulfill his lecture tour, ITA asked if I'd take it over. I told Pedro I didn't think I could fill his shoes, and he just laughed and said, with that beautiful Pedro accent, 'Of course you're not going to fill my shoes.' People picture him giving me the okay on his deathbed, this big emotional moment passing of the torch, but it wasn't like that at all. Pedro told me, 'Just tell them what it's like to live with me. You're like them—white, middle-class, straight. They'll relate to you. It'll alleviate the pity-factor I always get.' He was very laid back about it. . . . That was also the last coherent conversation I had with him—he got really sick after that. So I took over his lectures, and they were always packed. It was very, very hard for me. Pedro was in serious but stable condition at this point, but I knew he wasn't going to get better. And the audience would always ask how he was doing, and one day I just told them, Pedro is not going to get better, he is going to die, and I just cried. I cry every time I speak about him.

"I was in the room when he died. It was me, Sean, Pam, Pedro's sister Mily, some of his brothers. His dad was in the lounge. Pedro wasn't on any medication at this point. He didn't want to put his family through what they'd been through with his mother's death from cancer, which was apparently really long and horrible. It was November 10th, at 9 P.M., and Pam suggested we not leave, like we'd been doing at night. She just had a sense. And we just sat there and listened to his breathing patterns, for the whole night. At 4:25 A.M., the nurses came in to change his position, so he wouldn't get bedsores, and he was gone. He stopped breathing. It was not so dramatic. He was here and then he was gone.

"What was incredible is that media all over the world knew within hours. We got a call from someone in Israel, who'd seen the news of Pedro's death three hours after he died, his impact had been that great. And I feel so bad he didn't get a chance to enjoy it. He was such a little media pig. I mean, he died the day after the last episode aired—what a drama queen! Oh, and at the funeral, it's a beautiful day. As soon as the cast of The Real World comes out of the limo, it starts to pour. They get back in the car, it stops. And it just kills me that Pedro wasn't able to enjoy this.

"Do I think he had a sense of the impact he had? Yes, I do, but he was also sick by the 12th episode. I just wish he'd had one more year to enjoy the celebrity. He did so much—and he didn't get a chance to enjoy it. If he'd lived, he would've become a politician, fighting like crazy for what he believed.

"My mail doubled with Pedro's death. They can't write to him anymore, so they write to me. I got a letter from a 50-year-old woman in North Dakota, a real Bible-thumper, who insists she hates gays but said she took pride that Pedro walked the earth with the rest of us—that there was something so special about him, she just can't believe he'll go to Hell. That's pretty powerful stuff."

CORY: "The whole thing with Pedro was really unexpected. I mean, first we have the experience of being on the show, which was surreal, then having it be aired, and he's really sick, and then he dies. You don't get a chance to solidify things. You're looking to TV images to tell you he cared about you, that you cared about him, because you're never going to have the chance to tell him that. We were in the house five months, and we had disagreements, which we'd resolve. But they'd show the shows, and there'd be this whole different spin on the disagreements, and you're like, 'Wait a minute, that's not the way I remember it.' In reality, things pass and you reach a new understanding, but the show didn't show that. And there was no time to tell Pedro it wasn't that way; that things hadn't happened the way they showed them on TV. I was really frustrated with that."

MOHAMMED: "One time we were talking about his experience after his mom died, how he got into the club scene, which is something I did when I was young. Pedro talked about how he was looking for love at that time and how he got it sexually. About how fascinating it had been to be with all these adults, to hang out with them. I had dated all these older women when I was hanging out, so I knew what he meant. We were just like little boys, reliving some of these times.

"You have to realize he was having a lot of sex with a lot of people. Pedro was way out there, meaning he was wearing whatever, having a lot of unprotected sex. On the show, he was this real clean-cut, attractive guy, and he was that, too, but he was also a very sexual being. When he found out he had HIV, he was devastated, like anyone would be, but he understood why he got it. And I think he took all that sexual energy he'd had and transferred it into his motivation to make sure no one else got it. I mean, every day, he'd receive 12-14 letters when we lived in the house, from friends he knew around the world and kids who had HIV, and he would respond to every single one of them. He did this every day. It was obsessive. I really think he transferred all that energy to get to all these people and let them know."

RACHEL: "I really loved Pedro. When I see the episode about him, it's really hard because I never imagined it ending like that. And I really regret not going to Miami when he asked me to. I didn't have any money, but I should've stolen it to get there. I regret it because I always felt I had an instant connection with him and his family. In the video that Alex took, I said in Spanish to his sister Mily, 'I'll bring him back, I'll change him, I'm gonna marry him,' and the whole family laughed. I did go to Miami, after he was in the hospital. I remember I was so hungry, and his family fed me Cuban food, these enormous sandwiches with meat and cheese and all melted. They were so delicious."

ALEX: "When he started getting sick, I thought at first the celebrity had gone to his head. He became detached, kind of withdrawn, and I mistook it for putting on airs. I almost said, 'Hey, Pedro, it's me,' but it turned out it was the infection. He had P.M.E. (Progressive Multifocal Encephalopathy), which is very rare and spreads very rapidly. When he was diagnosed with it, they gave him two months, and that's about what it was. When he was sick, I made a point of reading every piece of mail when he was lucid enough to listen. I mean, he had letters from 13-year-old girls and 80-year-old grandmothers, letters from Europe. I am not in touch with Sean, unfortunately. He needed time to grieve on his own, I guess, to get on with his life and work. I feel badly about it, but I understand."

SEAN: "I get stopped every where I go. People are very excited about the whole MTV thing, then they're very sorry about Pedro, so it's actually kind of interesting. I watch people go through this total array of emotions from 'Oh, my God, it's someone who's been on television!' to 'But wait a minute, this is the person whose lover died.' It goes from excitement to condolences most of the time."

PAM: "I've met a lot of HIV positive friends and there's the knowledge that in the next decade I'm going to have a lot of friends going through some really hard stuff, although you can never know. It's intense. It's a weird thing to be aware of—to be in your twenties and be so aware of mortality. AIDS is becoming a younger problem."

MATT KUNITZ, COORDINATING PRODUCER: "Pedro was so special, at least to me and I'm sure for George Verschoor [producer/director] too—I mean we loved him as much as the cast did. We felt so close to him. And we had to witness what he went through. But yet, unlike the cast members, we couldn't go up to him and hug him and be there with him.

"After the show was over, and he was dying, and he was in the hospital, George and I went. He wanted us—it was very important to him that we film everything. He did not want it to be, 'Happy Pedro has AIDS.' He wanted it to be seen—AIDS kills. He wanted to be seen in the hospital, literally dying. His mind had gone off somewhere else. He could talk, he was still there, but he could hardly make a sentence.

"George was filming, and I was standing behind him. We're right at the bed. And George is crying and I'm crying. George asked him, 'Are you scared?' He was saying that he was scared. Half an hour later George and I had to go to Tami's wedding. We had our tuxedos in the hospital. We had to say good-bye to Pedro in our tuxedos, not knowing if it would be the last time we would see him. He was there enough to know who we were. We hugged him. He smiled. It was funny to him to see us in our tuxedos. In fact it was the last time we saw him."

London 1995

THE REAL WORLD

Name: Jacinda
Born: 2/8/72
Hometown: Brisbane, Australia
Education: Studied at Hamburg University; received pilot's license in London; also has a boat license
Career Goal: "I want to do a million things."
Job: Modeling
Living Situation: Always traveling
Favorite Song: None
Favorite Group: None
Favorite TV Show: *Mother and Son* (Australian)
Favorite Snack: "I'll eat anything."
Romantic Involvement: Boyfriend, Paul
Car: "I'd rather have a plane."

Name: Jay
Born: 12/7/75
Hometown: Portland, Oregon
Education: Grant High School, 1994
Career Goal: "I'm only 19."
Job: Performer/playwright
Living Situation: San Francisco
Favorite Song: "Hook," Blues Traveler
Favorite Group: Blues Traveler, Fred Astaire, Ice Cube
Favorite TV Show: *The Wonder Years,* and "OJ updates"
Favorite Snack: Teriyaki chicken
Romantic Involvement: Girlfriend, Alicia
Car: 1994 Trek 930 mountain bike

Name: Kat
Born: 6/13/75
Hometown: Yelm, Washington
Education: Junior at New York University, majoring in anthropology
Career Goal: Publishing and writing; anthropologist
Job: Student
Living Situation: Apartment at NYU in Greenwich Village
Favorite Song: "Africa," Toto
Favorite Group: Light Bright Overdose ("my brother's punk band")
Favorite TV Show: "I like *Sesame Street* and *Thomas the Tank Engine* but I get those on tape. I don't watch TV–I bought a stereo instead."
Favorite Snack: Saltine crackers and coffee
Romantic Involvement: "None–and don't want any"
Car: 1988 Sprint Metro

Name: Lars
Born: 10/5/70
Hometown: Berlin, Germany
Education: BA, communications and North American studies
Career Goal: To be in the music and club scene
Job: Student, club promoter, DJ
Living Situation: Back in Berlin
Favorite Song: "The Beautiful Ones," "Baby," Prince, "The Bomb," Kenny Dope
Favorite Group: Prince, house music
Favorite TV Show: "I only watch movies on TV and two hours of the news every day when I'm in Germany."
Favorite Snack: Pasta
Romantic Involvement: Girlfriend, Janette
Car: Volkswagen Passat

Name: Mike
Born: 7/17/73
Hometown: St. Louis, Missouri
Education: "Absolutely brilliant"
Career Goal: "Keep racing cars, run a team, become the next Frank Williams"
Job: "Right now, I'm trying to find money to continue racing. And I'm going back to college. I'll be a junior–again–this fall."
Living Situation: "With folks, for now. I'll get a place at school."
Favorite Song: "Growing up, 'Rhinestone Cowboy,' by Glen Campbell. Now, everything but country. I like what they play on MTV Prime Time."
Favorite Group: Red Hot Chili Peppers, Pearl Jam, Pink Floyd, Zeppelin, The Doors
Favorite TV Show: Car races, ESPN, movies
Favorite Snack: Dill pickles, vanilla wafers, and milk
Romantic Involvement: None
Car: 1992 Isuzu Rodeo

Name: Neil
Born: 1/31/71
Hometown: Keynsham, Near Bath, England
Education: BA, PPP, philosophy and psychology at Wadham College, Oxford. Currently studying for Ph.D. in cognitive psycholinguistics at Oxford
Career Goal: "Professional piss taker"
Job: "Research scientist and part-time rock star"
Living Situation: "Abject poverty"
Favorite Song: "22 Going on 23," The Butthole Surfers, "If I Was Your Girlfriend," Prince, 2nd Movement of Shostakovich's 10th Symphony, "1-800-SUICIDE," The Gravediggaz, String Quartet No. 3 by Alfred Schnittke, "Avalanche," Leonard Cohen
Favorite Group: Butthole Surfers, Gravediggaz, Leonard Cohen, Big Black
Favorite TV Show: *Grange Hill*
Favorite Snack: Cheese Hula-Hoops
Romantic Involvement: "No comment"
Car: "Can't drive. I have a nice bicycle, though."

Name: Sharon
Born: 5/11/74
Hometown: Collier Row, Essex, England
Education: Frances Bardsley School For Girls
Career Goal: To be a singer/songwriter
Job: Singer
Living Situation: At home in London for now, but moving to LA
Favorite Song: "Primitive," Annie Lennox, "Rock in This Pocket," Suzanne Vega, "Strong Enough," Sheryl Crow
Favorite Group: Sting, Bjork, Tori Amos, Suzanne Vega
Favorite TV Show: *Roseanne* ("I like her acerbic wit.")
Favorite Snack: Hummus and tomato on brown bread
Romantic Involvement: Single
Car: "Haven't got one at the moment"

EPISODE 1: Mike, Kat, and Jay travel from the States to join their international roommates. Everyone is excited by the prospect of living with such varied people: a fencer, a race-car driver, a model, an Oxford student, etc. Jacinda and Jay bond as she gently coaches him on dealing with his faraway girlfriend.

EPISODE 2: A flirtation blossoms between Kat and Neil, despite Neil's girlfriend of five years, Chrys—and the possibility of Mike's interest in Kat. The roommates remain hushed on the subject until jealous Mike spills the beans, prompting a rift between him and Kat.

Kat and Neil become closer and closer (episode 2)

EPISODE 3: Neil antagonizes the roommates by his demand to intellectualize. Mike is out of place in London, as he can't find ranch dressing. Neil receives a pig's heart for Valentine's Day from an angry Chrys. The roommates see Neil perform with his band, Unilever. Because of Chrys, Kat and Neil decide to be just friends.

EPISODE 4: The roommates find Sharon's overuse of the phone problematic. Lars tries to establish a career as an "event organizer" for the club scene, working for the radio station KISS-FM. Sharon must have surgery on her throat for nodules, which could jeopardize her singing career. Despite doctor's orders, Sharon has a hard time being quiet after the surgery.

EPISODE 5: Mike's

Neil's Valentine (episode 3)

attempt at getting sponsorship for his racing prove futile. He appeals to his wealthy father, but is turned down. After a pep talk from her mother, Kat finds a fencing salle in London, prepares, and then heads back to the States for the Junior Olympics. A disappointing finish proves inspirational to her, causing her to train harder.

EPISODE 6:

Kat competes in the Junior Olympics (episode 5)

Jacinda takes us through the modeling world, exploring both the inanities of being asked to "walk" for numerous castings, as well as the glamour of photo shoots. After lasting one day as a waitress, Sharon finds success as a saleswoman at a home expo. Mike begins to teach rollerblading, showing a softer side of himself.

EPISODE 7: Neil's tongue is bitten by an angry fan at a Unilever gig, rendering him almost speechless. He is forced to rely on notepads and a computer voice to communicate. In the process, his relationship with Chrys is strengthened. Jay struggles with insomnia attempting to adjust to London. Meeting his idol John Popper of Blues Traveler ignites Jay, as he begins to look for ways to perform his play.

EPISODE 8: Jacinda's boyfriend, Paul, also a model,

Jacinda models (episode 6)

visits, giving us a look at their complicated relationship, complete with arguments and make-ups. Along the way, Jacinda buys an adorable Shih Tzu pup, Legend, much to the delight and dismay of the other roommates. Mike struggles to find love in London and ends up "hooking up" with an old German friend, Mai, after a party. Mike struggles to explain his views of relationships to a puzzled Jay.

EPISODE 9: Mike's dad, Duke, stepmother, and half brother come for a visit. After Mike worries if his father will help him with his sponsorship money, a trip to a racing factory prompts Duke to pull out his wallet. Jay's first love, Marisa, comes for a visit, prompting Jay to question whether remaining the same for his Portland girlfriend is the right thing to do. He decides it is. EPISODE 10: The honeymoon is over. Tensions boil over as the phone is cut off due to lack of payment; Legend continues to remain un-house-trained; and Lars' bike is stolen. An attempt to clear the air through a "slam game" is only a temporary salve. EPISODE 11: The kids travel to idyllic northern England for an "Outward Bound" weekend, where teasing of Sharon crystallizes, prompting Jay to ask her when she "became the house joke." Other tensions arise as Lars and Mike get into an argument with Jacinda over her lack of respect for others' property. In the end, Sharon triumphs over most of the physical challenges but is left with much to think about in the way she is viewed by others. EPISODE 12: Mike finds a racing deal with the colorful Redgrave family. All of the roommates (except Kat) travel to see Mike race, cheering loudly for their cohort. Mike is disappointed by his finish, but enjoys the support of the others. Jacinda continues studying for her pilot's license, successfully completing her first solo flight. EPISODE 13: After learning he cannot perform his play in theaters due to his visa, Jay takes Mike's suggestion to mount it in

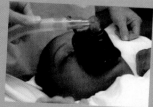
Sharon
in hospital
(episode 15)

the loft. With Sharon on the lights, Lars on sound, and Mike as all-around helper, Jay performs the show to a roomful of flatmates and their friends. Along the way, we learn of Jay's complex relationship with his biological father. EPISODE 14: The party rages on after Jay's play, as the roommates bond in new and unusual ways on the dance floor. Mike is the life of the party,

flirting with numerous women before settling with Sharon's friend, Hannah. Kat, meanwhile, is forced to contend with a drunken date, Lee. Mike then struggles to casually date Hannah, while his roommates rake him over the coals for his treatment of women, while Kat looks for love, first with her school friend, Josh, then with the outgoing bike rider Sebastian. EPISODE 15: Sharon continues to be the focal point of teasing in the loft, prompting a tearful heart-to-heart with a good friend in which she reveals "no one wants to be a joke."

After she falls seriously ill with tonsillitis, the roommates rally around her, taking care of her, as well as visiting her in the hospital. A toughened Sharon returns home, now firing back zingers and one-liners with authority. Kat, meanwhile, struggles with finals, encompassing her post-modernism paper, a drawing class, and a monologue for her drama class. In the end, Jacinda buys her a kitten to cheer

The confessional
(episode 17)

her spirits. EPISODE 16: Jay prepares for a trip to Portland, Oregon, to visit his girlfriend Alicia. Jacinda takes Jay shopping for a gift for Alicia—lingerie. Jay's trip makes him only more homesick for home and Alicia. Meanwhile, Jacinda gets more mischievous, crank-calling random people and streaking with Kat. Ultimately Jacinda outdoes herself when she gets her tongue pierced. EPISODE 17: A special episode focusing on the confessional, and the unique insight it gives into day-to-day life in the house. EPISODE 18: Love is

Kenya (episode 21)

blooming in the house again. Lars falls for Jeanette. Kat begins a relationship with Spencer, but has difficulty with his reserved manner. Mike finally meets the right woman, Nina. His roommates are surprised by the change in Mike, who will not let a coarse thing be said about Nina. EPISODE 19: Sharon and her band have a falling out, which culminates in their breaking up. Lars' plans for a party go awry, but he bounces back by

becoming the first German DJ to spin at London's premiere nightclub. Lack of funds forces Neil to get a temp job where he has to wear a suit and tie. EPISODE 20: Mike heads home to St. Louis to enter a big race, qualifying first. Back on the British racetrack, continuing his success, he performs better than he expected. Jacinda goes to Italy for a modeling shoot, where she's put in an uncomfortable postion. EPISODE 21: The roommates head off for a trip to Kenya. They are overwhelmed by the beauty of the country and the kindness of its people. The best part of the trip is when they get to attend

a Masai wedding. EPISODE 22: As move-out day approaches, the roommates reflect on their five months together. Kat is especially touched when the roommates buy her a dress for her birthday. Sharon accompanies Kat and Jacinda to the airport for a tearful good-bye. Mike heads off to Wisconsin for a race, and Jay heads back to Portland to be with Alicia. Lars, who plans to head home to Berlin, decides to keep a place in London. Neil heads back to Oxford, and Sharon moves back to Essex.

Moving out
(episode 22)

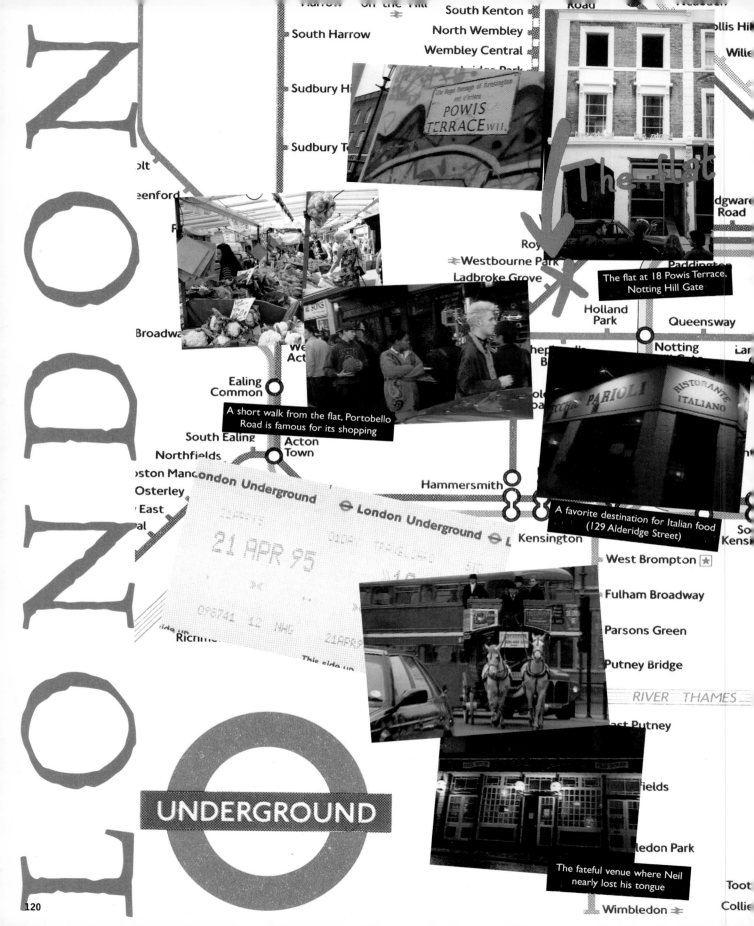

LONDON

South Kenton
North Wembley
Wembley Central

South Harrow

Sudbury Hi

Sudbury To

POWIS TERRACE W.11.

The flat

The flat at 18 Powis Terrace, Notting Hill Gate

Westbourne Park
Ladbroke Grove

Holland Park

Queensway

Notting

RISTORANTE ITALIANO
PARIOLI

A short walk from the flat, Portobello Road is famous for its shopping

A favorite destination for Italian food (129 Alderidge Street)

Ealing Common

South Ealing

Acton Town

Northfields

Osterley

London Underground   London Underground

21 APR 95

Richmc

This side up

Kensington

West Brompton ★

Fulham Broadway

Parsons Green

Putney Bridge

RIVER THAMES

st Putney

ields

UNDERGROUND

ledon Park

The fateful venue where Neil nearly lost his tongue

Wimbledon

Toot

Colli

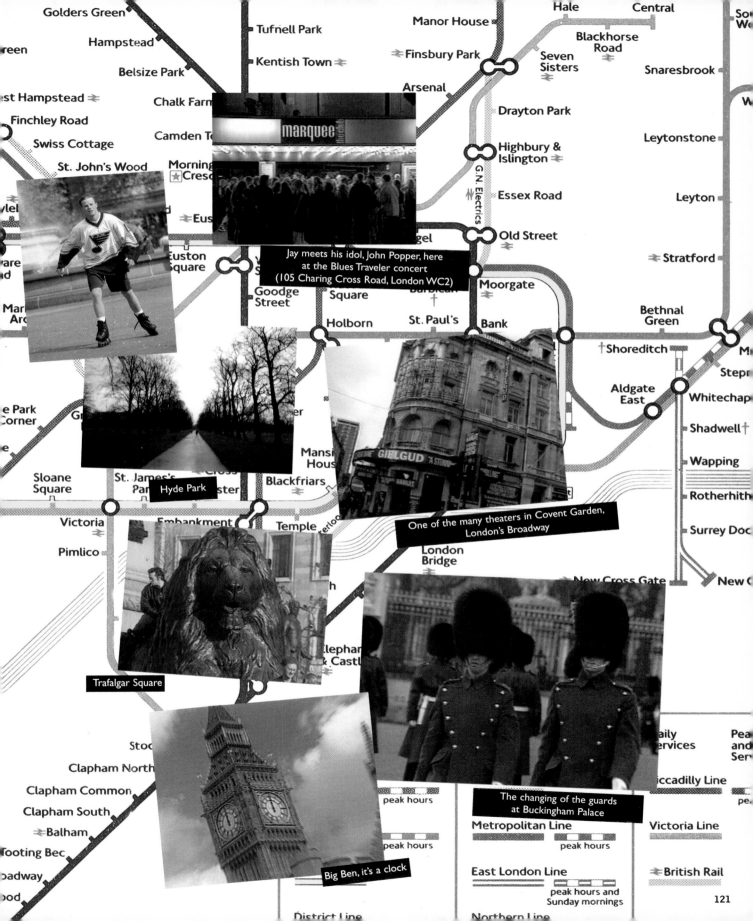

Golders Green
Hampstead
Belsize Park
een
st Hampstead
Finchley Road
Swiss Cottage
St. John's Wood

Tufnell Park
Kentish Town
Chalk Farm
Camden T
Morning
★ Cres

Manor House
Finsbury Park
Arsenal

Hale   Central
Blackhorse
Road
Seven
Sisters
Snaresbrook

Drayton Park
Highbury &
Islington
Essex Road

Leytonstone

Leyton

marquee

Jay meets his idol, John Popper, here
at the Blues Traveler concert
(105 Charing Cross Road, London WC2)

Eus
Euston
Square
Goodge
Street
Holborn

Square
St. Paul's

Old Street

Moorgate

Bank

Stratford

Bethnal
Green

Shoreditch

Step

Whitechap

Aldgate
East

Shadwell

Wapping

Rotherhith

Hyde Park

Mans
Hous

Blackfriars

One of the many theaters in Covent Garden,
London's Broadway

Surrey Doc

New C

e Park
Corner
G

Sloane
Square
Victoria
Pimlico

St. James's
Par
ster

Embankment

Temple
erlo

London
Bridge

New Cross Gate

GIELGUD

Trafalgar Square

lephan
& Castl

aily
ervices

Pea
and
Ser

iccadilly Line

pe

Stoc
Clapham North
Clapham Common
Clapham South
Balham
ooting Bec
adway
od

peak hours

peak hours

The changing of the guards
at Buckingham Palace

Metropolitan Line

peak hours

Victoria Line

East London Line

Big Ben, it's a clock

peak hours and
Sunday mornings

British Rail

District Line   Northern Line

121

To fully immerse oneself in English culture takes years and requires intimate knowledge of the combinations of slang. For example, "Look at that geezer, all lagered up and lairy, he's talking complete bollocks to that bird and she's eating it up, the slag!" is a valid sentence. However, "Wank off you chunder face!" will only be greeted with bemusement.

Neil's Dictionary

Arse: like American ass, without the confusion with donkeys. See also **bum**.

Bird: girl.

Bitter: dark beer.

Bloke: regular guy. Kind of like John Doe in the States, but less inclined to blow up buildings. See also **geezer**.

Bollocks (pl): 1. testicles. 2. nonsense, e.g., "He's talking bollocks!"

Bonk: to shag, popular with Britain's tabloid newspapers.

Bum: see **arse**.

Cheers: all purpose social lubricant covering the gamut from good-bye to thank you. Used without a trace of mock sincerity.

Chunder: vomit; to vomit.

Cupboard: closet (which British politicians rarely emerge from).

Fag: cigarette. To be used judiciously in the States.

Flat: apartment.

Futtock: an imbecile or buffoon, e.g., "The prime minister is nothing but an overblown futtock!"

Gaffer: head bloke. See also **guv'nor**.

Geezer: see **bloke**.

Guv'nor: see **gaffer**.

Intellectual masturbation: study at Oxford.

Jizz, jism: ejaculate.

Knackered: 1. orig. meaning: to be exhausted from sexual activity, now more frequently used to describe general tiredness, e.g., "I was up all night pissed as a bastard, chundering everywhere, and now I'm knackered." 2. to be in a nonfunctional state, e.g., "That car is knackered."

Lager: beer, also verb, e.g., to get "lagered up."

# of British Slang

Lairy: to be in a state of agitation, near to violence, e.g., "Look at that bloke, he's all pissed and lairy!"

Loo: toilet.

Lush: 1. verdant. 2. drunk. 3. encapsulating shaggability.

Peaky: to feel unwell, e.g., "I got all lagered up last night and now I feel a bit peaky."

Piss: 1. urine, to urinate. 2. indicates a state of drunkenness, e.g., "Look at him, he's as pissed as a bastard!" 3. also used to denote sarcasm, e.g., "He's taking the piss." Very important part of British culture/humor. Note: pissed people are not commonly angry in Britain.

Plum: general insult on the order of wanker, e.g., "What a plum!"

Quid: a pound, e.g., "Lend us a quid."

Rubber: pencil eraser.

Shag: to indulge in sexual intercourse. See bonk, e.g., "He/she needs a good shaggin'." (colloq.: "Fancy a shag?" Chat-up line used highly successfully by a few women, and highly unsuccessfully by a large number of men.)

Slag: 1. Woman of ill repute. 2. General insult.

Snog: to kiss (often indulged in when pissed). Not recommended when recipient is a psychopath.

Tosser: see **wanker**.

Wank, wanker: to masturbate; **-er**, one who masturbates (insult generally applied to men). Interesting that you can insult an Englishman by accusing him of an activity indulged in by a majority of the world's population. See also **tosser**.

Jacinda

"Jacinda I wouldn't call an Australian because she's been traveling for so many years, she's sort of international." –Lars

In her cousin's ball room dress, age 6

"Jacinda's really mischievous. She's a lot of fun that way. She pushes you a little. Some friends challenge you, and she's one of those people." –Kat

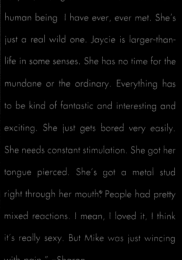

"Jaycie, that girl is the most mischievous human being I have ever, ever met. She's just a real wild one. Jaycie is larger-than-life in some senses. She has no time for the mundane or the ordinary. Everything has to be kind of fantastic and interesting and exciting. She just gets bored very easily. She needs constant stimulation. She got her tongue pierced. She's got a metal stud right through her mouth. People had pretty mixed reactions. I mean, I loved it, I think it's really sexy. But Mike was just wincing with pain." –Sharon

On location, Langkawi Island, Malaysia

London
PHOTO
Name of hold
MR/M S
Valid for u
shown wit
bearing the

G 4

"I didn't have too many preconceived ideas about the show. I'd only ever seen a couple of episodes. In Europe, it's not that big, and it doesn't even get to Australia. I was in Germany, and I saw that they were casting for one in London. At that point, I was just really fed up with modeling. I'd just been doing it for so long, and it was starting to get to me. I'd been traveling, traveling, traveling, working the whole time, and modeling just gets to be so empty. Once you know what you're doing, it just gets to be the same thing—for me, anyway. I wanted to do other things, but I wasn't really sure what; I wasn't ready to sit down and settle and stop traveling, so I thought, that looks interesting, why not? I'd always wanted to live in London. I didn't really know what I was getting into. I still don't, really. Say like Jay or Mike or Kat, they have a full awareness. Even though they say they don't watch the show, it's on there, it's an American show. • I didn't know what to expect. I didn't know where I would be living, not the address, not the people I'd be living with. I didn't know anything about the formalities and what I specifically had to do: that I'd have to check in, that I had to do interviews every week. So I thought, it's gonna be interesting, it's gonna be a challenge. Sometimes it was really fun, and sometimes it was just like hell. When it was a hassle—and it's not all the time—it was because of the whole process. I've lived with so many different people, but I didn't have to spend time with them. Here, you have house night every week, you have to go and do stuff and make an effort; have to analyze how you feel and talk about it; and have somebody there when you sometimes don't want somebody there. It's funny, because in the beginning, you don't mind the camera being there if it's something you feel worthwhile. But if you're just sitting there eating your dinner, and there's a camera that close to your face, it's just unnecessary. But things like that go away really quick. You just get so used to having them there all the time. It's cleaning your teeth or walking down the street or eating. It doesn't really matter anymore. • If I had it over, I'd do it again because this process is a one of a kind. A lot of people say, 'I couldn't handle someone invading my privacy like that,' but you get to a point where you think, people know that about me, so what? It doesn't matter. All it means is that you're going out to a lot more people than you would normally. Instead of just my realm of people knowing about me, there's gonna be a lot more people knowing about me. • As a whole, I think the seven of us got on well. When we'd have fun, we'd have real fun, and when we got fighting, we'd end up all ragging each other. But from what I heard, other shows have kicked people out. It was never even a possibility. There was not one person we could've all gotten together and said, 'Let's kick this person out.' • The thing I enjoyed most about living in the house is taking the piss out of people, joking. I just like to. It's the way I've always been. My mom's like it, too. It rarely backfires on me. Somebody said to me once, 'I've never seen somebody do what you do to people and not get beaten the sh*t out of.' I've been lucky it hasn't happened to me. I mean, often I'll take the piss out of somebody straight to their face and not cop anything from it, which is pretty amazing. The worst thing about being in the house is when you just want to be left alone, and you have to deal with somebody being there. And not having any control about what's gonna come out, which is strange. I'm used to having control. • I don't know if being on the show will impact my life, 'cause we never talk to the crew about after; they don't want to change our reality by talking about what's coming after. I talked to [codirector] Bob Fisher yesterday, and he said how he walked along with cast members from the other three seasons, and every third person was coming up to them and saying things. [My boyfriend] Paul kept saying to me, 'Oh, you're gonna get harassed, and it's big and everything in America,' and I just kept saying, 'Look, you're overreacting. It's not that big a deal.' I really don't think it is that big a deal. But then all these huge shows and publications flying over here to do interviews makes me start to realize, maybe so. Yesterday was my very first day out of the house, and I thought, God, what if I want out now? I can't. Its just been set running, and there's nothing I can do about it. • There's a bit of hoopla about people saying, 'Oh, yes, you're my best friend, we'll keep in touch,' but whether things actually happen is a whole nother kettle of fish. Even in Kenya people were taking phone numbers of people who were there. Why bother? That's something I've learned from traveling so long: it's the rare occasion that you really keep a strong friendship."

London, June 1995 "It's kind of a roundabout way I got onto the show. I wrote this play. It's a one-man show called *Bedroom*, and I won a couple of awards with it my senior year in high school. One of those was a Presidential Scholar Award. [Producer] Jon Murray called the White House and asked for a list of Presidential Scholars. I got a letter in my mailbox from MTV saying, 'Do you have compelling reason to be in London?' I'd made a bunch of money performing my play, and I was sitting at home with this money and this sports car and nothing to do for the year and figured if something came my way I'd go for it. So I went down to my basement and turned on my video camera and talked for 12 minutes about my play. I thought, what a perfect thing, I got nothing better to do with my life. So I sent in the tape.

"When I started all this, I had seen the show once. One of my buddies was like, 'Let's just watch a coupla these,' and I sat in that basement for about three hours, just engrossed in this show. I was fascinated with these people. Okay, they seem to be acting really real, but there are cameras there—who do they think they're fooling? That was the only time I saw it because I don't have cable. That's one of the things I said in my tape. When I was eight years old, someone broke into my house and stole the cable box, and it was probably the best thing that ever happened to me, 'cause if I would've had cable, I wouldn't have ever written a play. The next time I saw the show was when they flew me to New York for the finals. They put me up in a hotel room where they had MTV. I saw the NY series, the episode where this guy gets into a fight with this girl and calls her a stupid bitch and there's this big argument, and I was like, what have I gotten myself into?

"When I got to London, I had a hard time. . . . They say just be yourself. Well, what's myself when I'm outside of my home, in a different country, living on my own for the first time, when I can't work, when I'm not supposed to perform for the cameras? At times, I felt I was at a terrible disadvantage, never having lived anyplace other than my own home. I had nothing to judge it against.

"When the show started, the catch phrase was, 'You live your life—we've got a job to do. Just be yourself, and we'll film.' And as things went along, there was a period when I felt we were supposed to get involved in each other's lives. When real-life situations would happen, it was kind of like, oh, that's what it's all about. You gotta take steps to break down some of the barriers about being filmed, and sometimes I didn't want to do that. But how much of me not interacting with these people is them, and how much of it is the show? Even if I'm not all that involved in the house, you can still tell my story. If this were in Portland, I'd spend very little time in the house. If Alicia were over here, I would spend a lot of time with her and do my own thing. As it was, I had very little means of escape.

"One funny thing that happened is Jacinda talked me into buying lingerie for my girlfriend. It's something I'd never do, especially knowing it's gonna come on TV later. My girlfriend's a tomboy, a soccer player; I'm best friends with her and her mom and her family. So, Jacinda drags me out to King's Road, and we have the best time the whole day shopping for lingerie, getting this cute little lace thing. George asked in the interview before I went home for a visit, 'Are you going to give this to her on-camera?' Well, I didn't do it on-camera, and it turns out it's too small anyway. So I put it in my backpack, never said a word about it to anybody. My mom visits me in London two weeks later, and I'm telling her the story. My mom's completely petite, and she was like, 'Let's see it.' The cameras aren't there, so I pull it out of my backpack, and she says, 'Oh, that's cute.' So I end up giving the lingerie to my mom. In the next interview, George asks, 'Whatever happened to the lingerie?' And I started laughing. I said, 'I've been trying to figure out how I'm gonna tell you this, but I stuck it in my backpack and my mom saw it. . . .' So he says, 'Jay, you're telling me you bought lingerie for your mom?' And I'm laughing, 'Yes, yes, I bought lingerie for my mom! And it's just *wrong!*'

"The writing's been a really strange thing to deal with. I don't know if I'd be writing if the cameras weren't around. As someone who's observed people my whole life, being watched is such an opposite way to live a life. I'm being filmed, and this is something I'll never go through again. I really think I need to go through it first, and then maybe I can come to some sense and write about it.

"I feel like I have a leg up on other people in the house because of other news articles on me last year, about my personal life and about my show and all about 'my feelings about being 17.' I've been through meeting people on the street who know what I went through my senior year of high school. So I feel I'm prepared. Still, when the cameras aren't there, I am so watchful of walking down the street and having people ignore me. I've burned it into my brain time and time again, because nobody else realizes it's not going to be the same."

"Some people think he's kind of like a turtle, pulling his head in, but I disagree. Jay is this really easy going guy. And he's written his play. Few people at the age of 17 realize how precious the experience you're having is, and to get it down requires quite a lot of maturity. But it was difficult for Jay in London because his visa wouldn't let him work. People were calling him a slacker because he was spending an awful lot of time in bed, staying up all night watching Fred Astaire videos." —Sharon

126

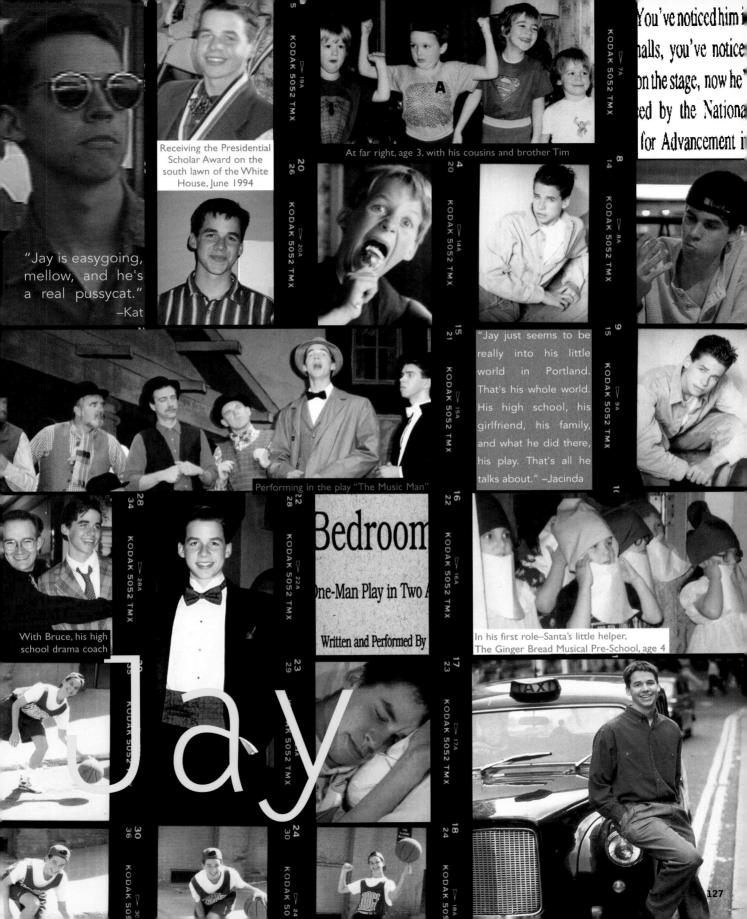

Receiving the Presidential Scholar Award on the south lawn of the White House, June 1994

At far right, age 3, with his cousins and brother Tim

"Jay is easygoing, mellow, and he's a real pussycat."
–Kat

"Jay just seems to be really into his little world in Portland. That's his whole world. His high school, his girlfriend, his family, and what he did there, his play. That's all he talks about." –Jacinda

Performing in the play "The Music Man"

With Bruce, his high school drama coach

Bedroom
One-Man Play in Two A
Written and Performed By

In his first role—Santa's little helper, The Ginger Bread Musical Pre-School, age 4

Jay

127

London, June 1995

"After high school I wanted to go as far as possible. My world had been so small, and I'd been so ready to go for so long, that it was overtrying. When I got to New York, I was working at the Gap and it was an okay job, but I was getting paid $5 an hour. That's originally why my friend Jeremy brought me <u>The Real World</u> flyer because I had mentioned to him that maybe I should be auditioning for commercials or sitcoms or something.

"Jeremy's an actor and a stand-up comedian, and he works in a skate shop on Broadway, and the casting people brought in the flyer. He said, 'Listen, I know this girl Kat and she fences and she's from Seattle.' They said, 'Call her and ask her if she wants to come in.' So Jeremy called me. My roommate Luna said, 'Listen, it's not going to be healthy for you.' My other roommate, Dawn, said, 'Why not try it?'

"I got up Sunday morning not sure I was going to do it. SOmeone put on Blur, and I thought, okay, I can handle London. I got dressed and I went. It just happened that one of my good friends, Craig, who was in town visiting me, was in the waiting room! Apparently he'd seen the flyer on my bed, written down the address, then quietly gone to the audition on his own, not thinking I was going to show up. I walked in and shouted, 'Craig!' really loud-it's kind of like a joke greeting among my friends. We were yelling in the waiting room. We were being so loud that they came out to see what we were doing. The casting guy said, 'Are you the fencer?' I was in really high spirits, and I said, 'Let me give you a fencing lesson!' We were being so loud and obnoxious that by the time I got in for my interview, I was on a talking jag. They threw me in this chair, and I was blah, blah, blah, blah.

"It was a whirlwind from the word go. I got a call back. Then they flew me back for an interview during Christmas break. I came really close to saying no. In the end I found out so late that I'd already paid my tuition. I called my mother from London to tell her I'd accepted.

"There's something about everyone in the house that I really, really like. We have such a shared experience, there's probably going to be withdrawal symptoms when we leave. Even Neil, who's like, 'No, I'm not going to miss you at all. I'm sorry, but I'm so sick of your face.'

"It was a good household. I don't know how it would be if we had to do it for another six months. Everyone in there is intelligent and thinks about things. I could have gone to Africa with so many people, but I had such a good time with that particular group, because no one was not thinking about things. When you've got seven strong people with seven strong viewpoints, it's so much fun, even when we bicker and don't agree. It's never wishy-washy. And no one's out to hurt anybody.

"Everyone in the house, with the exception of Jay, is pretty moody. I don't think there have ever been the kind of fights where you're slinging mud at each other. We tend to keep it in.

"I'm seeing Spencer, and it's definitely shown in that relationship. He's not comfortable. He's like, 'I really like you but we can only get to know each other so far,' while for me that inhibition has been broken down."

With dad and baby sister Ruth

There once was a girl named Kat,
who was a tear on the fencing mat.
From Tacoma she came
to make herself a name

Wishing you all the best, Jay

Greetings from Janette.

"The first day I saw Kat, she was wearing this big, thick, woolen jumper and this scarf and then these shiny red shoes. Her clothes said different things about her. She is mercurial. She's just a different person all the time. Her moods can sway up and down. She can give really strong and sensual and 'I am woman' vibes, and the next day, she's this terrified little pussycat in the corner." -Sharon

"One night at about 4 A.M., Jacinda asked me if I wanted to go for a jog around the block. I said, 'Nah, I know the cameras will come along.' She said, 'Not if we go naked!' Of course the crew were listening to us the whole time. We opened the front door wearing our raincoats, and there they were. But I hate backing down. We made a break for it, got to the corner, dropped our raincoats, and ran. When we got around the last corner, there they were with the cameras. Some bewildered guy was standing there, and we said, 'Er, it's for a movie!' and ran toward the cameras. We'd carried oxford shirts in our hands, so we had something to put on.

"We act like we're God's gift now. All of us became so aware of how we carried ourselves and presented ourselves as soon as we got on the show, so now everyone has good posture. It's odd, we noticed the other night, Sharon's like, 'People still stare at us, and we don't have cameras.' I said, 'Well, we're acting as if people should stare at us.' We act as if there is a glass wall around us. We don't move out of the way for people on sidewalks anymore, because we're used to having a crew of four people behind us. And so we're driving people off the sidewalk, and Sharon says, 'Why are people staring at us?' I say, 'We are ploughing down the middle of Portobello market! People are going to stare at you if you're doing that.' Or when the seven of us go out together, there's such an attitude. Jacinda said, 'We look like such a group of freaks. I would stare if I saw people like us walking together.'

"I guess I never expected to be recognized. I don't see myself as having a look that stands out. I live in New York City, which is a place with a lot of famous people, so to me, on the scope of say, Susan Sarandon, I may be an ant."

"Kat's so sweet to everybody, she's such a nice person, and it's nice to be with her, but she is a lot younger than me. I'm 23 and she just turned 20. This is her first time to be someplace by herself. There's a lot of things she's never experienced before, so if I were to come asking for advice or if I were having a sh*tty situation, Kat would listen and it would be nice to talk to her, but she wouldn't necessarily have been through it." —Jacinda

At space camp the summer before high school

versation

it confus
As p confuse s
rs come fro form
fusion and
reall expl k when I talk
ou hear the same things I
I guess it doesn't matter, no one listens to words anyhow
ly tone and inflection, equates to what you'd like

I suppose hurts. I don't like to remove the andages

Its too hard playing second string
to a world you'd like to appear in perfection.

Dear Neil
I'm thinking about you, honey
LOVE KAT
P.S. Meet me tonight at the goldfish bowl

Age 14

"I always felt that me and Kat had a special bond because we met each other first and we grew up so close together and we're the closest in age. Nothing but good feelings about Kat." —Jay

OPEN 'TIL LATE
CALL ME

YOU KNOW WHERE TO FIND ME....
STUNNING MISTRESS

"Lars is funny. He's so blunt. Sometimes truth is a thin veil for hostility, but at the same time you know what he's thinking." –Kat

Age 1

Baby Lars, with Mom and Dad, 1971

MINISTRY OF SOUND

PASSPORT TO FREEDOM

Lars with his mother

Kiss 100 fm
VISITOR
CODE No. _____ DATE 2.2.2.

"Lars was into a completely different thing than me. He was into techno clubs the whole time. I didn't find Lars interesting, I just didn't. He didn't do anything for me." –Jacinda

"We nicknamed him Queen of the Night because he just lives out, every night. The only German thing about Lars—everybody who meets him thinks he's American because of his accent—is that he's very proud. He can come across as very arrogant sometimes, but that's only because he doesn't like mistakes. He's just very precise. Not very tolerant of mistakes. If you ever point out something to him, he just doesn't find it funny. It's not him. But I really, really like Lars. He's a whole person. It's a bit of a weird thing to say, but he is." –Sharon

"For his casting interview Lars came in about an hour and a half late, then he just sat right down and lit a cigarette. He was just sort of blowing smoke in my face. I turned on the camera and said, 'First of all, you're an hour and a half late, and there are three people waiting after you, so do you have anything to say for yourself? And second of all, what gives you the right to come in here and start smoking like this?' He said, 'You know, I have respect for people, but I also like to do my own thing,' which was a good answer. He answered my challenge. There was something interesting about the guy." –Laura Ganis, associate producer

The Real World before, asking me if I was between 18 and 25 and if I speak perfect English, and I said yes, yes, yes. He said, we're having a casting tomorrow, and we'd like you to come. The next morning there was a huge queue, 30 people in front of me, and I said, 'I'm not waiting, either you let me in now or I'm not doing it.' So they let me through. I talked to this German guy called Michael, then I talked to Laura, then at night she called me and asked me to come in for a video interview. The next day I came in. I was 1 1/2 hours late. I hadn't taken a shower, I hadn't had breakfast, nothing. I felt terrible, I looked like sh*t. I think she was a bit upset. • I really wanted to come to London. I've always been wanting to live in London because for every club promoter or DJ, it's the place to be. I wasn't sure if I wanted to do this show, and I think that's the main reason the seven of us are here. No one except for Jacinda really wanted to be on it, and therefore everyone was pretty genuine during the casting interviews. • I think it's quite ridiculous to come up with huge cultural differences. All four countries are so Western. They really are not so different. I spent more than a year of my life in America, I study North American studies, I know a lot about America, so the three Americans, they couldn't shock me, they couldn't teach me anything. • England I hadn't been to before, but since it's Europe, and it's not too far from Germany, and since I spent a lot of time reading about the music and club scene, I pretty much had an idea, so Neil and Sharon weren't very different for me either. • Before my casting, I hadn't seen a single show. I don't have cable back home. I've seen the German equivalent, Das Wahre Leben. I sort of had an idea because the cast of the German Real World show came to one of my events in Berlin with all their cameras and so forth. So, I'd seen it in action. But the American show I hadn't really seen. • I knew what the apartment in Das Wahre Leben looked like, so I thought, yeah, it might be a bit civilized. But the thing that shocked me when I came into the house was color! Every room is a different color to the other rooms, and every sofa and every pillow—everything is so colorful! It was like aaaagh! You should see my apartment at home—it's all black and white and gray and steel and metal. • And then the fact that you are supposed to spend the night at the house. You know, before I met my girlfriend, there were other girls that I met—I mean, for my girlfriend, things are easy, she has her own apartment and no one is there—but other girls maybe still live at home or live in some dormitory or something, and it's a bit difficult, you know. Can't go to my place, can't go to your place. So I spent some nights in hotel rooms, you know, blew 70 pounds on a hotel room just to get laid, basically. • And then coming in at like ten in the morning and, like, 'Where were you all night?' And I'm like, 'In a hotel.' 'You're not allowed to do that! Not even my parents would say that! • Nightlife: that was my life here. I knew the big-name DJs, the big clubs, and the big record labels. I'd heard of all that before, but I hadn't been to a single club. The first two or three months I went out almost every night because I thought I had so much catching up to do. • I had an event planned for late May. The German booker, the New York booker, and the DJ all agreed and all wanted to do this event. Then the London booker said no. So then I had to cancel the whole thing, and at that point I got really frustrated. It was a weird point. And I met this woman that I fell in love with. And they were filming me trying to establish a relationship with a girl. And I almost quit. It was almost too much for me. But anyway, I didn't. I thought about it, but I never made the decision because I just didn't want to give it up. I wanted to stick with it. And it was good that I did. I really don't regret it; I'm glad I went through the whole thing."

"Mike was really funny when he first moved into the house, 'cause he was just a ball of energy. He was talkin' a mile a minute, talkin' all loud. I think I said to him, 'If you're jet-lagged, then I'm gonna have to move out. I'd hate to see when your body adjusts.' " —Jay

Age 3

"He didn't have to open his mouth. I knew he was American. He's that all-American boy. The first time I saw him, he had his white round-the-neck on, his hair down. And we immediately clicked." —Sharon

MIKE!

"Someone like Mike, the first day I came in there I was like, white fraternity boy, upper-class, conservative American. That was my first impression. I'm like, oh not my type, can't handle that. I've changed my opinion a lot. He's been very open-minded over here, and I think in fact he's the one who got the most out of this experience, not living with his parents and not hanging out with the people he usually hangs out with. He, for the first time, met a lot of people who are non-white or who are gay or who are different in some way. Someone like Mike would have shocked the hell out of me if I didn't know Americans, but they chose someone like me who has already been to America. Neil and Mike, I think are the ones that I became best friends with. And these are like the two I'll have the most contact with, I think, I assume." —Lars

132

With Mom and Dad at
class of '91 graduation

TDR
TEAM DUKE RAC-
ING

London, June 1995

"Okay! I'm the dude they call Mike. One morning I was lying on my futon, and I got this phone call. 'Hello, this is Laura something from MTV's The Real World. We've called the St. Louis International Raceway, and they gave us your name and number as a race-car driver who might be interested in going to London to be on The Real World.' Like, would you be interested? And I said, 'Sure, nothing else to do, right?'

"I had a great time, but I'm definitely ready to go home. You know, if this was The Real World in St. Louis, I probably wouldn't want it to end. But it's The Real World halfway around the world, and I'm ready to get back to my life kind of thing.

"I don't want to be walking down the mall shopping for Christmas presents come around Christmas time and have people coming up to me saying, 'Hey, you're Mike, right?' And me going, 'Yeah.' And them going, 'You're a real dick head!' That's the only thing I fear.

"Right now I'm a different person than what I'm going to come off like on the show—I'm five months older! And people are going to say, 'Oh, you were such an a.' And that's scary.**

"Mike I'm just horribly fond of. We have our spats—we have a very sibling like relationship. From the rumours I hear about the first couple of episodes, something about Mike being jealous of me and Neil, I think they mistook the way we relate, which is very siblingesque. More than anyone else, you'll hear us telling each other to f*ck off, and then the next minute it's fine. I don't know why that is. Anything Mike has said about me in confessionals, I know he's said to my face." –Kat

"I've heard that in the first episode I get jealous of Neil and Kat's relationship. As far as I knew, I was never jealous. I was mad that Kat was lying to everybody. I thought that if Kat wanted to be with Neil, that's great—just tell somebody. I know inside that they got together, and I didn't know why they were lying to us. I don't care anymore, but there was this part of me that—you kind of want girls to like you. And even though I never had any intention ever of wanting to hook up with Kat, being with Kat, going out with Kat—it still was kind of like, maybe it would be cool, you know?

"And there's other things. The night of our party and Jay's play, Jacinda and I were both pretty well intoxicated, and Jacinda was saying stuff like, 'Come on Mike, lets go to my room and . . .' do this or that, 'cause that's the way she is. And I was completely giving it back to her: 'You don't need Paul, he's nothing, he's a dork. Let's go up to your room and go for it. Come on, you know you want to!' You know, the same hammed-up stuff. But it turns out that I talked to Sharon yesterday, and she's like, 'You really liked Jacinda that one night.' No! The whole thing was a big hammed-up joke! We were both drunk and having fun and laughing.

"I'd seen the show the most. I remember when the New York episodes came on, I hated the show. The one time I really watched it, honestly, was during an LA marathon. I turned it on right when that guy David pulled off what's-her-name's thing. And I was like, 'Okay, what's going to happen next?' I was so mad at them, furious that they threw that guy out. I ended up watching four straight episodes, until the new guy came on, and then it was like, 'I'm going out to dinner now.'

"I'm not so curious anymore. Though one night we snuck off in the car. Jay and I were watching a movie up at Lightley's, a local mall kind of place, and there was a TV there, and the TV had MTV on, so we caught the channel guide and notice that The Real World was on at nine. So that night Jay, Kat, Jacinda, and I were like, yeah, we're just going to a movie, and the cameras went with us. The crew ended up filming us watching the show. It was weird."

29
ort Sleeve
Shirts

w neck
g in
ted
es and
s. 4-7.
2.99.

Mike's early modeling career

133

"Nobody got kicked out and nobody slept together."

LONDON, JUNE 1995 "Someone from <u>The Real World</u> stopped me on the street in Oxford. I had orange hair at the time. They said, 'Do you know the show?' I said, 'Yes, it's sh*t.' They said, 'Do you want to do a screen test?' I said okay. And then I did lots of interviews. They kept asking me back. Fools! They like the English-intellectual thing.

"I lost money doing this, I lost $7,000 worth of grant money. Oxford wasn't too keen on the idea of the show. The initial idea was that I was going to commute and continue studying, but they basically said, 'No, you're going to be filmed being a sleazy rock-'n'-roller. We don't want to be a part of that.'

My biggest worry is appearing pretentious.

It's a danger, because they're trying to get genuine emotions, which is something I'm not all about. I'd spend 59 minutes taking a piss and one minute actually saying something. Is that the minute they're going to show? The danger is that you'll come across as really sincere kind of guy most of the time—ripping the sh*t out of people. I just hope that the people who see it know that I'm taking a piss much of the time and having a laugh with it rather than being deadly serious.

"I have no idea what the reaction will be. It may seem that I don't like America much—I spent two and a half months in New York, and a couple of weeks in Atlanta. I just didn't like it. Let's just say I don't intend to start hanging around American fraternities. If I do go to America now, it might be a bit dangerous.

"I don't think people here watch the show. The word will get out that I'm an Internet junkie, and I'm a bit apprehensive that I'll be working on my thesis on the computer, and all that will be right there staring me in the face, and I'll be tempted to read it.

"I'm looking forward to dying my hair. I've had blond hair for 20 weeks, which is the longest I've had the same hair color. For editing purposes, the producers like you to have a kind of uniform image, because they're interested in stories rather than in narrative. So a story could take six weeks for only that one episode, so if my hair changes every week from pink to green to orange, then it would begin to look pretty strange."

UNILEVER

Age 3

Age 10

"Neil and I bite each other's tails, but when it comes down to it, he's a huge softy, though he sometimes wishes he weren't. But I've never seen anyone sucker out over a kitten like he did—never. It was embarrassing to watch. Sharon walked in and he was holding it on his bed saying, 'You're the most beautiful cat in the world and I love you.' Sharon was like, 'Neil!' and he was really kind of embarrassed." —Kat

Arriving at Oxford, October 1989

Chrys and Neil's graduation, Oxford, March 1993

The Slacker Collection

DEAR MUSIC CONSUMERS
Please treat my CDs with respect. I'm getting a bit pissed off with finding them out of their cases and lying around getting scratched. Please be more considerate.

Thank you *Neil.*

"Neil's got a very unique sense of humor. It's very English. He just likes to shock and loves to provoke and get a rise out of people. He's very prickly, thorny, a 'You can't get next to me unless I let you, unless I deem you worthy' exterior. But he's such a soft, mild, gentle guy. He really is." —Sharon

Neil's nipple ring

Sharon

"I found out about the show after I finished working at a camp in Vermont. I'd come out to New York and was staying with my grandmother and I saw about three or four episodes of the New York series. The main thing that stayed with me was the apartment and the decor, and I just remember thinking it was a very interesting concept. I had never seen anything like it before. When I was back in London, my friend was spotted in a bar by one of the MTV casting agents and asked to come in, so I went with her. I was in the reception area, and the receptionist asked if I would like to apply, and I was like, 'Hell, yeah.' I'm always open to suggestions and game for anything. I was also at a point in my life where I'd come as far as I could come on my own.

I needed something new. And so I really put in a strong prayer for something to come up. And within two days of that, I found out I was on the show. Definitely many higher sources at work.

"I knew the roommates would be between 18 and 25. I knew I would be filmed in everything I did outside the house. I didn't know that we were going to have monitors inside the house. But I really didn't struggle too much with being observed continually.

"The main problem for me was we weren't allowed to have any interaction at all with the crew. None whatsoever. No more than a 'Hello, how are you?' kind of thing. For me, it's difficult because I'm a very social person. Being English, as well, we've got this politeness thing bred into us. Having a person standing there filming me and not being able to acknowledge them in any way, I did struggle with that. It took me about a month to get over the fact that I wasn't being rude by ignoring them. I was meant to ignore them.

"I thought it was astounding to move into the center of town with six people in a fantastic house, and these six people are from all over the world. Three continents lived in that house for five months. Initially, our phraseology was a lot different; everybody had to find out about that. The most flippant comment, like, 'I can't be bothered,' to an English person would be nothing, whereas the Americans found that incredibly rude. Some of the boys in the house used the term <u>bitch</u> very casually, as a reference for any female, not even necessarily in a negative way, and that offended the English people. We'd say, 'Hang on, now, that's a real huge insult.' Then just little things. We have 'knickers,' Americans have 'panties.' We say 'blokes' for guys. And 'slog.' The Americans had never heard of a slog. It's a kiss with tongue.

"You know, we were very different–politically, theologically, philosophically. Finding things in common was difficult, but I'd say social differences have a lot to do with it. But we appreciated each other's differences. And I really have to say, I'm so glad I accepted this project. It really was a good thing to do."

"Sharon, one-on-one, when she's being mellow, is incredible. I love her most when she's sleepy and tired and so mellow. You can absolutely rely on her. If I had a bad day and I called her from somewhere and I was crying, she'd come immediately, no matter what she was doing." —Kat

Age 9

Age 2 1/2

"Sharon can be so sweet when she wants to be, but she can be demanding and stuff, too. I'm sure Sharon's gonna be good for keeping in touch, 'cause she loves the phone, she loves gossiping." –Jacinda

"Me and my Mum, Christmas 1991"

Snog: to kiss (often indulged in when pissed). Not recommended when recipient is a psychopath...

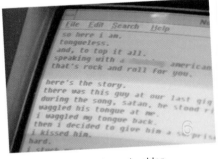

1 Neil performing at a local pub, The Camden Falcon, before snogging a heckler **2** Neil backstage at the club awaiting the ambulance after the drunken heckler has bitten through Neil's tongue **3** The ambulance rushes Neil to hospital **4** Neil displays his stitches **5** Neil is forced to communicate without speaking—writing notes is arduous **6** A computer with voice module is arranged so Neil can communicate without having to write longhand. The joke is on Neil–the computer has an American accent! **7** Chrys and Neil's relationship is strengthened by the ordeal

"I was really impressed with the way he handled himself. I went out of my way not to speak with him." —Jay

"What an unexpected and horrific injury. And the crazy thing is, it all came out of a joke." —Sharon

"Neil came with me when I had my tongue pierced. I don't think he thought I was gonna do it. He nearly passed out. But he'd had his tongue ripped off earlier. Still, Neil's into that kind of stuff." —Jacinda

THE WOUND·TINGLES

ALL THIS IS MINE

Neil and Chrys snogging

TO PULL MY

TYING OFF
BLOOD VESSELS
HURTS

S RECEIVING STICHES
HERE'S NO LOCAL
HERE

IT)   IT F*CKING
HURTS

"Neil and I are quite different people. He's a bit like Madonna—he doesn't want to <u>live</u> off-camera. He's been desperate to be famous since he was in diapers. For me, the last six months were one part genuine amusement to two parts horrified fascination to three parts utter nightmare.

"Once the sheer weirdness of being dogged day and night by some poor suckers carrying heavy equipment had worn off slightly, I found Neil in the throes of a minor nervous breakdown <u>and</u> suffering a serious lapse in taste. And, no. Neil and Kat didn't have a ground-movingly passionate affair behind my back.

"So the Valentine wasn't really about Kat specifically, more about how being placed in a confined space under pressure was making Neil psychotic, and I was damned if Our Relationship was going to pay for it. Out here in the <u>real</u> world, I was going mildly insane myself, trying to write a master's thesis two weeks late and without a lot of crucial materials, and my shallow, fame-hungry boyfriend decides to go psychotic and starts snuggling up to some teenage hippie child for comfort. It was almost more than a girl could take.

"It did all get worked out eventually. Neil woke up and realized just how much rope he'd wound around his neck, and I decided to stop worrying and love <u>The Real World</u>. But no sooner had things begun to settle into amicable normality than Neil decided to tickle some heckler's tonsils with his tongue, nearly losing it in the process. I have to confess I went into defensive overdrive.

"In the aftermath of The Tongue Incident, everyone—cast, crew, directors—gradually became more human-sized. I found they actually gave a sh*t whether Neil would ever speak again. Not just because their show would be f*cked if he couldn't, but because, hey, they didn't all have those cloven hooves, horns, and tails. So, gradually, I <u>did</u> stop worrying and learned to laugh at the process of <u>The Real World</u>. I breathed a sigh of relief when the cameras packed up and went home, but it was also sad to see everyone disperse. I actually got quite fond of The Kids in The House, and good times had been had despite tongues, crushes, and unprecedented invasions of privacy."

—Chrys (Neil's girlfriend)

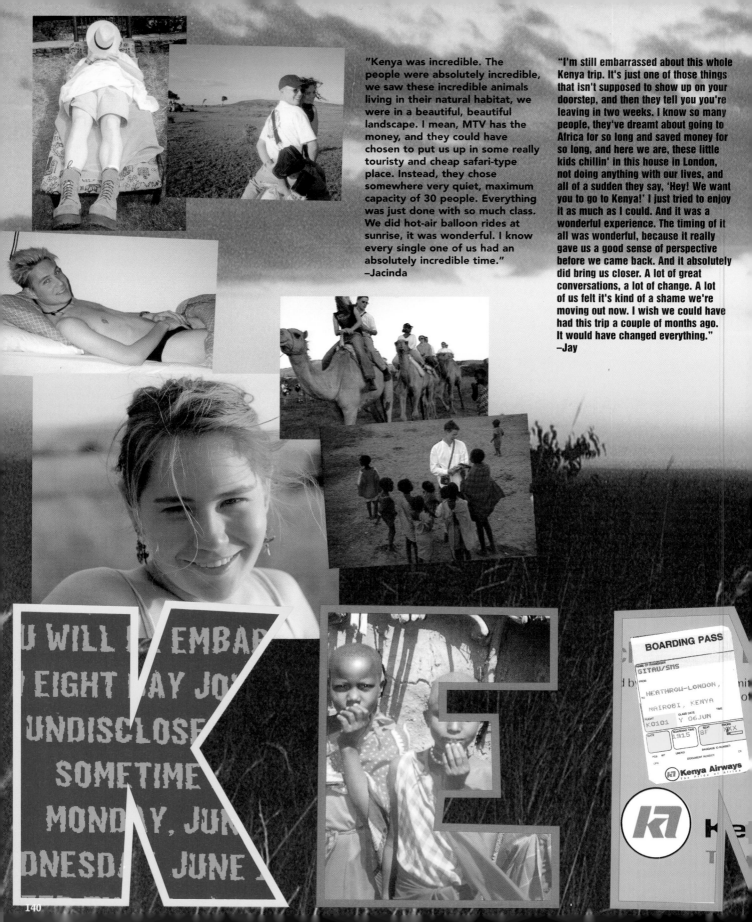

"Kenya was incredible. The people were absolutely incredible, we saw these incredible animals living in their natural habitat, we were in a beautiful, beautiful landscape. I mean, MTV has the money, and they could have chosen to put us up in some really touristy and cheap safari-type place. Instead, they chose somewhere very quiet, maximum capacity of 30 people. Everything was just done with so much class. We did hot-air balloon rides at sunrise, it was wonderful. I know every single one of us had an absolutely incredible time."
—Jacinda

"I'm still embarrassed about this whole Kenya trip. It's just one of those things that isn't supposed to show up on your doorstep, and then they tell you you're leaving in two weeks. I know so many people, they've dreamt about going to Africa for so long and saved money for so long, and here we are, these little kids chillin' in this house in London, not doing anything with our lives, and all of a sudden they say, 'Hey! We want you to go to Kenya!' I just tried to enjoy it as much as I could. And it was a wonderful experience. The timing of it all was wonderful, because it really gave us a good sense of perspective before we came back. And it absolutely did bring us closer. A lot of great conversations, a lot of change. A lot of us felt it's kind of a shame we're moving out now. I wish we could have had this trip a couple of months ago. It would have changed everything."
—Jay

U WILL EMBAR
EIGHT DAY JO
UNDISCLOSE
SOMETIME
MONDAY, JUN
DNESDA JUNE

BOARDING PASS

GITAU/SMS

HEATHROW-LONDON,
NAIROBI, KENYA

KQ101   Y 06JUN

L915   8F

Kenya Airways

"I don't care if I come across as the biggest slag that ever lived—this whole thing was worth it just for that trip."
—Kat

"It was worth it just for the trip. It may be disappointing, there's not a lot of skin—it wasn't Hawaii, which was a relief. I am not a beach person." —Neil

"That was just the most amazing thing, that they took us there. I know it was a dream of quite a few people in the house. I had a personal interest in Kenya as well, because my father's from there. I'm half-Kenyan. It is incredibly beautiful. As soon as we touched down at Keekoric Airstrip, I did a 360, and the entire horizon was unbroken. It was a fantastic experience for us. We did a balloon safari, we rode camels, we camped out with the Masai. These warriors would protect us in the middle of the night with spears from lions. I mean, we really did the African thing." —Sharon

The Last Supper

(and ᴛʰe AFTERMATH)

where are they going?

Neil: Well, I've got to go back to Oxford and write my thesis on childhood language acquisition. I take an anti-Chomskyan position. I've got till Christmas to write 50,000 words on something I haven't thought about for 20 weeks.

Jacinda: I'm going to LA, I have not had my own set place in five and a half years. I've got [my dog] Legend, I've got so much sh*t, and all the things I want require that I have a place. I know I want it to be somewhere hot, and I have to be able to speak English for everything I want to do, so that means not in mainland Europe. I'm not interested in chasing after modeling at all, but I've got a lot of people, agencies and stuff, that'll have my card. They'll book me direct from my modeling book and then I can just do what I want. I have a billion ideas of things I want to do. Flying was just one of many, it was just something I decided to do in London. I mean, there's so many things I could do. But I hate having a set plan. I've made plans before, but I never end up sticking to exactly that, so I take everything as it comes.

Lars: I'd much rather live in London now than in Berlin. But I still want to finish my education back home, so I'm going back. I have four papers to write this summer, so I'll come back here every other weekend to, like, spin at Peach on Friday, to host Satellite Club on Saturdays, and then to like do two days of office work on Monday, Tuesday, and then go back home again. And that way I'll see my girlfriend. I'm studying Communication and North American Studies, so becoming a journalist has also been a thing that's been on my mind for a number of years. I'd like to somehow be a journalist in the musical club scene.

Kat: I have a list in my notebook of things I want to do in my life. I want to write a book. I want to learn to fly—I wanted to before I met Jacinda. I want to go back to Kenya. Just some abstract ideas. Suddenly I know so much more of what I want, and it's not so set as what I wanted before. I was all set to settle down and live in NYC for a couple of years after graduation, now I'm looking at it and going, why? It's time to do something new. I'd like to go to Italy. I came here with my head not quite screwed on right about fencing. I feel like I have more drive towards that. I'm interested in film. I'll graduate with an anthropology degree then take a few years off. Eventually I do want to work in Kenya, almost in the area where we were at, and I don't know if I want to do archaeology or cultural anthropology. I used to know, but then I went to Kenya and visited.

Sharon: My first task is to just get my voice back on track. Once I've done that, I guess the thing to do would be get back to producing my work. Then again, having done this experience, I've become interested in film. It's fascinated me. But music is definitely my primary interest. But I've been really worried lately. While I was in Kenya, my band split up. It's kind of been, what am I going to do? Who do I phone? I know I'm capable of singing and songwriting, but you need to have more assistance. It's nothing you can do yourself. You have to rely on so many factors: being in the right place at the right time, finding the right people to work with. So, it's worrying. But, it's all I've ever wanted to do, so I'm going to do it.

Jay: My plans are just to go back home for the summer and hang out with the people I've hung out with most of my life and my girlfriend, and hopefully if all that's cool and things are cool with my family, then the opinions of millions of strangers around the world won't carry too much weight. As far as career, I'm doing my play in Portland this summer, and I'll probably do it again a couple of times and make enough money to live next year and make it to the East Coast and audition for musical-theater schools.

Mike: Tomorrow I fly straight to a qualifying race in Racine, Wisconsin, a really big race. I do all my races, then I go home, see my family for about a week, then head to the lake in the Ozarks where I live in the summer. My goal is to race Tour of the Atlantic or Indy Lights in the next two years and be at the Indianapolis in three years. Full-time race-car driver, that's the plan. What I really want to do in the future is maybe ride and manage a team. I'm extremely interested in engineering, in business and marketing, and the whole corporate side of it, you know. It's not just that you go out, go in circles, and drink some beers. Once you get to the high levels you're building race cars. Who knows? I want to go as far as I can racing. I know I'm probably not the best in the world, but it's like once I get in a car, I start going real quick, you know?

144

Behind the scenes

WE REGRET
THE CREW GYM
AND JACUZZI
ROOM IS NO LONGER
AVAILABLE.

Operators!
Assists!

Your country asks...

What tape is that?

Please - check how
many tapes have been
shot with your camera
before you make a mistake!

Mary-Ellis Bunim
& Jon Murray
Executive Producers 6/95

"I [Mary-Ellis] had been a soap opera producer for years. MTV asked me to develop a serial based on an idea they had, and although I told them from the beginning that it was too expensive to produce, we developed it for a year before they dropped the project. At that point Jon, who was a news and documentary producer, and I pitched them an innovative way to achieve a serial, by crossing documentary with a soap opera structure. We had just produced a series for Fox titled *American Families* where we had mixed genres and thought if we could add a hip, cutting style and top-40 music, it would play to the MTV audience. The head of development, Lauren Corrao, loved it, saying she could immediately see the dramatic possibilities since she had lived in a loft with five other people when she first came to New York.

"We made the pitch at breakfast, and it was okayed by lunch. We took some time casting six cast members. The shoot was over a long holiday weekend in New York. When the pilot was tested, the approval rating went through the roof, but it still took MTV every day of its nine-month option to commit to doing a season.

"MTV then ordered 13 episodes to be shot in New York. It was difficult to cast because the applicants didn't know what the show would look like. We narrowed the finalists down to seven but couldn't choose one to give up, so we went with seven instead of six. It was a grueling first season for the cast and crew. The cast worried whether it would be a fair depiction since it had no control over what would and would not be filmed. As for the crew—we never wanted to leave because we were afraid we'd miss something.

"We devised a system where a staffer would call the cast every day to ask what their plans were, and then we'd decide where to send our cameras. Of course, sometimes the cast didn't tell us what they were up to, and we'd find out later that they'd gone off on a great date.

"The original concept of the show was that if not enough happened, we would encourage the drama by 'tossing pebbles into the pond,' so to speak. MTV wanted that guarantee. So our first 'toss' was to ask Peter, a cast member from the original pilot, to invite Becky out on a date. We'd pick up the tab for the date. But Becky found out and was very uncomfortable being set up like that. The same thing happened with Eric, who'd appeared in Bruce Weber's *Bare Pond* book without clothes. We planted the book in the loft, and Heather teased Eric, and this added to the paranoia. We realized we couldn't manipulate what we were going to get. We stopped 'tossing pebbles' and promised not to use the footage. Besides, the unprompted drama that was happening was much better than anything we could set up.

"We certainly had a lot of drama that first season, in front and behind the camera. One of the original directors, Bill, had been flirting with Becky for weeks, and when the girls went to Jamaica, Bill and Becky had a quick affair. We asked him to resign, and the cast became very upset. They'd grown attached to him, and they threatened to quit. It was finally ironed out, much to our relief.

"We've tried to learn from our mistakes. Since the second season, we hired staff who don't want to be 21 again. They're interested in the cast but don't feel the need to be part of the cast. Things ran smoothly with the crew the second season, but not so on the cast side of things. The cast battled from the moment they walked through the door.

"The second cast had seen the first season and thought they were supposed to fight. We had to tell them not to fight for the show's sake. But there were other problems. For instance, Beth S. hid the fact that she was an aspiring actress. She was constantly trying to create a character, posing in each shot. It was weird and inappropriate. The cast picked up on it and started calling her 'Drama Queen.'

"The most memorable fight that season was, of course, Tami and David. When some of the cast asked us to kick David out, we told them it had to be a cast decision. They voted to do it, and David thought it was completely unfair. He asked to use the videotape, to prove that he hadn't done anything wrong. But we never show tape to the cast before it goes on the air. It would be like inviting them to participate in the editing, and that would be chaos.

"We'd never anticipated someone being kicked out of the cast, and now it's happened twice. We asked both guys, David and Puck, if they wanted cameras to follow them after they left the cast. Dave let us for a while but wasn't real comfortable with it, and Puck wanted us to continue right to the end.

"Both David's and Puck's story lines were edited so there was a balance; we didn't take one side over the other. We try to let the audience make their own decisions about who they think is right.

"And we don't want to see anyone hurt by the show or the experience. It's not like normal TV, where the viewer's emotions and reactions are manipulated by a writer. These are real people, and we care about what happens to them after they leave the house—their careers, families, marriages, kids, ups and downs.

"Losing Pedro was the most profoundly affecting thing that ever happened to the cast, or crew. And it still brings us together. Just recently there was a Hollywood clinic named for Pedro, and all of the cast members who were on the West Coast were at the dedication ceremony with staff and crew members from different seasons.

"Puck wasn't there. . . . Puck was offended that he wasn't invited to Pedro's funeral, too. But we didn't make up the guest list, Pedro's family did. And it was pretty obvious that Pedro and Puck weren't what you'd call 'close.'

"Puck has tried to work the show to his advantage. And he has every right to do that. Some of the cast have thought doing the show would lead to other opportunities in the entertainment business, but with the exception of Eric, it really hasn't. We tell everyone who applies to this show not to do it for the fame or exposure; do it because it's an incredibly cool experience."

George Verschoor
Producer/Director 7/95

"I'd worked on dramatic shows and music videos and comedy and things like that, and I'd worked with Jon Murray and Mary-Ellis Bunim before on other shows. When they sold this to MTV, they asked me to come to New York and figure out how to do it. For me, it was the opportunity of a lifetime. There's such a purity in this premise. When I told it to friends and other people, they all thought I was out of my mind. Who would come to watch seven strangers living in a loft for 13 weeks?

"When I was on my way to New York to do this show, a friend said to me, 'You'll never be the same again, trust me,' She was right. It's like going to the moon—words can only describe so much of it. That's why I think it's formed such an incredible bond between us—the crew—and the roommates who do this because the cast knows we *know*—we've lived through it with them. It's like family.

"That first season in New York, no one knew where we were going. When those kids walked through the door of that loft at Broadway and Prince, the paint was still drying on the walls. It was pretty bumpy. A lot of people think that there is this big curtain, and behind it Oz is pulling all the levers—but behind the curtain there's just me and my crew.

"In New York, we initially tried to be like the Palace Guard, where under any circumstances the crew does not talk to the cast. You cannot blink. You cannot move. After about three weeks of this bullsh*t, I said, we're going to lighten up. These people have to trust us or else they're not going to show us their lives. One night we—the crew—snuck out without the MTV people knowing and went out to dinner with the cast, just to lighten up and talk and share a little without any cameras around. We had some margaritas and chilled out. We all felt like we were sneaking off and having an affair.

"You just have to have faith in the people that you've selected, that their lives will be interesting enough without manipulating them. The temptation to manufacture drama is intense because you have right at your finger-tips the ability to just be the puppeteer, to drop little pebbles in the pond. There's an insecurity—if we wait long enough, will something happen? And it does. You go for a walk with Gouda, and Gouda drags Heather down the street. That's what we want to see, not these packaged blind dates and this and that. It's those moments in life when you feel like nothing is going on. A cameraman will say to me, 'Why do you want me to go in there? He's just lying on the bed listening to music.' I'll say, 'Trust me.' This show has the opportunity to focus on those things. They add up to who you are as a person. They explain the struggle.

"So many stories happened behind the cameras. When Heather and Julie met Larry Johnson, the basketball player, well, it was two hours after the game that they finally got to meet him. By then there was no one in the stands and they went outside the Meadowlands and closed the door, and there was nothing left in the parking lot—no buses, no taxis, nothing. It was snowing like hell. They looked around for a bus, a telephone. We roamed around out there for two hours. Julie finally looked at me and said, 'George, give me your cell phone!' I just looked at her and shook my head. The crew was so pissed at me because we were in knee-high snow trudging through the Meadowlands, filming these two lost souls going up and knocking on windows. Finally some security guys caught us. They threw us in a security van and took us all down into this holding tank until they called a cab. We didn't

get out of there until four in the morning.

"In New York you could see these cables like spaghetti all over the floor. For LA, we came up with a remote feed system where you could transmit from the camera back to the control room. But one day this little old lady who lived next door in Venice came up to me and said, 'I just love that furniture in your house!' And I said, 'What are you talking about? How do you know what's in my house?' She said, 'Aren't you from that MTV show? I get it on my TV. It's channel 31.' I said, 'Ah, right.' So we had it fixed, and it hasn't hap-pened since. But we ended up giving her those chairs at the end of the show as a gift because she loved them so much.

"In LA, Glen and Jon had a habit of going to play basketball at the court on Venice Beach at one in the morning, and it's not a good idea. I was distressed and thinking, I can't let them go alone, because they're going to get mugged. One night we were down there following Jon and Glen, and I notice these two gang-bangers standing there watching us. This was two in the morning. Jon and Glen are com-pletely oblivious to these things. Jon's from Kentucky, he doesn't know what a Blood or a Crip looks like. The two guys go away, and then they come back with two more. Again they go away and come back with another guy. Then there's six guys around us, and it's starting to get hairy. The crew knows because we're all from LA. It's one of the rare times that I just stopped the cameras, and I said, 'Jon, Glen, we're going home.' They looked at me like, George, this is so unlike you! I just shook my head toward the guys, and they went, 'Oh, we've seen those guys in movies. Are those the guys we saw in *Colors*?' I said, 'Yes, and that blue bandanna means we are now in trouble if we don't leave their turf.' We all just bailed out.

"One day one of my assistants came in and said, 'George, there's a huge, suspicious-looking suitcase out on the front steps, and it's really heavy.' So I went out with a couple of people. We tried to pick it up, and it felt like there was a dead body in it. We were all laughing. I suspected somebody was in it, try-ing to sneak into the show, so I told my assis-tant, 'Take it down to the garage.' I had them drag this body or whatever it was down into the garage and told my assistant, 'Call the cops.' (Wink, wink.) The suitcase made some rustling noises while we pretended to call the cops. I unzipped the top of the bag really

slowly, and this hand popped out like a hand coming out of a grave, holding this video camera. I tore it away and zipped the thing back up. We didn't expect this camcorder to come slam-ming out of there like Freddy Krueger's hand!

"We were all just laughing. We harassed him a bit with some jokes while he was inside the suitcase. We're just busting up. I said, 'Let's leave him in here for a couple of weeks, put him in the corner with the rest of the garbage.'

We all slammed the door and stood there. You could hear him in there, mumbling away. We were laughing hysterically. Finally I unzipped it, and this kid pops out. He has these wraparound sunglasses on, and this bandanna across his face like he's this video pirate. He was from the art school just around the corner, and he was doing a video project. I just cracked up, but at the same time I told him, I don't want this. He was good-natured about it.

"I give the cast a great deal of credit for their courage. It takes an incredible amount of char-acter to accept the truth. When you're 22 years old, you don't necessarily live by the truth, you live by what's going to get you through the day. *The Real World* is a difficult mirror to look into. And here I am asking them, 'Please tell me everything about your life, the good, the bad, and the ugly, whatever you can tell me. I need the complete picture in order to paint an accurate portrait of your life. If you turn your back to me, you're going to see your butt.'

"It's been tremendously rewarding for me and our dedicated staff to tell so many stories over these years through these young peoples' lives. We've captured issues ranging from leaving home to family illness, romance, racism, roommate relations, living with AIDS, looking for work, abortion, or simply pulling practical jokes, slacking, or sticking your finger in the peanut butter jar. These everyday human experiences have taken us from New York to London, Jamaica, Hawaii, Ireland, Miami, Phoenix, San Francisco, Kenya, Las Vegas, Mexico, Berlin, St. Louis, Portland, Italy, Los Angeles, Paris, to Owensboro, Kentucky. We've all given a great deal of our own lives to the show, but it has in return given a hell of a lot back to us and our viewers.

Matt Kunitz
Coordinating Producer   6/95

"I'm Matt Kunitz, I'm 26 years old, and this is my third year. I did Los Angeles, San Francisco, and London. I started as a production coordinator, then associate producer, and now I'm the coordinating producer. The crew is really young. We can relate to the roommates. We like the same things they like. We're all just a bunch of young kids.

"We've filmed from hot-air balloons, trains, planes, boats, cars, trees, and helicopters. We've filmed on skis, Rollerblades—we had a bike cam in LA with a mounted seat that you could sit on backwards. It had shocks, because we're on Venice Beach—it took thousands of dollars to build it, You could sit and they could roll behind you. We had motorcycle cameras, like when Puck was riding. We filmed from horses, we filmed from camels, we filmed underwater, we filmed on race cars; we've had cameras mounted on Mike's race car, Puck's soapbox car, Jacinda's plane. When she did her solo flight, we mounted a tiny cockpit camera because it's solo, so you can't have someone filming in there.

"Most of the time, how it works is that one of them will call me up and say, 'I'm going to dinner in five minutes at Joe's Steakhouse.' And I will hang up the phone and hit the intercom button, and I will say, 'George, the ball's in motion.' They start pulling out the equipment, while I call up Joe's Steakhouse and say, 'Hi, it's Matt Kunitz, I'm with MTV. Can I speak to a manager, please?' The manager comes up. 'Hi, I'm with MTV and we're doing a documentary and we're following the lives of seven different people. Basically, we just film everything they

do. They decided they want to come to your restaurant tonight, and we'd just like to know if we can come and film.' And the guy says, 'Is it a big crew?' I say, 'Oh, no, we're flies on the wall. You'll hardly know we're there. Please don't treat them like anybody special, don't give them a free meal.' 99.9 percent of the time they let us in.

"We are at the restaurant in five minutes. We are filming instantly. There is nothing to set up. We have a battery belt and what's called a box of light, which is a little teeny box that's the size of a napkin holder. We just throw it on the table, and we are filming within 10 minutes of the phone call.

"This restaurant could be totally full. We don't make such a big scene. Once in a while, there'll be a table that'll be a little close, and I'll personally feel like we're interrupting them— not the roommates, but the crew—so I'll buy them a bottle of wine, just as a gesture.

"One of my main responsibilities is to get releases signed. In LA, the very first day, Beth S. invited all the roommates to a party in Beverly Hills that she wasn't invited to. They go, and they get kicked right out. It's a great scene. But the crew did not get a release from the person whose party it was, and we didn't figure that out until many, many weeks later, during editing.

"I called Beth S. and said, 'Beth, whose party was that?' She said, 'I don't know, but it was my friend the drummer who . . .' So I called the drummer: 'Do you know whose party that was?' The drummer says, 'Well, actually it was the guitarist's girlfriend's sister's brother.' So I called the girlfriend, and the sister, and the brother, and finally figure out that it was this girl. I call up and her parents say, 'That was her going-away party. She's traveling around the world for a year now.' Well, I tracked this girl through Israel, through Egypt, through Afghanistan. I finally reach her. To make a long story short, she finally did sign the release.

As cast liason, it's my job to be calling everybody three or four times a day. Once, during the first three weeks in LA, I called Beth S. and asked, 'What are you doing today?' She says, 'Oh, nothing. What's everybody else doing?' I said, 'Irene and Jon are going bowling.' So Beth says, 'Okay, I'm going bowling, too, then.' I'm like, 'Okay, cool.' I'm young and naive. I call Dave, and he, too, says, 'Well, what's everybody else doing?' So I did this with all seven people. I was so proud of myself. 'George,' I said, 'all seven roommates are going bowling.'

"It became a huge incident. Irene was upset because it was supposed to be just Jon and her. Dave was just belligerent, and he and Dominic got into a big fight. They all blamed me and rightfully so. I learned.

"One night it was four in the morning in San Francisco, and George and I are in the control room, just kind of sitting and talking, closing up. On the monitor, we see a taxi pull up to the front door. Hmm? What's that all about? George looks at me, and I look at him. We didn't have to say anything. He grabbed the camera and grabbed a bag, and we ran outside and got in the cab. And here comes Puck, walking down to the cab. He thought

we were gone. He gets in the cab and there we are saying, 'Where you going, Puck?' He says, 'F**k! I can't believe you guys!'

"He was planning on going over to this girl's house to go and sleep with her, but he didn't want to tell us. But we were there, and we filmed until it was appropriate.

"Most of the time it's like a firehouse. You're waiting and waiting and waiting, and then it happens all of a sudden. We're in the last two days of shooting in London, and Jacinda calls, and she's going to jump in the parachute right now. She hasn't jumped yet because the weather's so horrible here. I was at home asleep. All the crews were out, and my crew wasn't coming in until six. She called at 5:15 P.M., and I said, 'Okay, we'll meet you there.' It's a big deal because you need a beta-cam to shoot from the ground; you need a small High-8 to go on the helmet of the guy who's going to jump out of the plane with her; and you need another High-8 to go inside the plane, and a tripod, sound mixer, etc. Luckily the soundman is there early. The cameraman shows up five minutes before the shift. We got the call at 5:15. At 6:05, we're on a train. At 7:30 she's getting on a plane and we're shooting it. By 7:45, we are filming her coming out of the sky and landing there, and it was just like, 'This is what it's all about. This is so cool—we pulled it off.' "

Laura Ganis
Associate Producer   7/95

"I've been working on the show three years. I started as the casting assistant during the LA season. When you do casting, you run into all sorts of people. Some can be quite odd. We do these prescreenings, these open calls where 300 people show up and you have one minute to spend with each of them. I have the interesting ones come to me; we kind of weed them out that way. In Berlin, this beautiful, striking Naomi Campbell look-alike comes in carrying a teacup poodle. We spoke for one minute—that's all we had. She was a singer, and she had a gorgeous, really macho boyfriend with her. I thought she was great, so I had her come to my hotel room the next day, where we do a longer interview and videotape. I asked her to bring some snapshots. She comes in and hands me her pictures—of a nice-looking guy. I hadn't realized it at all. He's Harvard educated and really has a lot going for him. I thought he'd be good for the show, so I brought him back, but I guess it was little far-fetched.

"Another time, we were recruiting people on the street in Los Angeles, having them come in for interviews, and one of the girls saw this really great-looking guy. She asked him if he wanted to be on *The Real World*, and he said, 'I already was.' It was Eric.

"I've worked as production coordinator in San Francisco and associate producer in London. Every season, we plan a trip. We had endless brainstorming sessions with George and Bob Fisher [co-director] trying to determine our destination—everywhere from Morocco to Hong Kong was thoroughly researched. In the end, we decided on Kenya based upon what we thought would challenge us and the room- mates the most. During those two months on preproduction, the cast would often ask Matt, 'Where's Laura?' They had no idea that I was spending 16-hour days planning their vacation. George and I ended up taking two scouting trips to Kenya prior to the actual trip. The logistics of getting the roommates and crew totaling 23 people in—and out of—Kenya were tremendous. Just trying to get a call or fax through to Kenya could take up to a day. We had extensive negotiations with the Kenyan government. Kenya had been recently burned by a negative documentary and had serious concerns allowing an unscripted, unstructured program free access to the country. They insisted on providing the production with a government 'minder' whose sole job was to observe the entire week's shoot. This was potentially disasterous, as there were issues of censorship and the potential of a third party telling the roommates what they could and couldn't do or say. We had to take thousands of pounds of equipment, and huge sums of cash because no one would take checks in Kenya, and fly twelve hours on two planes to reach the Masai Mara game reserve. With all of these concerns, we came close to changing our destination several times, but we knew that Kenya was going to be very special. When the roommates stepped out of the plane on the tiny airstrip in the middle of the Mara, literally jumping up and down with excitement— even Neil—we knew we'd made the right decision. Even though we put in several 20-hour days, it was the adventure of a lifetime for all of us, cast and crew."

Laura Folger
San Francisco Casting Director, U.S.
Casting Director for London 7/95

"When you're casting, you're not looking for people who've watched the show a thousand times and think they know what you're looking

for. We're not. We're looking for people with- out an agenda, people who wouldn't normally look to do this. And you have to hope they'll trust you enough to let you know the real person. The hardest thing about casting is you can only achieve a certain marriage, so you wind up losing people you love. It's a mix you're going for—it's very organic. It requires a lot of energy and focus and staying with the heart.

"We got a huge contrast of people during the casting process, especially in San Francisco. We conducted a giant outreach because the city itself is so diverse. We'd be at a gay bar till four in the morning and a cotillion the next night. We searched schools and rehabs; we spoke with secretaries and cyberpunks and psychics. We'd have casting calls, and the outpouring was enormous: 1,200 people in Boston, hundreds and hundreds of tapes in Omaha. New York was the most insane. It was an open call at The Palladium, and we'd asked people to bring in a photograph. There was this group of drag queens trying to better their odds by convincing anyone who hadn't brought in a picture that they had to leave.

"We've had people send in artwork, shoes, logs. One time, we got the torso of a mannequin but nothing else. A year later, we found an application inside the mannequin, and it was really creative! She was an art director, and she'd fabricated an amazing application. All that work, and we hadn't even called her! So I tracked her down and asked if she wanted to reapply for London. She sent in the mannequin's leg; inside were a videotape and a bottle of British beer.

"I found that most applicants were looking for a way out, or for an opportunity to connect with people or change their life. It was always fascinating to hear what they were willing to talk about. I felt people were really courageous— they really opened themselves up. I remember talking to one young guy from a very well-to- do family, and as the interview progressed, he started feeling sad and lost. He had all these advantages, but when I asked him what he wanted to do with his life, he had no idea. It was really very moving. A lot of the kids spoke about the alienation they were feeling. They were looking for a camaraderie they weren't getting at home, or with their peers."

Oskar Dektyar
Editorial Director 7/95

"We have 60 to 80 hours of tape to make a 24-minute show. They shoot that in a week, and some of the episodes, like the first one in San Francisco, take 16 weeks to edit. We observe situations—we sit and absorb with our hearts. What are the specifics and the essence of these people, of this family? We try to see where the drama is, where the comedy is, what's exciting. You have to be careful of their feelings and not be exploitive. We never tell them what to do; we don't create anything for them. How can you create a better script than Puck being arrested two hours before he's supposed to meet everyone at the house? If you really trust in life, then amazing things happen.

"Great theater is always best when you can relate to it in some way—that's what makes great film. So what could be better than work- ing with real people? It's the best reward. It's like *My Fair Lady*: you do something and then you fall in love. I compare it to some of the classic experiences I had in Russia. When I'm watching these young kids, they seem to me like Romeo and Juliet. These people, they become your heroes, your friends. It's a surrealistic experience to finally meet them— it's amazing. It's the most satisfying, the most challenging show I've ever worked on."

Billy Rainey
Technical Supervisor 7/95

"I get here a couple of months before the roommates show up and get the house ready for them technically, in terms of all the camera elements and the sound; all the good stuff that's behind the walls that they don't get to see. There are a ton of lights, a ton of cable. There's probably about three or four humans' worth of electrical intestines in here. The roommates are told there will be cameras around 20 hours a day, seven days a week, but I don't think

any of them really believe it. We outlast them.

"We go through 50-something AA batteries a day, 30-something 9-volts, and two to three loaves of bread. That's *The Real World* diet: toast, batteries, and coffee.

"You're not allowed to talk to the cast. I mean, you say, 'Good Morning,' but there are a lot of different ways to say good morning, depending on someone's mood. There's 'Morning!' or just 'Mornin',' if they're all hungover and you're hungover. Maybe that's a bad example—it sounds like we're always hungover.

"There's a rapport you get with them. For every big event, we're there. And they become comfortable. When a new camera guy comes in, they're like, 'Who the hell's that?' They figure out, like anyone figures out, 'Oh, you're cool. I'd like to hang out with you,' or, 'You, I don't want to be with. You're a dork.'

"From behind the cameras, we see the same issues arise every year. You sit there and think, wow, didn't we hear this same conversation last year? It's usually sex, masturbation, drinking. And there's always heated political debate—'Welfare: Right or Wrong?' It's kind of funny, hearing seven different people's takes on things.

"We can't interfere, but I'd be a liar to say I would never want to. Like Kat. For the entire season, she'd say, 'I have to go to American Express to get some money.' So we film her going to American Express. Well, there's an American Express three blocks from here, and we've been walking down to Harrods every day for a season. So it was really nice the other day, to say in a good-natured way, 'By the way, Kat, did you know . . .'

"We have fun, too. It's such a commitment, that if you're not having fun, it's just not worth it. San Francisco, especially, is one of the most positive experiences I've ever had—career-wise, professionally, emotionally, everything. Especially after doing so much bad TV for so long before *The Real World*, where all the shows I do—no one's learning anything from them. If someone can learn something, laugh, and have fun at the same time, then we've been doing a good job.

"Finally getting to talk to the San Francisco roommates was so amazing. I don't know what the vibe was, if it was San Francisco hippie-free-love, but it was amazing. That first time I

saw the roommates when we were done, Cory just came across and tackled me. George is standing there and I said, 'Is this okay, George?' He said, 'Yeah.' I'm right there, saying, 'Come here girl.' And then I grabbed Pedro, 'cause he was the one I'd been waiting to really talk with. It was the same this year. Just having a good time, having some beers with the guys. It's great, because we've been there every day with them. I've moved them into this house, and I've moved them out."

Dave Albrecht
Associate Producer   7/95

"You're constantly being approached by people saying, 'What're you doing? A documentary? Can I be in it?' And you say, 'Well, no, it's about them. We're documenting them.' I frequently do some of the audio mixing, which is good—you can sort of hide if you have headphones on. Still, people come up, and it can be frustrating. 'What are you doing? Can I watch? Can I be in it?' One of the roommates finally said, 'It's a documentary on herpes. Want to be on it?' That was Puck. Sort of seems right for him. He was certainly an interesting one.

"Sometimes the cameras will attract people, sometimes it'll repel them. I'm surprised that we don't have more shots of people looking into the cameras passing by, thinking, what the hell is that? Because it is like that. There are these huge crews just walking backwards. I was working with the cameraman one time, and I sort of grabbed his hips so he could snake back toward me. And there's the soundman walking backwards, and another crew person. And I thought, how does this look to people? Four people walking backwards through this crowd, up stairs, down escalators. And all along, just following two people talking.

"Everyone's taken a pratfall. Bob Fisher plunged into the Pacific Ocean. Billy Rainey nearly fell down Lombard Street snagging his Armani shorts on a shrub. Actually depantsed himself on-camera. He was just walking. You have to walk backwards half the time. He was

wearing these big, baggy shorts, they got caught on this tree, and he just goes head over heels, and the shorts came tearing off. The cast just sort of ground to a halt and said, 'That's not supposed to happen.'

"There's always things that go wrong. Once in San Francisco, we were following Mohammed to an African-dance class at a college on the other side of the Bay. It took us quite a while to get this arranged because a lot of teachers, understandably, aren't too comfortable with cameras coming in. So we'd gone through quite a bit to get it arranged. We trundled on over to somewhere in Berkeley, probably a 45-minute drive, zipped around, threw open the van—and there's no camera. Everyone sort of looked at each other. We said, 'Well, today is just a scout of the location.' I don't think anybody outside of the crew noticed it.

"As carefully as we plan things, so much of the show is still up to chance. Like going to see Neil's band play. Bob Fisher and I were the only ones on that night. Suddenly, it turns into this debacle. There's blood everywhere. The two drunk people who were involved in it are running around screaming. That was a time we should have had a full crew with us, but who knew? Bob and I stood there saying, 'Well, what can we do?' Part of you wants to film because it's good TV, but certainly we were trying to figure out what was going on, whether this was a serious wound or not. We put down the gear and sorted out what was happening. Neil's girlfriend, Chrys, was quite upset at first because she thought we were just rolling tape. That's not the case. Something like that we have to stop. We can't just pretend we're a news crew because we are involved. We are and we're not, but you can't help but take a personal interest because you are there every day, and you have to be there the next week, the next months.

"It's interesting how comfortable the roommates get being on microphone and on-camera. You'll hear them start talking about us. 'Are we out of range?' 'I think so. I think we've lost them.' And we're still two cars behind chasing them down the street. That happened in Hawaii, when Mohammed and Judd picked up a couple of girls and went off on this midnight chase. They turned their microphones off for five minutes. Then they turned them back on again, and they were saying, 'Yeah, I'm feeling pretty tired. Let's just do a little more sight-seeing, then we'll go back to the hotel.' And I'm going, hmm, okay, sure. It was such a transparent thing—the microphones go off and the guys come back on with this little scripted, 'Let's go home now.' 'Good idea.' We're driving around, it's pitch-black; they have no idea where they're going, neither do we. But we found them—they did not escape!

"It's been really strange, at least it has been for me 'cause you're always trying to start a friendship. But you're already so far ahead of them, as far as knowing what makes them tick because you hear them talking to Mom and to each other and whispering at night. You know so much of them and they know nothing of you. Where can you start? I haven't become close friends with anybody, but I certainly do miss them because I know what they're up to and what they want to accomplish."

REAL WORLD

HEATHER

NORMAN

THE REAL WORLD London

MTV SEEKS INTERESTING 18-24 YEAR OLDS

TO STAR IN MTV'S REAL LIFE SOAP OPERA

"THE REAL WORLD"

MTV MUSIC TELEVISION

The Making of London

2. While part of *The Real World* staff interviews thousands of young hopefuls, the other part scouts for a location to house the lucky seven. Most times, the space chosen is gutted and completely renovated.

1. Casting is the first step in creating *The Real World*. Some casting is done through specific outreach and the rest through general casting calls, using fliers like the one above.

3. After several months of sawing and hammering, *The Real World* crew creates a masterpiece destined to become the visual backdrop for five months of drama.

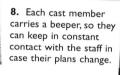

8. Each cast member carries a beeper, so they can keep in constant contact with the staff in case their plans change.

7. A typical day begins with a required call to Laura Ganis (above) or Matt Kunitz to report the day's list of activities.

9. Throughout the course of a 24-hour day, there can be anywhere from one to three video crews simultaneously active. One will cover the house; others will follow the cast throughout the day. Here Greg Blanchfield, Joe Petrowski, and Chris Merry are suiting up for their shift.

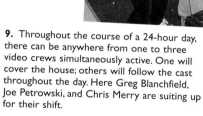

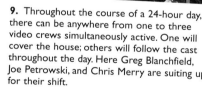

10. Although it seems impossible, the cast eventually gets used to eating dinner with three or more cameramen several feet away recording their every bite.

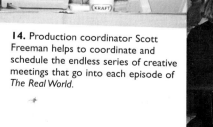

14. Production coordinator Scott Freeman helps to coordinate and schedule the endless series of creative meetings that go into each episode of *The Real World*.

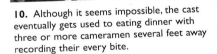

15. Post-production also involves watching hours and hours of tape to identify and finalize narrative story lines. Here Toni Gallagher, Dave Rupel, and Gordon Cassidy brainstorm story lines.

16. Editorial director, Oskar Dektyar, verifies that the story line on paper is as strong on screen.

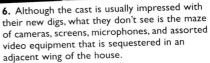

4. The search for the season's cast starts with over 40,000 applicants and narrows it down to 10 or so finalists, who go through a series of very personal interviews to determine who's got what it takes.

5. Once the final cast has been selected, they fly in from all over the world to arrive at 18 Powis Terrace with heavy bags and open minds.

6. Although the cast is usually impressed with their new digs, what they don't see is the maze of cameras, screens, microphones, and assorted video equipment that is sequestered in an adjacent wing of the house.

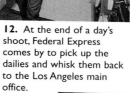

11. Meanwhile, directors George Verschoor and Bob Fischer are the wizards behind the curtain, as they view all the monitors and determine where the action is taking place.

12. At the end of a day's shoot, Federal Express comes by to pick up the dailies and whisk them back to the Los Angeles main office.

13. Post production starts in the Los Angeles offices. Here Brendan Murphy and Steve Lichtenstein log all the footage shot.

17. After story lines are established, Bob Sarles line edits the 77 hours of footage into 24 minute episodes. The average is 154 minutes of tape for each minute of show time.

18. When the final show has been edited, Russell Heldt and Dan DiPrima lay music onto the sound track, pulling from the current and coolest hits.

19—21. Before parting ways forever, cast and crew gather for the wrap party. This is often the first opportunity that the cast and crew have had to freely communicate (and boogie), after months of living in such close quarters.

HOW TO Get on The Real World: (From the Producers)

To apply to be on <u>The Real World</u>, you need to show us that you are an open, honest, and sincere person who's dealing with issues of concern to <u>The Real World</u> audience. How can you do this? Read on for step-by-step directions.

1. Call <u>The Real World</u> hotline: (818) 505-7795

This number will give you the latest information on applying. It will tell you where to send your application and when the deadlines for the next season are. Be sure to call this number first to get the most up-to-date information.

2. Write a cover letter

We want you to tell us a little bit about yourself and what you plan to do in Miami. (Yes, the fifth season of *The Real World* will be filmed in Miami, Florida.) Why do you want to spend six months there? What activities will you pursue? Please also include a snapshot of yourself with this cover letter.

3. Make a videotape

We would like to see you as well as hear from you. Make a ten minute videotape of yourself talking about whatever you think makes you a good candidate for *The Real World*.

Remember, we want to see if you are a person who is open and willing to express what is important to you. Sometimes the best videos are very simple: someone sitting on their bed talking about what makes them tick. Try to be honest and sincere. Don't overthink it. (Also make sure there's enough light on your face and that you are close enough to the mic to be heard.)

4. Fill out the enclosed application

Answer all of the following questions as best and as honestly as you can. Please keep your answers to a paragraph in length. You can use additional sheets of paper if needed. Please be sure to type or write your answers legibly. **For examples of applications that worked, look at the sample pages from previous Real Worlders' applications included (see pages 158-171).**

APPLICATION FORM

NAME

ADDRESS

PHONE

BIRTHDATE   AGE

SOCIAL SECURITY NO.

PARENTS' NAME

ADDRESS

PHONE

SIBLINGS (NAMES AND AGES)

ARE YOU OR HAVE YOU EVER BEEN A MEMBER OF SAG/AFTRA?   HAVE YOU EVER ACTED OR PERFORMED OUTSIDE OF SCHOOL?

EDUCATION: NAME OF HIGH SCHOOL   YEARS COMPLETED

NAME OF COLLEGE   YEARS COMPLETED AND MAJORS

OTHER EDUCATION

WHERE DO YOU WORK? DESCRIBE YOUR JOB

HOW WOULD SOMEONE WHO REALLY KNOWS YOU DESCRIBE YOUR BEST TRAITS?

HOW WOULD SOMEONE WHO REALLY KNOWS YOU DESCRIBE YOUR WORST TRAITS?

DESCRIBE YOUR MOST EMBARRASSING MOMENT IN LIFE

DO YOU HAVE A BOYFRIEND OR GIRLFRIEND? HOW LONG HAVE YOU TWO BEEN TOGETHER?
WHAT DRIVES YOU CRAZY ABOUT THE OTHER PERSON? WHAT'S THE BEST THING ABOUT THE OTHER PERSON?

IS THERE ANY ISSUE, POLITICAL OR SOCIAL, THAT YOU'RE PASSIONATE ABOUT?

DESCRIBE A MAJOR EVENT OR ISSUE THAT'S AFFECTED YOUR FAMILY

WHAT IS THE MOST IMPORTANT ISSUE OR PROBLEM FACING YOU TODAY?

DO YOU HAVE ANY HABITS WE SHOULD KNOW ABOUT?

WHERE WERE YOU BORN? WHERE DID YOU GROW UP?

WHAT DO YOU DO FOR FUN?

DESCRIBE A TYPICAL FRIDAY OR SATURDAY NIGHT

WHAT WAS THE LAST UNUSUAL, EXCITING, OR SPONTANEOUS OUTING YOU INSTIGATED FOR YOU AND YOUR FRIENDS?

DO YOU SMOKE CIGARETTES?

DO YOU DRINK ALCOHOL? HOW OLD WERE YOU WHEN YOU HAD YOUR FIRST DRINK? HOW MUCH DO YOU DRINK NOW? HOW OFTEN?

DO YOU USE STREET DRUGS? WHAT DRUGS HAVE YOU USED? HOW OFTEN?

DO YOU STILL KNOW A LOT OF PEOPLE WHO DO DRUGS, OR NOT? WHAT DO YOU THINK OF PEOPLE WHO DO DRUGS?

ARE YOU ON ANY PRESCRIPTION MEDICATION? IS SO, WHAT, AND FOR HOW LONG HAVE YOU BEEN TAKING IT?

DESCRIBE YOUR FANTASY DATE

WHAT ARE YOUR FAVORITE MUSICAL GROUPS/ARTISTS?

HAVE YOU EVER BEEN ARRESTED? (IF SO, WHAT WAS THE CHARGE AND WERE YOU CONVICTED?)

WHAT IS YOUR ULTIMATE CAREER GOAL? WHY? DO YOU HAVE A GAME PLAN AS TO HOW TO ACHIEVE WHAT YOU WANT?

ARE YOU LIVING ALONE RIGHT NOW, OR WITH A ROOMMATE?

IF YOU'RE LIVING WITH A ROOMMATE, HOW DID YOU HOOK UP WITH THEM? TELL US ABOUT LIVING WITH THEM

HOW IMPORTANT IS SEX TO YOU? DO YOU HAVE IT ONLY WHEN YOU'RE IN A RELATIONSHIP OR DO YOU SEEK IT OUT AT OTHER TIMES?

HOW DID IT COME ABOUT ON THE LAST OCCASION?

DO YOU BELIEVE IN GOD? DO YOU PRACTICE A RELIGION?

OTHER THAN A BOYFRIEND OR GIRLFRIEND, WHO IS THE MOST IMPORTANT PERSON IN YOUR LIFE RIGHT NOW?

WHAT ARE YOUR POLITICAL BELIEFS?

WHO HAVE BEEN YOUR ROLE MODELS? WHY?

WHAT IS YOUR GREATEST FEAR (AND WHY)?

WHAT ARE YOUR PERSONAL GOALS IN LIFE?

DESCRIBE A RECENT MAJOR ARGUMENT YOU HAD WITH SOMEONE; WHO USUALLY WINS ARGUMENTS WITH YOU? HOW?

HAVE YOU EVER HIT ANYONE IN ANGER OR SELF-DEFENSE? IF SO, TELL US ABOUT IT (HOW OLD WERE YOU, WHAT HAPPENED, ETC.)

WHAT BOTHERS YOU MOST ABOUT OTHER PEOPLE?

IF YOU COULD CHANGE ANY ONE THING ABOUT THE WAY YOU ARE, WHAT WOULD THAT BE?

IF SELECTED, IS THERE ANY PERSON OR PART OF YOUR LIFE YOU WOULD PREFER NOT TO SHARE?
IF SO, DESCRIBE (E.G., FAMILY, FRIENDS, BUSINESS ASSOCIATES, SOCIAL ORGANIZATIONS, OR ACTIVITIES)

ARE YOU NOW SEEING, OR HAVE YOU EVER SEEN A THERAPIST OR PSYCHOLOGIST? IF SO, WHY?

	RATING	COMMENT

PLEASE RATE THE FOLLOWING ACTIVITIES/PASTIMES USING THE FOLLOWING SCALE:
N: NEVER
S: SOMETIMES
O: OFTEN
A: ALWAYS

Activity	RATING	COMMENT
READ BOOKS		
SLEEP 8 HRS		
WATCH TELEVISION DAILY		
SHOP		
GO OUT/SOCIALIZE		
SPEND TIMES WITH FRIENDS		
SPEND TIME ALONE		
WORK/STUDY		
TALK ON THE PHONE		
COOK		
CLEAN		
ARGUE		
WRITE		
READ NEWSPAPERS		
STATE OPINIONS		
ASK OPINIONS		
CONFIDE IN YOUR PARENTS		
VOLUNTEER		
PROCRASTINATE		
EAT		
DRINK ALCOHOL		
DIET		
SMOKE		
CRY		
LAUGH		
CINEMA		
THEATRE		
CONCERTS		
CLUBS		
PARTIES		

LIST 4 PEOPLE WHO HAVE KNOWN YOU FOR A LONG TIME AND WILL TELL US WHAT A GREAT PERSON YOU ARE (EXCLUDING RELATIVES)

NAME	ADDRESS	PHONE	HOW DO THEY KNOW YOU?
1.			
2.			
3.			
4.			

SIGNED _____ DATE _____

Hi! My name is Pedro "Peter" Zamora. I am a 21 yr. old, gay, Cuban American living with HIV/AIDS. I came to Miami in 1980 along with 125,000 other Cuban refugees. I found out I was HIV+ during a high school blood drive. I was 17 yrs. old and a Junior in high school at the time. During the past 3 yrs. I have visited countless schools, educating my peers not only about the facts surrounding HIV/AIDS but also sharing how it feels to live with it.

So why should I be on The Real World? Because in the real world there are people living productive lives who just happen to be HIV+. I think it is important for people my age to see a young person who looks and feels healthy, can party and have fun but at the same time has to take 5 pills daily to stay healthy.

On one of your episodes this season you had an HIV+ guy come in and talk about HIV/AIDS with the group. He was there for a few hours and left. I wonder what kind of issues would have come up if that HIV+ guy would be living with the group, sharing the bathroom, the refrigerator, the bedroom, eating together. Every day for six months. Things that make you go hmmm.....

Even though I am HIV+ and it is a big part of my life, it is not all that I am. Coming from a large Hispanic family (which is extremely supportive of me and my work) I am used to sharing both my living space and my life with others. At a very early age I learned how to get my feelings and ideas across without stepping on too many toes. However, being the youngest of 8 brothers and sisters sometimes it meant being confrontational. There were a few swollen toes.......

I know that being on the "Real World" would mean exposing the most intimate details of my life on national television. How comfortable am I with that? Well, I do that through my job every day. If I can answer the questions of an auditorium full of 5th graders with inquiring minds, I am sure I could do it on national television.

What would I do in San Francisco for 6 months?

① Find a job with a local AIDS organization (in all probability San Francisco AIDS Foundation)
② Do presentations on living with HIV/prevention at local schools.
③ Find a doctor (visit every 1½ months)
④ Find a support group for HIV+ individuals (once a week)
⑤ workout at the Gym.
⑥ Bowling, roller blading, movies, dancing, playing dominoes (which I'm willing to teach the others)
⑦ Very Important !!! Find a Cuban restaurant and a place that sells Cuban coffee.
⑧ Maybe take one class at a local university.
⑨ Last but not least and most important of all DATING.

JUDD WINICK

9/27/93

TO THE GOOD PEOPLE OF "THE REAL WORLD",

I SAW YOUR AD AND I WOULD VERY MUCH LIKE TO BE A PART OF THIS INSANITY. SO, YOU WANT TO KNOW "WHY WE SHOULD CHOOSE YOU." SIMPLE. PITY. PURE UNCUT PITY. HAVE ANY OF YOU LIVED ON LONG ISLAND? ITS HELL. ITS AMY FISHER, SERIAL KILLERS AND LAWN CARE, I NEED HELP AND I NEED IT FAST. FOLLOWING MY GRADUATION FROM COLLEGE I SPENT A YEAR IN BOSTON BUT NOW I'M BACK ON THE ISLAND OF MY BIRTH. GOD HELP ME I'M TIRED OF BILLY JOEL.

I ENCLOSED A RESUME, FORGIVE ME, IT SEEMS LIKE I DON'T SEND BIRTHDAY CARDS WITHOUT A RESUME. MY RESUME IS IMPORTANT IN THIS CASE BECAUSE WHAT I DO AND WHO I AM, SEEM TO OVER-LAP. I'M A CARTOONIST (I'VE ENCLOSED SOME, ENJOY) IN SOME PEOPLE'S OPINIONS CARTOONING IS THE LOWEST RUNG ON THE ARTISTIC LADDER. MAYBE SO, BUT WE'RE A HELL OF A LOT MORE FUN AT PARTIES.

Judd's cover letter

JUDD WINICK

(2)

YOU EVER TALK WITH ABSTRACT SCULPTORS? A FUN BUNCH, I ASSURE YOU.

ME, I LIKE DEALING WITH PEOPLE. I LIKE WATCHING THEM, TALKING WITH THEM, BUYING THEM LINGERIE, ETC. WHAT I DO IN MY LIFE COMES OUT IN MY WORK. NOW, IS THIS REASON ENOUGH TO PUT ME ON YOUR SHOW? I DON'T KNOW. IF ITS ANY HELP I SPENT SEVEN SUMMERS WORKING AT A DAY CAMP SO I'M FAMILIAR WITH HANDLING BICKERING CHILDREN. WHICH, TO MY UNDERSTANDING, IS AN ONGOING THEME TO THE SHOW. (EXCEPT THE CHILDREN ARE IN THEIR 20's) BUT, I DO KNOW ALL THE BEST LINES TO DEAL WITH THESE SITUATIONS:

- "DO I HAVE TO SEPARATE YOU TWO?"

- "DON'T MAKE ME COME OVER THERE."

- "IF YOU GUYS CAN'T PLAY NICE THEN YOU SHOULDN'T PLAY TOGETHER."

- "THE POOL IS NINE FEET DEEP."

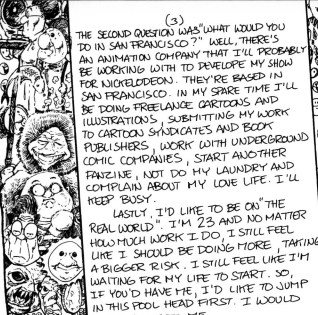

(3)

THE SECOND QUESTION WAS "WHAT WOULD YOU DO IN SAN FRANCISCO?" WELL, THERE'S AN ANIMATION COMPANY THAT I'LL PROBABLY BE WORKING WITH TO DEVELOPE MY SHOW FOR NICKELODEON. THEY'RE BASED IN SAN FRANCISCO. IN MY SPARE TIME I'LL BE DOING FREELANCE CARTOONS AND ILLUSTRATIONS, SUBMITTING MY WORK TO CARTOON SYNDICATES AND BOOK PUBLISHERS, WORK WITH UNDERGROUND COMIC COMPANIES, START ANOTHER FANZINE, NOT DO MY LAUNDRY AND COMPLAIN ABOUT MY LOVE LIFE. I'LL KEEP BUSY.

LASTLY, I'D LIKE TO BE ON "THE REAL WORLD". I'M 23 AND NO MATTER HOW MUCH WORK I DO, I STILL FEEL LIKE I SHOULD BE DOING MORE, TAKING A BIGGER RISK. I STILL FEEL LIKE I'M WAITING FOR MY LIFE TO START. SO, IF YOU'D HAVE ME, I'D LIKE TO JUMP IN THIS POOL HEAD FIRST. I WOULD MEAN A LOT TO ME.

JuddWinick

(4)

THANK YOU FOR YOUR TIME AND I'M LOOKING FORWARD TO HEARING FROM YOU SOON.

BEST REGARDS,

JuddWinick

P.S. LIVING IN SAN FRANCISCO SOUNDS GREAT. TOM HANKS CALLED IT "THE MOST BEAUTIFUL CITY IN THE WORLD." HE'S GOT BAD HAIR LIKE ME SO I TRUST HIM.

WHERE ARE YOU FROM ORIGINALLY? DIX HILLS, NY. WHICH IS WHERE I'M TEMPORARILY RESIDING UNTIL I MOVE TO MANHATTAN.

WHAT DO YOU MISS MOST ABOUT WHERE YOU GREW UP? WHAT DO YOU MISS THE LEAST? I MISS MY PARENTS. I MIGHT ALSO SAY I MISS "BIG HAIR", THE SMELL OF A FRESHLY TARRED DRIVEWAY, GIRLS WHO SAY "YOUSE GUYS", DISCUSSIONS ON LAWN CARE, GUYS NAMED ANTHONY, AND 17 YEAR OLD GIRLS WHO DRIVE B.M.W.'S, BUT I DON'T REALLY MISS IT. I JUST MISS MY FOLKS, I SUPPOSE.

WHY WOULD SOMEONE NOT LIKE YOU? I'VE ALWAYS FOUND IF PEOPLE DON'T LIKE ME IT'S FOR ONE OF THE FOLLOWING REASONS: ① BY THE COMPANY I KEEP ② THEY MISINTERPRET SOME OF MY SHYNESS FOR ARROGANCE OR SNOBBERY (IS THAT A WORD?) ③ I DON'T LIKE THEM ④ I DON'T LIKE SHARING FOOD.

WHAT DO YOU DO FOR FUN? WELL, FOR TRUE FUN, I GUESS CAUSING TROUBLE (NOT REAL TROUBLE, NOT ILLEGAL TROUBLE) JUST STUFF THAT WILL MAKE ME LAUGH, AS WELL AS THE FOLKS I'M WITH. I KNOW THIS IS VAGUE BUT FUN IS A SERIOUS MATTER TO ME AND I DON'T THINK I CAN COVER IT HERE.

DESCRIBE A TYPICAL FRIDAY OR SATURDAY NIGHT 5:00 PM - START SHAVING BACK 5:20 MAKE SOCK PUPPETS OR BEGIN INTERPRETIVE DANCE 5:45 PRANK CALL ... (WHO HIT ME IN 5TH GRADE) 6:00 CONTINUE SHAVING BACK 6:45 EAT CEREAL 7:00 QUIETLY REFLECT ON THE LIFE OF BETTE DAVIS 7:30 NAP 9:30 FINISH SHAVING BACK 10:00 TRY ON SEVERAL EVENING GOWNS AND ATTEMPT TO MATCH SHOES 10:30 FRIENDS ARRIVE, ORDER PIZZA, WATCH "HEATHERS". THIS IS A SILLY QUESTION.

DESCRIBE YOUR FIRST LOVE. ...WE WERE BOTH IN SIXTH GRADE. SHE BROKE UP AND GOT BACK TOGETHER W/ ME FOUR TIMES BEFORE SHE FINALLY SHATTERED WHAT WAS LEFT OF MY 12 YEAR OLD HEART. SHE WAS MY FIRST KISS, I WAS HERS, AND SHE WAS EVERYTHING TO ME. YEARS LATER SHE WOULD DEVELOP A MUSTACHE PROBLEM. I FELT VINDICATED.

Judd's application

161

HOW DID YOUR PARENTS TREAT EACH OTHER? (DID YOUR PARENTS HAVE A GOOD MARRIAGE? WHAT WAS IT LIKE?) My parents... they've completely, totally in love. I've never seen them fight. My Dad's a commercial fisherman, so he's gone 6 months out of the year. I know their marriage is something they both take seriously and put a lot of value on. They tease each other a lot. They hold hands. One day, they were supposed to pick me up from school. I came out and — ↱ they were making out in the car.

WHO HAVE BEEN YOUR ROLE MODELS? WHY? My Grandma and my Mom. They're high powered, intellectual women who are married because they love their husbands, not because they need them. I've also always admired genis and poetry in people. Paul Simon is phenomenal. I pattern myself after him in that I try to cultivate what I'm strong at — and to do good with it. Martin Luther King is another person I admire. For strength.

WHAT ARE YOUR PERSONAL GOALS IN LIFE? Personally? Okay. Well, I want to keep growing. I want to be able to know when to walk away from something. I want to be wealthy enough to found a scholarship for "The Second Child in College" scholarship. I want to be honest. I don't want to ever screw someone over for money. I want to be married only once.

DESCRIBE YOUR FIRST LOVE. Oh geez. We met in, marching band, freshman, no, sophomore year of high school. He was a drummer – into that Seattle sound music. He had his own band. One of those alternatively "cool" guys. We dated for a long time. He was probably the only nice guy I dated in high school. We're still friends. I'm a lot taller than he is now, yep...
I thought we were going to go out forever. I still think he's cool though.

DESCRIBE THE WEIRDEST OR MOST INTERESTING PERSON YOU'VE EVER MET. There's this guy... He's a junkman, and he grows German Shepards in his back yard. He never bathes, and is always bringing me broken bicycles and puppies. He fixes up broken toys for poor children. He loves junk, and he is proud of being a junkman. He wants a whole planet full of junk. He's about 60 yrs old. My Dad met him at a gas station & brought him home for dinner.

DO YOU PLAY ANY SPORTS? Yes! Fencing, collegitely and judo as a club sport.

DESCRIBE HOW CONFLICTS WERE HANDLED AT HOME AS YOU WERE GROWING UP (WHO WOULD WIN AND WHO WOULD LOSE, WHETHER THERE WAS YELLING OR HITTING, ETC.)? Conflicts at home: we all scream & let it out – and no grudges or guilt trips were held. I won a lot 'cause I'm persistant, loud, and my brothers are push-overs. With my parents – they refuse to fight. They get nice and sweet on me and I lose my steam. So I never win. They're so frustrating. They just say "But we love you honey" ARGH! When I fight with my sistr (she's three) she wins. She's tough and stubborn and she can scream loud. My brothers will do anything to make her shut up.

HOW IMPORTANT IS SEX TO YOU? DO YOU HAVE IT ONLY WHEN YOU'RE IN
A RELATIONSHIP OR DO YOU SEEK IT OUT AT OTHER TIMES? HOW DID IT
COME ABOUT ON THE LAST OCCASION?

    Good--no, great sex is very important. But a great person
is more important. Right now, I only have sex with **my boyfriend**,
although I have had sex outside of the relationship. Sometimes
we've been broken up, sometimes not. I need GOOD sex if it is
outside of a relationship. The last time I had sex was on the
"set" of my MTV <u>REAL WORLD</u> application video.

DESCRIBE A TYPICAL FRIDAY/SATURDAY NIGHT

    Get home from work. Turn on the TV, but don't watch it--
make phone calls, find out about the parties or bands playing
somewhere for cheap. Snack a bit. Go have an evening latte at
the local coffeehouse. Pick up some alcohol, have people come
over for drinks. Go out to parties or clubs and dance, etc.
Roll home around 4 am. Saturday: nurse hangover, eat huge greasy
brunch. Shopping. Try art, movies, music or plays that night.

WHAT'S THE BEST THING ABOUT BEING OUT ON YOUR OWN? WHAT'S THE
WORST THING?

Best: Cable TV! Worst: Cable TV! haha!
    The best thing is that I can express myself freely, and I
get to do and be what I want. Nobody cares if I'm home at 4 am.
    The worst thing is...Nobody cares if I'm home at 4 am! I
could be bleeding in a gutter somewhere! I suppose it's a
reflection that being on your own is being alone, and being
accountable for yourself. It's tough.

DESCRIBE A MAJOR EVENT OR ISSUE THAT'S AFFECTED YOUR FAMILY
My family has really struggled with racial identity issues.
My father came from China, and grew up in Thailand and Singapore;
he speaks four Oriental languages. My mom is Chinese, but she
grew up in St. Louis, Missouri, when there were almost NO other
Chinese people living there. None of the four girls in my family
speaks a word of Chinese. We were raised to be totally American.
We can't even speak to our grandmother. We have--GASP--white
boyfriends! At the same time, we grew up with all kinds of
traditional Chinese values and "family things." I'm still trying
to find out how I can resolve these two worlds.

WHO HAVE BEEN YOUR ROLE MODELS? WHY?

    My father has been my strongest role model. It's pretty
obvious considering my career choice. I'm the "eldest son"
equivalent since there were no boys in my family...it's okay that
I follow my dad's footsteps. I wish I had more of his attitude.
I also admire the beauty and spirit of the famous female jazz
singers like Ella Fitzgerald or Billie Holiday. My most recent
role model was a very tiny, very tough, excellent Asian lesbian
surgeon. It's the first time I ever had a teacher that looked
like me! Wow, it really makes a difference.

WHAT IS YOUR GREATEST FEAR?

    I fear mediocrity. I fear being run-of-the-mill or
unremarkable. I fear waking up as a doctor in six years, with no
sense of my former self. Run screaming from the medical training
cookie cutter! Run screaming into the void! Run screaming into
the void!

DESCRIBE YOUR FIRST LOVE

    My first love was for my best friend in Junior High & High
School. He was a confident, creative, impeccably dressed ballet
dancer, blonde, effervescent, arrogant, with grades ALMOST as
good as mine. He brought me pink Azaleas at school, with the
stems wrapped carefully in wet tissue and foil. I carried them
like trophies all day. We wrote notes in class; we kissed hello
and goodbye; we called each other baby. I finally confessed my
love to him in a 70 page letter during our Senior year in high
school. He took me to picnic on the traffic islands in the
middle of Chandler Blvd., where he confessed that he was in love
with someone else...that he was gay. We still went to Prom
together, and I still love him.

DESCRIBE YOUR FANTASY DATE My fantasy date is lighthearted, fun and romantic. I love good food, the ocean under moonlight, and kissing. My dream date would probably be with someone like Isabella Rossellini.

HAVE YOU EVER BEEN ARRESTED? (If so, what was the charge and were you convicted?) Yes, once. I was driving through a logging town in Oregon with a bright pink liscence plate reading "downtown LA"! They falsely arrested me for ~~exte~~ allegedly going 115 miles an hour, running from the officer and resisting arrest. All charges were dropped in court. They don't like Californians in Oregon.

WHAT JOB OR CAREER DO YOU ASPIRE TO? WHAT DRIVES YOU TO PURSUE IT? DO YOU HAVE A GAME PLAN AS TO HOW TO ACHIEVE WHAT YOU WANT IN YOUR CAREER? I would like to open a used clothing store, and eventually design casual clothing. It will hire women from shelters, a certain percentage of proceeds will go to local battering shelters, and clothes will be donated to low income women. I feel compelled to help women heal. It is the only way we can learn to help heal our brothers and our earth. It all starts with each individual. I also enjoy clothing, fashion, and a good bargain. I would be able to express my creativity, my political beliefs, and healthfully pay my bills. My game plan is neatly filed in my file cabinet.

ARE YOU LIVING ALONE RIGHT NOW, OR WITH A ROOMMATE? I have a room-mate from heaven.

IF YOU'RE LIVING WITH A ROOMMATE, HOW DID YOU HOOK UP WITH THEM? TELL ME ABOUT THEM AS A PERSON. DO YOU GET ALONG? WHAT'S THE BEST PART ABOUT LIVING WITH THEM? WHAT'S THE HARDEST PART ABOUT IT? We originally met at age 5 & 6. But were re-aquanted in LA at our work place (a health food restaurant). She is an angel on earth, a true ray of sunshine. What would life be without her - not as happy, not as fun. We have lived together over two years and argued only two times. We get along so well. We are like the saturday night live show seven days a week. The only hard part about living with her is when I'm home and she's not.

HOW IMPORTANT IS SEX IN YOUR RELATIONSHIP? HOW IMPORTANT SHOULD SEX BE IN A RELATIONSHIP? HOW DO YOU FEEL ABOUT SEX IN GENERAL?
Sex is a biggy for me. Sex for me is important because now that I'm with women I enjoy it. It's great to be with someone you are shaking with passion for. In general sex isn't everything, it's not the big picture, but it sure helps ease city life. :")

DO YOU LIKE KIDS? WOULD YOU LIKE TO HAVE KIDS ONE DAY? IF SO, TALK ABOUT WHY. IF NOT, EXPAND ON THIS. I like children very much. They are the beginning of life. I do not wish to have childrens. I feel that my life will be dedicated to hard work in healing the earth, and racial oppression. I will not have time to raise my own children. However I'm sure there will always be children in my life.

DESCRIBE YOUR MOST EMBARRSSING MOMENT IN LIFE. I have not had to be embarrassed to often. There was one time however when a few of my friends and I were drinking on campus - we decided dont ask how -, to take off all our clothes and climb trees and buildings (this is a common thing in oregon, land of free loven hippies). So I get on top of this house and get bight fright. My friends had to wake the people in the house to get a ladder and help me down. They fortunatly were understanding hippies and got a good laugh out of it.

DESCRIBE YOUR FIRST LOVE. I guess the first man I was really in love with was... He was a 50's rockabilly. He played in a band and went to college. I thought he was the world. I even ended up dating him again years later.

167

DESCRIBE YOUR FANTASY DATE <u>Cindy Crawford.</u>

We go out. We have a great time. Turns out she's been a big fan of mine for a long time. She confides in me that she wants to be with me instead of Richard Gere. She dumps him. We get along famously. We have a great time. We go home and have sex for 2 weeks straight. She still likes me. All this happens somewhere exotic. PS Don't tell TRACEY.

WHAT ARE YOUR FAVORITE MUSICAL GROUPS/ARTISTS? I changes every week. I've always liked STONES, FACES, U-2. Right now my 'favs' are STIKKITY, 4-NON BLONDES and SCREAMING TREES.

WHO'S THE MOST IMPORTANT PERSON IN YOUR LIFE RIGHT NOW? IF YOUR ANSWER WAS YOUR BOYFRIEND OR GIRLFRIEND, THEN WHO'S THE NEXT MOST IMPORTANT PERSON TO YOU? TELL ME ABOUT THEM. I don't know if there is. My Mom, family, brothers, TRACEY, my friends Mac and Kirt, my DOG. That's a tough one.

WHAT'S THE BEST THING ABOUT BEING OUT ON YOUR OWN? WHAT'S THE WORST THING? Free to think, Free to RELAX, Free to run round the house naked if I want. I spend very little time on my own so I can't think of a worst thing. On a desert Island I'd probably change that response.

WHAT'S YOUR GOAL IN LIFE?
(1) To be happy and content.
(2) To be respected in whatever I do.
(3) I figure for 1 and 2 to happen I'll need a sh*tload of money.

IF YOU COULD BE ANYTHING IN FIVE YEARS, WHAT WOULD IT BE? In 5 years I'd like to Be
The Dominic Griffin Corporation.
(my conglomerate)

WHAT'S A GOOD AGE TO GET MARRIED? It's nothing to do with age. One
DID YOUR PARENT'S HAVE A GOOD MARRIAGE? WHAT WAS IT LIKE?
Yeah, I guess. They're still to-gether,
but thats Ireland. They raised 4 cool
children. My father's moodier than me,
My Mom puts up with him. She's
a SAINT

WHAT ARE THE MOST IMPORTANT ISSUES FACING YOUNG PEOPLE TODAY?
Involvement - People need to get involved and
interested in their future. Abortion - make sure it
isn't abolished. Economy - make sure it starts working.
Environment - make sure it's still there when and if we grow
up. CRIME pisses me off.

**IN YOUR EXPERIENCE, HAS YOUNG PEOPLE'S TREATMENT OF SEX IN THEIR LIVES CHANGED
SINCE AIDS, OR NOT? AND IF SO, HOW?** Yes but not enough. "I don't practice
safe sex but I have an aids test every 6 mths." Big f**king
deal. Aids test are important but they only confirm you've
got the disease. It's a little late when the test comes
positive. Aids tests won't save your life.

Dominic's application

WHAT DO YOU MISS MOST ABOUT WHERE YOU GREW UP? WHAT DO YOU MISS THE LEAST?
I miss cowtipping, chicken plucking, and watching my Polish cousin slaughter pigs to make Kielbasa. HA! But seriously, I miss my friends. They're all settling down, buying houses down the street from their families, getting married, having babies. Everyone thinks I'm absolutely out of my mind for moving here. But I know I wouldn't be happy living a simple life. I need excitement!

HOW WOULD A FRIEND DESCRIBE YOU? A good sense of humor, very caring, very intelligent, and extremely intriguing. She goes after what she wants until she gets it. When she has a project she's extremely detailed and does it "big" and extravigantly. A definate Drama Queen. Her life is always a soap opera.

DO YOU BELIEVE IN GOD? ARE YOU RELIGIOUS? Yes I believe in God but I don't go to church every Sunday. Ever since my father died, I stopped going because we used to go together. Pretty soon it will be 10 years since he died. My family thinks I'm not religious because of that and because I've never been to my father's grave.

WHAT KIND OF FAMILY DID YOU COME FROM? DO YOU MISS THEM, OR ARE YOU GLAD TO BE AWAY FROM THEM? My parents were born in Poland and escaped to move to the USA in 1950. My father died when I was 13. I love my mother but we aren't close at all. My sisters grew up in a different decade and I can along, probably as a mistake. We have a hard time seeing each other eye to eye. I do miss them and I wish I could find a way to be closer with my family but I have to start my own life now.

HOW DO YOU EARN A LIVING? HOW DO YOU FEEL ABOUT YOUR JOB? TELL ME ABOUT THE OTHER PEOPLE WHO WORK THERE, THE GOOD AND BAD POINTS OF THE JOB ITSELF AS WELL AS YOUR CO-WORKERS. I work freelance doing work for directors and producers. Sometimes I work on music videos which is really fun. I worked Guns N Roses a few times and that was a major culture shock. Some people are nice, some are f**ked up on drugs, some are on power trips but I just take the good with the bad. Since I work freelance I don't work everyday so it gives me a lot of free time.
WHAT'S YOUR GOAL IN LIFE? To be successful in the path I choose to take with my career and give my mother more than she gave me.

HOW IMPORTANT IS SEX IN YOUR RELATIONSHIP? HOW IMPORTANT SHOULD SEX BE IN A
RELATIONSHIP? HOW DO YOU FEEL ABOUT SEX IN GENERAL?

Sex is REAL. I think two people should be able to please each other sexually and with every time, they should take their partner higher and higher.

Sex shouldn't be the only basis for a good relationship. The two should share more intimate things - their likes/dislikes - their hobbies. General conversation and just touching/kissing should be pleasing as well

I LOVE SEX WHEN ITS RIGHT

DO YOU BELIEVE IN GOD? ARE YOU RELIGIOUS? I believe in GOD/Higher Power. I AM BUDDHIST - I chant every morning at 8:30 for world peace and inner peace and serenity.

WHAT KIND OF FAMILY DID YOU COME FROM? DO YOU MISS THEM, OR ARE YOU GLAD TO BE
AWAY FROM THEM? Strong - Proud Mom. I'm still very close to my mom. She was 15½ when she had me, so we basically grew up together. I love her - All that I want to be is so that I can take care of her.

WHAT'S YOUR GOAL IN LIFE? To achieve spiritual gratification and to be a successful vocalist so that I may take care of my mother so that she doesn't have to work. To make tons of money and have every materialistic thing I've ever dreamed of.

AIDS STATISTICS

- Fifty percent (50%) or half of new infections are occurring in persons under the age of 25. One quarter (25%) of new infections are occurring in teens (persons under age 20).

- Since 1 in 5 reported AIDS cases is diagnosed in the 20-29 year age group, and the incubation period between HIV infection and AIDS diagnosis is many years, it is clear that large numbers of people who were diagnosed with AIDS in their 20s became infected with HIV as teenagers. (Through June 1994, more than 15,000 persons aged 20-24 and more than 60,000 persons aged 25-29 have been diagnosed with AIDS.)

- More than 75% of new AIDS infections are contracted through sexual intercourse.

- Among adolescents reported with AIDS, older teens, males, and racial and ethnic minorities are disproportionately affected.

- The proportion of females among U.S. adolescent AIDS cases has more than doubled, from 14 percent in 1987 to 32 percent in June 1994.

Source: The Center for Disease Control. Data is current as of June 1994.

"If you want to reach me as a young gay man, especially a young gay man of

color, then you need to give me information in a language and vocabulary I can

understand and relate to. I will be much more likely to hear the message if it

comes from someone to whom I can relate . . . I needed positive messages about

my sexuality. I needed to know about condoms, how to use them correctly and

THE PEDRO ZAMORA MEMORIAL FUND

where to buy them. I needed to know that you can be sexual without having

intercourse. I needed skills to negotiate relationships. I needed to know how to

say 'I don't want to have intercourse, I just want to be held.'" —Pedro Zamora

AIDS ACTION CREATED
THE PEDRO ZAMORA
MEMORIAL FUND IN
1994 AS A LIVING LEGACY OF
PEDRO ZAMORA'S ADVOCACY
WORK IN HIV PREVENTION.

Thousands of individuals from all walks of life were touched by Pedro's life and his work, which was conveyed to millions of television viewers through MTV's *The Real World*. Financial contributions from many of these individuals have already been made to the Fund in memory of Pedro. It is AIDS Action's intention to continue to increase the fund by soliciting contributions from individuals, corporations, and foundations to be utilized to support the objectives outlined below.

GOALS:

To strengthen adolescent and young adult HIV prevention programs through broad policy education and empowerment of adolescent advocates.

OBJECTIVES:

- ESTABLISH a Pedro Zamora Fellowship Program at AIDS Action Council to train four young people annually in HIV/AIDS policy advocacy.
- EDUCATE policy makers about the need to prevent HIV transmission among youth and young adults by augmenting federal HIV prevention programs in the schools and in communities. Such programs must be unencumbered by restrictions on content.
- SUPPORT increased participation by adolescents and their service providers—especially adolescents of color and gay youth—in planning and implementing HIV prevention programs.
- EDUCATE community members and the media about adolescent HIV prevention policy concerns through outreach, dissemination of written and audio-visual materials, and other communications strategies.
- SUPPORT stronger interagency and interdepartmental coordination on HIV prevention efforts among adolescents and young adults.

A portion of the proceeds from the sales of this book will be donated to the Pedro Zamora Foundation. If you, too, would like to make a donation or get more information, please contact the Pedro Zamora Fund at the following address:

THE PEDRO ZAMORA FOUNDATION
AIDS Action Council
1875 N. Connecticut Ave.
Washington D.C. 20009

CREDITS AND SOURCES

Grateful acknowledgment is made to the following people and institutions for permission to reproduce photographs and artwork:

Ewing Galloway: pages 10, 11, 43, 100 - 101. **Courtesy Julie:** pages 12, 16, 20, 21, 25. **Jay Strauss:** pages 12, 15, 16, 18, 22, 24, 25. **Chris Carroll / Onyx:** pages 14, 21. **Dimitri Halkidis:** pages 13, 16, 17, 24, 33, 34. **George Verschoor:** pages 16, 28, 42, 118, 148, 151, 152, 153. **Courtesy Heather:** page 18. **Deborah Thornhill:** page 20. **Frank Couch:** page 21. **Connie Eckles:** page 32. **Malik Yusef:** page 22. **Staci Rodriguez:** page 22. **Courtesy Kevin:** pages 22, 23, 33. **Clint Cowen:** pages 24, 25, 34, 35. **Bettmann Archives:** page 26. **Kim Bancroft - Thomas:** page 34. **Frank Micelotta:** pages 36, 70. **Jeff Kravitz:** pages 42, 44, 46, 47, 49, 51, 52, 53, 54, 55, 56, 57, 58, 60, 66, 67, 77, 108, 109, 151. **Courtesy Beth A.:** pages 46, 47, 68, 69. **Courtesy Beth S.:** pages 48, 49, 66. **Don Hohman:** page 48. **Auintard Henderson:** pages 50, 66. **Courtesy Jon:** pages 52, 55, 59, 60, 151. **Courtesy Tami:** page 60. **Courtesy Glen:** pages 54, 55. **Courtesy Irene:** pages 56, 57, 67. **Kurt Schmidt:** page 57. **Katie Brennan:** pages 58, 59, 70. **Alan L. Mayor:** pages 58 - 59. **Lucy Baldoc:** pages 60 - 61. **Tom MacDougall:** pages 64, 65. **Anitra Silverton:** page 67. **Susan Robinson:** page 68. **Harold Hechler:** page 70. **Judd Winick:** pages 78 - 79, 84, 85, 86. **Courtesy Cory:** pages 80, 81, 82, 83, 84, 85, 86, 88, 90, 91, 92, 93, 95, 99, 102, 103, 107, 110. **Courtesy Jo:** pages 77, 81, 82, 95, 102, 103, 107, 151. **Courtesy Rachel:** pages 81, 82, 86, 93, 94, 95, 99, 100, 101, 103. **Marty Sohl:** page 86. **Courtesy Mohammed:** page 86. **Courtesy Pam:** pages 88, 89, 98 - 99, 109. **Alex Escarano:** pages 90, 91. **Courtesy the Zamora Family:** pages 90, 91. **Courtesy Sean Sasser:** pages 91, 103, 105. **Bruce Kramer:** pages 92, 96, 110. **Michael Howley:** pages 94, 95. **Leslie Fratkin:** pages 32, 118, 134, 142 - 143, 145, 151, 153. **Peter J. Fox:** pages 118, 124, 127, 128, 129, 130, 131, 132, 134, 135, 136, 144, 147, 152, 153. **Courtesy Sharon:** pages 119, 132, 133, 136, 137, 140, 141. **Courtesy Jacinda:** pages 124, 127, 130, 140. **Steve Shaw:** page 124. **Nick Ferrand:** page 124. **Colleen M. Cahill:** page 127. **Courtesy Jay:** page 127. **Courtesy Kat:** pages 128, 129, 130, 132, 134, 140, 141. **Courtesy Lars:** page 130. **Bruce McDonald:** pages 130, 132. **Courtesy Mike:** pages 130, 132, 133. **Courtesy Neil:** page 135. **Ken Probst:** page 146. **Mike Beale:** pages 148, 151. **Mary-Ellis Bunim:** pages 149, 152, 153. **Courtesy Laura Folger:** pages 149, 151. **Courtesy Bill Rainey:** page 150. **John Chater:** page 151. **David Vance:** page 172.

ADDITIONAL CREDITS

Eric on *The Faith Daniels Show* — **courtesy NBC News Archives.** New York City subway map and token — **Used with permission by New York City Transit Authority.** Page 28 — **Courtesy *New York Post.*** Page 30 — **New York Newsday Inc.**, Copyright ©, 1992; Courtesy *Total TV*; Copyright ©*The Fresno Bee*, 1992; *PEOPLE Weekly* is a registered trademark of Time Inc., used with permission; Courtesy *Los Angeles Daily News*; Courtesy *Detroit Free Press*; Courtesy *TV Host Weekly*; ©1992 *The Washington Post*, reprinted with permission. Page 31 — **Courtesy *Contra Costa Times*; Courtesy *Los Angeles Times*; Courtesy *Boston Phoenix*; Courtesy *The Atlanta Journal*;** Copyright ©1995 by The New York Times Company, reprinted by permission; Reprinted with permission from *TV Guide*, Volume 40, #21, 1992; Courtesy *Evening Telegram*; Courtesy *Star News*. All Glocks Down CD single — **Courtesy Pendulum Records.** Vibe Magazine — **Photograph by Reisig and Taylor; Art Director: Diddo Ramm.** recognize — **Published by Harlem River Press, an imprint of Writers and Readers Publishing Inc., cover photograph by Carl Posey.** Page 35 — **Courtesy *Entertainment Weekly*.** Tami on *Studs* — **Courtesy 20th Century Fox.** Los Angeles and San Francisco maps — ©1995 by Rand McNally, R.L. 95 - S - 205. Jon Brennan Fan Club newsletter — **Courtesy The Jon Brennan International Fan Club.** Sassy article and logo — **Courtesy Sassy Magazine, photograph by David E. Williams.** BAM article — **Used with permission by BAM Magazine and writer Aidan Vazari.** Thrasher stickers: Thrasher logo is a registered trademark owned by HSP, Inc. — **Courtesy Thrasher Magazine.** Tattoo care — **Courtesy Ed Hardy's Tattoo City, San Francisco.** Pedro Zamora Memorial Fund — **Courtesy AIDS Action.** London Underground Map — ©1995 London Regional Transport, Reg. user # 95 / 2274. Ministry Of Sound Invitation —**Courtesy Ministry Of Sound.** Team Duke decal — **Courtesy Team Duke Racing.**

THIS BOOK WAS PRODUCED BY MELCHER MEDIA
170 FIFTH AVENUE, NEW YORK, NY, 10010
UNDER THE EDITORIAL DIRECTION OF CHARLES MELCHER

EDITOR: Sarah Malarkey
EDITORIAL ASSISTANT: Erin Bohensky
ART DIRECTION: Carol Bobolts and Deb Schuler, Red Herring Design
DESIGN ASSISTANTS: Adam Chiu, Adria Robbin
PHOTOGRAPHY EDITOR: Leslie Fratkin
PHOTOGRAPHY COORDINATOR: Mary Anderson

SPECIAL THANKS TO: Lisa Berger, Mary-Ellis Bunim, Lynda Castillo, Gina Centrello, Ian Corydon, Juli Davidson, Kelley Drucker, Amy Einhorn, Tina Exarhos, Scott Freeman, Lisa Hackett, Marcy Hardart, Julie Insogna, Sheryl Jones, Andrea LaBate, Judy McGrath, Jonathan Murray, Ed Paparo, Renee Presser, Jack Romanos, Gail Shapiro, Robin Silverman, Sabrina Silverberg, Donald Silvey, Van Toffler, George Verschoor, Jill Wallach, Kara Welsh, and Irene Yuss.

AN ORIGINAL PUBLICATION OF MTV BOOKS/POCKET BOOKS/MELCHER MEDIA

POCKET BOOKS, A DIVISION OF SIMON & SCHUSTER INC.
1230 AVENUE OF THE AMERICAS, NEW YORK, NY 10020

ISBN: 0-671-54525-6

First MTV Books/Pocket Books/Melcher Media trade paperback printing November 1995

10 9 8 7 6 5 4

Pocket and colophon are registered trademarks of Simon & Schuster Inc.
Printed in the U.S.A.